I0659563

DID GOD LOVE

Lucifer

AFTER THE FALL?

.

Did God Love

Lucifer

After the Fall?

A NOVEL BY

Nia Miah

Copyright © 2017 by Nia Miah

All rights reserved. No part of this book may be used or reproduced, distributed, or transmitted in any manner, including photocopying, recording, or other electronic or mechanical methods, whatsoever without prior written permission. For information or permission requests address:

Creative Energy, LLC
NiaMiahWrites@gmail.com
Fax (888)266-0445
www.CreativeEnergy.co

Printed in the United States of America

ISBN -13: 978-1-945372-01-8

This is dedicated to the strength, the resiliency and the resolve inside of each of us to rebound from any situation or circumstance. This book is dedicated to a future that is destined to survive lifes journey's through hills and valleys. This book is dedicated to hope. That little thing that keeps life going.

May comfort and encouragement ensue you.

In service and in love,
Nia Miah

Chapter 1

Troy

I listen as the church soloist sings how he is thankful that he has a God of a second chance. The song moves me and I want that, that second chance. Then I remember, I had a second chance and messed that one up too. *What kind of a God do I need?*

Here I am divorced with two children and another on the way, and I don't even know if it's mine or my best friend's. I saw the woman I love, kiss another man and watching the words 'I love you' leave her lips and fall on his ears was like watching the grim reaper's sear steal the life from me. I stare at the wooden cross on the pulpit and ask myself, is there a God of a third chance, a thirty-third chance. I know I've fallen. Did God still love Lucifer after the fall? I want to stand back up, but not to just fall again, so my life doesn't move. I stand still, staring at the cross. Is there a God of a 99th chance?

I look around and the church is empty. A few people are lingering behind laughing and chatting with each other and I sit still. I fix my gaze back at that cross. The words "I want my family back" leave my mouth as whispers yet voraciously rip through my soul re-opening the painfully sealed scars on my heart.

"Troy." I hear someone call my name. I break my eyes from the cross as I look around searching for a recognizable face. I look up and see the man that my wife has fallen in love with - Rick. I look back at the cross and question whether God is showing me love or disdain. I don't acknowledge Rick at all. I just stare at the cross.

"You're a good man Troy. I was wrong for kissing Sojourn as a married man."

He doesn't say anything else. We don't make eye contact, just sit in silence.

I break the silence, but don't look at him, "Sojourn's mine. You can't have her."

Rick remains still, but his words manage to intrude on my space, "Neither one of us has any control over who she gives her heart to Troy."

I feel him shift his gaze on me, but I don't move. "I just want you to know, that kiss was not about you or disrespecting you. You're a good man Troy." He waits for a response. The anger and resentment I feel for this man has sealed my mouth shut. I give him nothing. He gets up and leaves. I feel the open wounds of my heart bleeding and I look back to the wooden cross. Can God still love a fallen angel? "I want my family back."

"Brother Troy." I look up and see Deacon Mitchell. He's a young guy about my age. We went to school together.

"Hey brother."

"What's up man? You waiting for next Sunday to come?" He says with a smile.

I want to smile back, and return the friendly gesture, but my lips feel too heavy. I continue to just sit staring at that cross, as if I'm waiting for a sign, a message. I wait, hoping the cross will get up sit next to me and speak. I want my family back.

"Troy, that cross ain't gonna come to you. You have to go to the cross, and the cross will embrace you. You have to make the first step."

"I don't want to fall again Mitch."

"If that's what you want, you might as well tell us all bye and go to Heaven now."

I look back at him.

"We all fall down man. All of us. All of us. You ain't the only one that's been on that ground."

"Walking to that cross means I'm ready. Ready to make better decisions, but I have so much anger and resentment in my heart. Man I want to destroy the brother that Sojourn fell in love with."

"Destroying him ain't gonna make her love you."

He leans back in the pew almost relaxing, "and walking to that cross doesn't mean you're ready or perfect. It just means you're moving closer to God and if you're moving closer to God, you're moving closer to the peace and the answer you need."

He looks at the cross and I follow his gaze and look back at it myself.

"Come near Him and He'll come near you Troy."

"I hate him Mitch." The words rip the tears from my eyes and send then down the back of my throat setting it on fire.

"No you don't. It's not him you hate, he ain't done nothing to you man. It's just easier to hate him."

He looks back at me.

"The only thing standing in the way of you and Sojourn is you. Figure out what part of you is keeping this relationship strained and if you can, remove it and if you can't move on man."

"You're a good friend Mitch."

"You've yet to let me down, when I needed you brother. We're there for each other."

He just sits with me in silence, we both stare at the cross.

Chapter 2

Carlo

"Honey, I have Sunday dinner ready at the house. I invited your sister over to eat with us. I hope that's OK?"

I know her intentions are well. Sadie treats me so good, she loves me and I love that she loves me. But every time I look at her and that baby growing inside of her a piece of me is angry with her. How do I love this baby, not knowing if it is mine or not? I feel my blood pressure rising just thinking about this.

"Carlo, did you hear me?"

"Yea, that's fine. Next time, tell me *before* you invite her Bella."

I don't know what's worse, knowing that this baby may not be mine, or knowing that the only other possibility that exists is that this baby may belong to Troy, my best friend. I can't even talk to him about it. Just the thought that he had his hands all over my woman's naked body and was inside of her, disgusts me. The thought that it may be his seed growing inside of her and not mine, disgusts me. The fact that he heard about the pregnancy before me and then told me about it before she did, disgusts me.

"What are you thinking about Carlo? Wait, let me guess, you want me to slide my big ass on that dick tonight don't you?"

Sadie always knows how to make me smile.

A small chuckle escapes out of the corner of my smile, "I like that thought, Bella."

She reaches over and grabs my thigh as I am driving to my apartment. She rubs her hand up and down my thigh. The one thing that Sadie can do well is make a man's body feel good. I glance at her as I struggle to keep my eyes on the road.

Sadie's words glide up to me, "Shhh. Just focus on the road, baby."

She unzips my pants and frees me. She grabs me and looks up to me with a smile. "How about an appetizer?"

I just nod my head yes. Immediately I begin to grow in her hands and my eyes follow her as she moves her body bending down in my lap. She wraps her entire mouth around me. She slides one hand down around the base of my dick and holds it there, tightening all my skin and the sensation of her mouth and tongue looping all around me is heightened. Umm, this woman feels good. I take one hand off of the steering wheel and rub my hand up and down her back and inside of her shirt. I move my hand around until I'm cupping her breast. I feel her hard nipple pressing through my fingers.

"Sadie." I whisper, "That feels good, Bella."

When my words fall down on her ears, she rotates her mouth around me with more vigor. The intensity keeps rising and rising. I can't hold it in anymore, "I can't hold it anymore Sadie, it feels too good. I've got to come to you."

She rotates her other hand around me and she keeps the other hand planted on my base and rotates her free hand in rhythm with her mouth and tongue and I can't take it anymore. Pleasure explodes. She doesn't remove her mouth or her hand. She swallows and licks me dry. She zips me back up dry and rises up.

Damn. "I love you Bella."

I pull into the apartment complex and see my sister's car in the parking lot. Sadie reaches in her purse and pulls out a mint and chucks it in her mouth. She looks back at me with a smile, "Are you ready for the main course? I cooked your favorite."

She walks over and greets my sister as I stand with the car door open and one foot propped up, on the railing of the car leaning over the car door. That woman is amazing.

My sister, Sojourn, walks to me and gives me a hug and a kiss.

"Well, are you just going to stand there? Let's go in," She wraps one arm around my waist and I wrap my arm around her shoulder. Sojourn is the one woman in my life who has always stood beside me, through thick and thin, no matter what. No one else is more important to me. No one.

"I've missed my brother, I haven't talked to you in a while." She looks over to Sadie, "Thanks for inviting me, Sadie. I really appreciate it. I know this was your idea and not knucklehead's over here."

My woman just smiles back at her, as she unlocks the door to the apartment. She walks to the kitchen and washes her hands as she gets ready to prepare the table. She looks back at me and tells Sojourn, "Carlo and I already had appetizers. I could offer you something if you're hungry. It should be only a few minutes while the food heats up."

"Oh girl, I'm fine. Thank you. I'm just going to sit here and catch up with Carlo a bit."

Sojourn looks back up to me. "How are you handling this pregnancy, brother?"

Sojourn, has never really spent time beating around the bush, and after all these years she still calls me brother. I'd much rather she call me friend.

"It's tough. It's real tough. It's hard to consider how this baby could actually be Troy's."

"Don't I know? This baby is either the sibling to my children with Troy or my niece through you. I'm struggling with this too. Either way, this baby is part of my family."

"It's tough Sojourn. Speaking of Troy, what's up? Are you working that out?"

Sojourn just sinks and her head lands on my shoulder. She takes a deep breath and says nothing.

"Sojourn, you know I like Rick. He's a good guy, but so is Troy. Rick needs to take care of his business."

She looks up to me, "I know Carlo. I like Rick too. You're right, Troy is a good guy and a terrific father."

She leans back on my shoulder. "You're going to have to make a decision Sojourn. I don't approve of you playing both sides of the fence."

She looks up at me and kisses me on the cheek, "Thanks for being you Carlo, and staying true to who you are with me."

"Carlo, Sojourn, you can wash up and come to the table now."

As Sojourn gets up, she releases my arm and calls back to Sadie, "My brother is such a good guy. Take care of him Sadie; he's one of a kind. You could search a lifetime and not find a better man than the one you have now."

Sadie nods her head in agreement; "I plan on serving him a real good dessert tonight." She answers with a smile.

Chapter 3

Tiffany

As much as I love my husband Richard, I really don't care if I never see him again. I walk around our huge home, listening as my feet fall on the hardwood floors in pace with the beat of my heart. The realization that starting all over will be just as difficult as salvaging this marriage and this pitiful man slowly and suddenly emerges as a car coming through a thick fog. How dare he cheat on me, as if I'm not woman enough for him? I realize I've started pacing the room and working myself up again. I want to call him, but know I shouldn't. He needs to still be on punishment. Even so, my fingers dial his number and his line rings.

"Hello Tiffany."

"Richard."

"What's up?"

"I don't know Richard, I think I want a divorce." Did those words just come out of my mouth? Did I just say that?

What am I doing? I don't know what I want.

"Okay. Okay I hear you. I can't have this kind of conversation over the phone. We'll talk. Do you want me to come by?"

Well, too late to back-peddle now. Why did I say I wanted to divorce? I don't know what I want.

"Yes Richard, that's fine."

"Bye Tiffany."

"Bye."

I continue to pace the floor of this huge house and look around. My gourmet kitchen, Richard designed and had built for me. A sorrowful smile emerges, why didn't I use it more? I look on the shelves and admire all of the collectibles we've acquired from our travels all around the world. Painful reminders of a wonderful past that is dead. Gone. Nonexistent. It has to go. All of it. The couch we picked out, the table, paintings, rugs, dishes from wedding gifts, holiday gifts to each other. I hate it. I hate it. Hate it. All of this was with Richard. What would my home look like without him? Can I make it without him? What kind of marriage would I have if I stayed with this man knowing he has shared a kiss with another woman? Who knows how he really feels about her or about me? Damn it Richard! My lungs are pumping my breaths faster as my mouth tries to catch up with the pace of my lungs. I then realize I am pacing the floor and walking in and around this house so vigorously a bead of sweat is forming on my forehead. Tears have formed in my eyes and pain has crept back up on me. I hate him and that woman is a bitch!

The doorbell interrupts my poisonous thoughts. I walk to the door and peep through the peephole and I see Richard. I wipe the tear and tear residue from my face and open the door. When I see his eyes something takes over me and I slap him across the face. My hand burns from the impact.

He just looks at me with hurt in his eyes.

"Tiffany, I'm sorry you're hurting."

"You hurt us Richard. Our families, our worlds. Nothing is the same anymore."

"I know Tiffany."

"Do you love her Rick?"

"Tiffany, I didn't come to talk to you about her, I came to talk to you about us."

"*She* is the reason we are where we are."

"No, Tiffany she is not. We had problems long before that night at the Coffee Bean."

"Richard, why? Why would you kiss another woman?"

"Tiffany. I am only going to talk about us."

"Richard that is us. You kissing her with passion and love is about us, you should be kissing me like that. I am the only one who has a right to those kinds of kisses. Just me."

"Tiffany what do you want from me, what do you want me to do?"

There's that question again, what do I want to do? I have no idea. I don't know if I want him or if I hate him. I answer him by turning away in silence.

"Tiffany, we have been unhappy with each other for so long, do you want to stay like this or do you want change?"

"Richard, you keep saying we again. I was happy with you. You were the only one unhappy and running around throwing your tongue down other people's throat. That was you, not me."

"Kissing Sojourn was wrong. You're my wife, that type of intimacy should only be for you. You're right."

"Me being right isn't doing anything for this marriage Richard."

He looks back at me, with a distant pain in his eyes.

"I'm sorry you're hurting."

"Try being sorry for your bullshit. Try being sorry for that Richard."

Richard just stares back to me blankly as if that's an impossibility.

"Tiffany, I never should have kissed her. I've told you that." "Yes you disrespectful asshole, you did. You never said sorry, meaning you regret what you did. Meaning you want to make amends, meaning you love me enough to say sorry for disrespecting everything we've built and that you want to attempt to recover."

I have no idea what this man wants. His face is empty. It feels as if his heart is empty.

"Do you want to be married to me Richard, to spend the rest of your life with me?"

"The next step we take is going to be hard either way Tiffany. I don't have an answer for you."

He walks towards me. I want to collapse in his arms. I need him to rescue me from this pain as he has done for me many times before. I need him, but I don't trust his arms or his heart to catch me. Instead I retreat to the kitchen table and sit in a chair.

"Can you tell me you love me Richard?"

"I love you Tiffany." He doesn't mean it, his words sail across the room and land on me like feathers, you can barely feel the impact - it's like he hasn't said anything at all. His eyes are empty. He's just appeasing me. Right now, I'm not loving him either, but the truth is I am loving him.

"Just get out Richard. I can't stand to be in the same room with you right now."

"Tiffany."

"Do you want me Richard?" My words topple out of my mouth like rocks. My heart is burning with pain.

His mouth is silent, I look into his eyes searching for an answer and I get lost in the emptiness. His coldness chills me. He can't feel any of my pain. I'm standing right here, barren, broken and his gaze follows me as if he is watching a western on television and not involved in the heat of the battle as a major party. He might as well have asked for the divorce himself. *I know. I* know I love him. Bastard! Why can't he love me back! His emptiness has infuriated me. My pain is too much for my body to contain. A wild fire rages inside of me and my mouth breaks free from the shackles of proper composure.

"LEAVE!" I scream at the top of my lungs.

"Get out Richard! Now!" flames out of my mouth, my eyes burn with pain.

He looks at me with guilty eyes and walks toward the door. Nothing else is said and I lock the door, sliding to the floor with my back on the wall. "I love that man. Why can't he love me back?"

Chapter 4

Richard

The drive to my house was hard, it gets harder every time I go and visit Tiffany. The vibration of my phone interrupts my thoughts. I pull my car over and search for my phone to answer the call.

"Hello?"

"Hey Rick."

"Sojourn. How are you holding up?"

"I'm ok." She answers me as if she was forced to give that answer.

"Rick, we need to get ready for the next recruiting visit. It is going to be a bit different from the rest, so I want to make sure we're prepared. I have sent some modifications to you early this morning. Look over them and get back with me."

"No problem."

"Rick, I hope through all of this we can remain friends."

"I would like that, Sojourn."

"How about a penny for your thoughts then?"

"Well that's simple Sojourn. I'm a married man and I can't stop thinking about being with you. I'd take you now if I could."

"Do you feel this way with Tiffany?"

"No. Not right now."

"Have you ever felt that way about her?"

"Our sex life was never the problem in our marriage Sojourn, it was everything else. Your turn, a penny for your thoughts."

"Well that's easy for me too, my thoughts are on Sadie and this baby. This baby will be part of my family no matter who the father is."

"Speaking of fathers, I saw Troy at Church today."

"Ouch. Awkward. How did it go?"

"It was a bit of an awkward moment, but I spoke to him."

"How did he respond?"

"He spoke back. We didn't have much to talk about, as you can imagine. Troy is a good man. In any other situation, we would probably be best friends. The only difference between him and me is that if you were married to me, I never would have let you go in the first place."

"That's what Tiffany is saying about you. Maybe that's why you're still married and not divorced."

I don't answer.

"You know Rick, if I were Tiffany, *I would hold on to you too*. In fact, I'd fight like hell to keep my marriage together."

"You see Sojourn, comments like that grow me closer to you."

"Tiffany is giving you those words in actions, you're growing closer to the wrong person."

"I seem to be growing closer to a woman that makes me feel good to be a man when I'm around her."

"Rick, don't do this. You know how I feel about you. We both need time to sort through things. My ex-husband wants to reconcile, I'm torn. Just like you."

"You miss Troy don't you?"

She responds back with a small chuckle, "I don't have a chance to miss him. We stay in pretty good contact, because of the kids."

"We see each other almost every day, yet there are times, that I miss you."

"You don't know what you want Rick. You need the space to figure that out. I do too."

"I'm heading to the office Sojourn, I'll review your changes and get back to you. I don't have internet set up in my apartment yet, so I'll probably be working at the office late tonight."

"Alright Rick. Troy has the boys tonight so call me when you send it over. I'm anxious to read it."

"No problem Sojourn. I'll talk with you later."

"Bye, Rick."

"Good bye."

As I drive into the parking garage, I try to focus on work and getting done what I need to do to get caught up. Thoughts of Sojourn and Tiffany swim in my head, circling around like a pack of sharks ready to attack any other thoughts that attempt to surface. I love Sojourn, but I'm married to Tiffany. Having feelings for another woman like this isn't fair to Tiffany. Not giving this marriage another shot with all of my effort isn't fair either.

As I walk in my office thoughts scatter away at the surprise of seeing my secretary Shannon.

"Shannon? What are you doing here on a weekend?"

"Hi Rick, I know things have been really difficult for you lately, so I started working on some of the projects that are late. We have new deadlines Monday."

"Shannon. Are you serious? But how, my work isn't your area."

"Rick, if you lose your job, I lose mine - so we have to take care of each other."

Words can't express how I feel about Shannon's support right now. I look at her like I am putty in her hands.

She smiles, "I may not have a degree in engineering, but I have the mind of one. Working around you does that to a person."

The only thing that manages to leave my lips is a "Thank You, Shannon."

"That's what I get paid for!" she says with a smile.

"You have a report due at the board meeting next week over your recruiting visits and three over-due reports based on your sites. I've worked on two of them and I'm completing the third."

She pushes a couple of buttons on her computer rotates the mouse and the tosses me a thumb drive.

"Here you go Rick, load these on your computer and finish the first two off. I'll have the third one finished for you in about two more hours. Oh, I'm ordering a midnight meal for two, any special requests."

"Shannon you are too much. Thank you for everything. You have already done way too much, go home and get some rest, I can take it from here."

She looks at me with a smile. "I'll leave when our work is complete."

She winks as I walk towards my office.

"Besides Rick, I love the overtime pay!"

"You deserve every penny Shannon."

I walk into my office and finally, I'm able to focus. I owe Shannon big time.

Chapter 5

Shannon

Rick has been a mess since he moved out of the house with his wife. And to think a kiss from Sojourn started it all. I look at the clock in the office realize I should have left hours ago. Someone around here needs to work, Rick just isn't able to focus right now. I've written so many reports with Rick in the past, I believe I can catch him up. The last thing he needs is trouble at work. I have a professional respect for Sojourn, but she needs to keep her eyes and her hands off of Rick. The last thing he needs is an ambitious female coming into his world attempting to destroy it.

I see a figure approaching the office and as it comes closer my heart warms as I recognize the figure and stagger as Rick's. He is an incredibly sexy man. Even though he greets me with a look of surprise on his face,

I'm not at all surprised to see him. With all of this work that needs to be done, this is exactly where he needs to be. As I update him on the progress I have made, I see a look of relief on his face, his eyes cry thank you to me. I'm happy to do it for him and I'd do a lot more if he ever gave me the chance. After we finish these last two reports, I'll order a romantic dinner and bottle of wine to celebrate, who knows what could happen once his inhibitions are relaxed. This will be an evening he won't forget. I hear my phone buzzing and search for my purse. It's a text message from Jason, my ex-boyfriend. *Jessica knows it was you. She's furious. Still on vacation.* Great. Just what I need last year's drama taking away my fun. Jason broke up with me to work things out with Jessica and we've both moved on. Why can't she? If her relationship falls apart, it's all on her. I'm long out of the picture. He needs to work that out. Either she's going to forgive and forget or remember and regret. Whichever, neither have anything to do with me anymore. I've moved on, Rick is about to be single, we have a great working relationship and I know he's ready to explore. So am I. I delete the text message from my phone, and try to delete it from my memory. My focus is all on Rick right now.

No phone, no one in the office, just me and Rick - exactly how I want it. I peek back and see Rick in his office typing away at the reports. This is my chance to set the mood. I call my contact and see if he can meet me with our dinner. Rick is going to be so surprised.

"Hey, Josh did your brother hook me up?"

"Yeah, he's boxing up the dinners now, I can bring them to you."

"Josh, if you could that would be great. Call me on my cell when you get downstairs."

"That's the least I can do for you since you saved me from losing my job. I'll be there in about twenty minutes."

"Perfect Josh, see you then."

I peek back at Rick and see him reach for his phone. Oh no, not tonight. I walk into his office and playfully grab it from his hands, as I look down at it, I see Sojourn's name pop up. She is not going to ruin my perfect night with Rick. Not tonight. When I grab the phone from his hands, I see the look of surprise on his face as if I have just crossed the line. I know I have.

"Focus boss. I'll take this and have it for you when you get ready to leave. No interruptions tonight. You and I need to finish."

"Looks like you're the boss tonight."

His acceptance warms me up and moves me closer to my target - a connection. "I just emailed you the third report. I'm moving on to the reports regarding the recruiting visits. These shouldn't take long. We finished the New York report already; the California report is near completion. It just needs to be cleaned up. Once those are done. We can enjoy dinner and go home."

I walk back out of his office and close the door. I quickly email him the last of the reports so I can get him where I want him, in my arms. I go to my closet and pull out my huge picnic basket. I completely clear off my desk and lay white linen tablecloths on the desk. I peak back at Rick and he is totally occupied by his work. Perfect, he won't notice a thing.

I set the table with a romantic centerpiece, place the long stemmed candles and light them up. I get a wine bucket, go to the lounge, fill it with ice and grab my bottle of chilled wine from the freezer. I almost skip to back to the office. Tonight is the night this man is going to fall in love with me. I grab my phone and run downstairs to check to see if Josh has made it and just my luck he is walking up to the door as I am approaching it. This night could not get any more perfect.

"Hey Shannon, you know my brother is one of the best chefs in the city, you should enjoy this."

"I'm sure I will Josh."

"You know lobster is a natural aphrodisiac so behave yourself." He says playfully.

"I definitely plan on not behaving myself." I respond back with a smile.

He laughs, "Well are we even now?"

"You bet."

"Ok, see you Shannon."

"Bye Josh."

I glide back upstairs and place the plates on the table. Things are perfect. I freshen my make-up so I glow in the candlelight and spray a hint of perfume on my neck and wrist.

Everything is set, now all I need is my man.

"Rick, you should be finished by now. Come out and share a celebratory dinner with me. We did it!"

Rick emerges from his office and his eyes are tired and red. He looks at me with a boyish smile.

This midnight meal is going to be the beginning of Rick viewing me as a woman and not a secretary. I eagerly pour our first two glasses of wine and we toast. I'm anxious for the natural vitamins in the lobster to begin to sexually stimulate his body. Even if we don't do anything, if he begins to desire me in this way, I would have made progress. The desire is half the battle.

Rick makes small talk with me as we eat, but I see his eyes sparkle. He wants me. I feel it. As we finish dinner, we move to the leather couch in the front of the office. He sits right next to me. Proximity, just what I've been waiting for. We drink more wine and I try to get inch closer to him, almost leaning my head on his shoulder when someone approaches our door. Damn.

Chapter 6

Troy

I go to children's church and pick up the boys. We load up in the car and head out. The only person missing in this picture is their mother.

"Alright fellas, what do you want for dinner tonight?"

"Daddy, please can we go to Granny's?" they both cry from the backseat.

"Yeah, no problem."

We turn into my mother's driveway and she is already standing at the screen door with both hands on her hips. The kids bust out of the car and you can hear her voice in the distance, "Are those my precious baby boys coming to see me?"

They run to her screaming, "Granny!"

I get out of the car and begin to approach my mom, "Troy you go on now, let me spend some time with my grand babies, you can come back in a while. I need some help in the garden in the back and they love working with me back there."

She kisses me on the forehead, "We'll talk tonight." She looks into my eyes and just her glance warms me. "Go on and take care of your business son. I love you."

The boys rush in the house and I walk back to the car.

Before I can pull out of the driveway my phone rings, I'm hoping it's Sojourn, but the caller ID says Tiffany.

"Hey Tiffany, what's up?"

"Troy, I need someone to talk to. My two best friends, and co-workers are too wrapped up in their own lives right now. Jess is on another vacation with her husband Jason, Sadie is wrapped up in this pregnancy and you're the next best friend in line. Besides that you might need a shoulder to lean on too."

"You must have just encountered Rick?"

"Yes. Can you come by?"

"Yeah. Sure why not? I only have a short time because I need to get my boys tonight."

"Thanks Troy. Hurry and get here."

I pull out of the driveway and head to Tiffany's house. The last person I want to talk about is Rick, but maybe this conversation will give me insight into what is going on with Rick and Sojourn. As I'm driving, Deacon Mitchell's name pops up on my caller ID.

"Hey what's up man?"

"Brother Troy, just wanted to check on you. I know you're feeling like your life is not in the best place right now."

"Mitch the place I'm in right now completely sucks."

"Well it may get worse before it gets better, so just prepare yourself. God wants all of the credit if it is in His will to restore your family."

"What do you mean?"

"Well he wants you and everyone else to be able to look at your life and say, 'only God could've put that family back together.' He wants the room to prove He's God."

"I hear you Mitch, but I don't need things to get much worse than they are right now. Really."

With that last comment, my mind jumps to Sadie and this pregnancy. I need to start preparing my family if this baby is mine. I look and see the house that Rick built in front of me and pull into the driveway. I can't get this man out of my world.

"Deacon, I'm pulling up to a friend's house. I'll give you a shout back."

"Alright, later man."

"Later."

I get out of the car and make my way down Tiffany's walkway leading to her door. It winds back and forth with perfect landscaping, bursting with color on both sides. She has a big hard solid wood door made from what looks like a Mahogany wood or wood stain. I knock on the door and the wood is solid, you can't really hear a thing so I reach to ring the doorbell. I smile as it plays a loud deep melody inside of the house, letting her know I'm here.

She comes to the door in a robe and when I look into her eyes they are puffy and red. She must have been crying.

"Hey." I say quietly. I feel a sting from the breeze of pain that runs out of the house when she opens the door. Tiffany looks up to me and falls into an embrace in my arms.

"Please, don't let go. I need this right now."

I just hold on to her and feel her vulnerabilities take refuge in my arms.

"It's been so hard Troy. I love him, but I'm the only one in love in this relationship. His love is lost. All that we have left is this commitment of marriage, but what good is it? He doesn't want me anymore."

Hearing Tiffany talk about Richard is killing me. He's not in love with her anymore because he is so in love with Sojourn. "He loves Sojourn," slides out of my mouth leaving a trail of pain the way a slug slides through mud. "No. That's not possible Troy. He's too in love with himself. He's completely smitten with his needs, his wants, his desires, his goals, and his future. There's no room in his heart to love anyone else. Not his wife or his mistress!"

She buries her head back in my chest, "I told him I want a divorce."

I just continue to hold her and listen. She releases her embrace and guides me to the couch. We both sit down. She lifts my arm and wraps it around her shoulder and she seeks comfort in my arms again. I don't mind. It feels good to shelter a woman; it's just a reminder of the fact that I am man.

"What are we going to do Troy? Are you still going to restore your marriage to Sojourn?"

"That's up to her Tiffany. The door is open, she hasn't walked through yet."

"You know Troy, the night that I was on stage with you and played the piano, we kissed. So maybe we are just as guilty as Rick and Sojourn."

"It was a different kind of kiss, Tiffany."

"I felt something in that kiss Troy, something I haven't felt with Rick in a long time."

"Tiff, it was just the energy of the night. All first kisses are the most memorable ones."

"You think it was because it was a first kiss?"

"Yeah, and the energy of the night."

Her head lifts off my shoulder and she grabs my chin gently turning it towards her and her lips lightly land on my lips and leave. I reach back to her and chase after another gentle kiss just like the one she just gave me and it is returned. I feel my body getting warm, light tingles of adrenalin begin to strike my body. She approaches my lips again and gently kisses me more passionately and her robe falls off her shoulder revealing her breast.

"Tiffany we..."

She interrupts me, "You felt it didn't you. You felt connected to me."

"Tiffany I feel like I'm going to lay you on this couch and take you in a minute."

"You felt connected Troy, admit it."

"Tiffany I feel sexually aroused. I need more than your body to feel connected, I need a woman's heart and her mind."

I lift her robe back over her shoulder and lean back on the couch, trying to relax my body before this sexual energy takes over.

"Well I'm aroused too, why don't we do something about it."

I think of Sojourn and my promise to save myself for her. I think about Rick and how sleeping with Tiffany would be the ultimate revenge. Then I look at Tiffany and realize that her pain is influencing her right now, she'll regret this later. Will I?

"Tiffany, if we do this we're no better than Rick and Sojourn."

"Forget about them Troy. They didn't have any regard for us when they did whatever they did."

She lifts up and straddles across my lap. Revealing that she has nothing on under her robe. One night of passion can lead to a lifetime of regrets. I look into Tiffany's eyes and she has already unbuckled my pants attempting to free my body from the restriction of my boxers and my pants. Her robe is barely holding on to her body.

"Tiffa....."

"Troy, forget about them. Just for one night, let's not let them drive our hearts and our minds. Can we just escape from this hell of trying to win the hearts of Richard and Sojourn, just for this one night?"

"Tiffany, it never ends up being just one night. If Rick finds out, it's over for you two."

"...and what Troy, if Sojourn finds out you get a divorce? Newsflash - worst case scenario is already here."

She topples off of my lap and falls backwards on the couch throwing her legs across my thighs. The flap of her robe falls to the side of her thigh revealing more of the nothing she's wearing underneath.

"Troy, we should be chasing and discovering what makes us happy in life, not chasing them, what has chasing them brought us?"

I think about that, and she's right. Trying to create a situation for Sojourn to fall back in love with me and the hope that she will has brought me nothing but disappointment. I look back down at Tiffany's thighs and her nakedness playing peek-a-boo with me.

"Tiffany, us having sex with each other may not bring happiness."

"We don't know what it will bring, let's see."

"You are a persistent, sexy something." I say as I lean over and kiss her on the neck. Damn! What am I doing? Shit. I need to be able to control this.

"You're going down tonight Troy. We both know it's going to happen. I just want you to give me all you got. So I need you to free your mind."

She walks over to the kitchen, pours two glasses of wine, turns on the music and walks back over to me.

"Let's experience harmony, you know that moment when the music and our movements are one."

She lies across my lap and loosens her robe.

"This is my glass of wine" She sets it on the table.

She holds the other glass in her hand and lies back across my lap. "This is your glass of wine. Do you want it?"

I look at her and nod my head. I feel like taking her, and it has nothing to do with who she is, her pain, or her beauty, this is about me. If I do this, it would punish Rick, back him off Sojourn. No. No, I can't use Tiffany like this. Damn. I want her.

"One rule, you can't drink it from the glass." She pours it down her chest, "Lick it up."

I watch as the wine rolls down her chest around her breasts and puddles near her belly button.

"Drink up, Troy."

Chapter 7

Carlo

"Carlo, are you coming with me to the next doctor's appointment to see the baby on the ultrasound monitor?"

"Sadie, you know I can't take off work."

"I know Carlo, but you aren't showing much excitement about the baby. I thought if you came with me to the doctor, it might make you feel more connected. Jessica has been coming with me, but she is out of town, on vacation right now."

I look at Sadie with resentment in my eyes. I keep my mouth shut because I know the next words that come out of my mouth are going to slice through her like butter. Why would I want to feel connected to something that may not even be mine? She just doesn't get that. She doesn't really understand how frustrating it is for me to know that the baby growing inside of her may belong to another man - a man that has explored every part of her body. And he's a man that is one of my best friends. Fuck! I turn my head back toward the TV in disgust.

"Carlo? You are excited about the baby aren't you?"

I try hard to pretend that I can't hear anything coming out of her mouth.

"Carlo?"

"Carlo."

She gets up and leaves, finally she gets my point.

I flip aimlessly through the channels and try to find something to watch to take my mind off this shithole of a situation I'm in. I see Sadie come out of the bedroom with the corner of my eye, but don't stop looking at the television.

She stands right in front of the TV and turns it off. I look up and she is standing in a beige negligee. Her belly is poking right through.

"Sadie, what are you doing?"

"I'm turning the TV off, so I can turn you on."

She turns on some soft music, turns the lights off and stands behind me massaging my neck.

"Carlo, please tell me why you look sick every time I bring this baby up."

Damn. More baby talk.

"Bella. I have a lot on my mind. That's all."

"Carlo. Look, I didn't ask for this to happen, but it has. We both have to learn to live with this."

"Sadie, you slept with my best friend." I slide away and look at her. When I move, her hands break off of my shoulders and I feel the tension surge back up my neck.

"How was I supposed to know you knew each other? When I told you I was reserving my body just for you, I meant that. We haven't been together since I committed to you."

"It's just a messed up situation, Bella. If this baby is not mine, what am I supposed to do? We both know Troy is going actively raise this child and he is not going to want another man's help. It's like I'll be a stranger in my own house. I can't live like that, Sadie. I'm not that kind of man."

I turn back around and lean back on the couch while she bends over the couch wrapping her arms around me in an embrace, resting her head on mine.

"Carlo. I don't have any answers. This is new for me too. My body is going through all of these massive changes. I didn't plan a pregnancy. You know we used protection. I don't know what is next. How am I going to work, go to school, raise a child and create a home for a family? I don't know if I may lose you over this. It's hard, Carlo. We both are just going to have to exercise some faith that this will all come together to work for our good."

"Bella, I admit I have been a bit emotionally selfish. I know I've only been concerned with how I feel." I kiss her on the cheek, "I'm ready to listen. Tell me how you've been holding up."

She walks around the couch, sits next to me and rests her head on my shoulder.

"I don't want to lose you, Carlo."

"I'm here, Bella."

"Let's fall in love with this baby together Carlo - as parents."

I reach across and touch the place on her body where the baby is growing. I touch her without thinking about who the father is, or how this happened. As I get ready to remove my hand from gently touching her, my body feels like the wind has just been punched out of my stomach. I can't pull my hand off, it feels as if the baby is grabbing me from inside of her stomach. My child. My body still feels weak as I begin to accept that this is *my* child. *My* child is reaching out to me. "I love you too." I quietly whisper to my baby through the touch of my hand.

"I'll be there Sadie. I'll come with you to the next appointment. It's time I met my child."

Chapter 8

Richard

As I turn my computer on and begin to load Shannon's thumb drive. I see her walk in through the corner of my eye.

"What's up Shannon?"

She walks over to my water wall, turns it on and turns on my CD player with the nature sounds.

"Just thought I'd try and focus your thoughts, in case life attempts to creep in and interrupt your flow. You think better when your office creates the right mood."

"Thanks Shannon. I guess you know everything about me don't you?"

"Well not quite everything, but I'm a quick study."

She walks out of my office and goes back to her desk. She certainly is what I need most, at the moment.

I load up the two reports she started and begin to clean them up. I see my phone vibrating in the corner and Shannon walks in as she hears it too. As I reach over to answer it, she takes it from my hand, I see Sojourn's name pop up on the caller ID.

"Focus boss. I'll take this and have it for you when you get ready to leave. No interruptions tonight. You and I need to finish."

I want to tell her to bring me back that phone, but I resist.

"Looks like you're the boss tonight."

She smiles. "I just emailed you the third report. I'm moving on to the reports regarding the recruiting visits. These shouldn't take long. We finished the New York report already; the California report is near completion. It just needs to be cleaned up. Once those are done, we can enjoy dinner and go home."

"Thanks Shannon."

Dinner, I'll enjoy. Going home. Not so much. I turn back to my computer and continue working on these reports.

When I look up, I realize I've been at this for hours, but I've finished all three reports, the recruiting visit reports and opened up Sojourn's proposal for our next recruiting visit. Something I am definitely looking forward to.

"Rick, you should be finished by now. Come out and share a celebratory dinner with me. We did it!"

I walk out of my office and Shannon has blown me away. She has set up her desk as a dinner table. Complete with a linen tablecloth, candles and a centerpiece.

"Shannon, how did you do this? When.."

"I slipped out while you were working Rick. Now let's eat. Steak, lobster tails, baked potato and grilled asparagus."

"Wow. How..."

"Connections." She smiles, "Our delivery boy, has a brother that is a chef at the hotel down the street. I saved his behind one day when he misplaced one of our deliveries, I just called in the favor."

She pours wine in both our glasses. I look at her like she is superwoman, "Shall we toast?"

She lifts up her glass to mine.

"To a wonderful secretary and a treasured friend. You're beautiful."

Shannon smiles, "I'll drink to that. Flattery will get you everywhere Rick."

"That's not flattery, that's truth."

I stop eating and look at Shannon, "I don't know how I could have made it without you."

She smiles with a sparkle in her eye.

"Shannon you have selflessly sacrificed for me. That means a lot to me. Thank you."

"That's what you pay me for boss." she says, and attempts to dismiss all of this as if it was nothing, as if it was in her job description.

"You weren't my secretary tonight Shannon, you were a friend. Your friendship is priceless."

"Honestly boss, I didn't think you would notice."

She gets up and clears both our "to go" plates away in the trash and goes over to the waiting couch in our office space. I get up and sit next to her. She pours more wine into our glasses.

"I noticed." I respond looking into her eyes.

"I have cheesecake. I know that's your favorite. I'm dieting so it's all yours."

I laugh out loud, "So you want me to be the big fat pig?"

She smiles with me and our light banter is interrupted by the figure of a woman standing in the doorway. As she walks through the threshold the light hits her face and reveals Sojourn.

"So you're throwing a party without me. That wasn't very nice."

My body begins to smile, "Hey Sojourn. What are you doing here?"

"Well, I've been blowing your phone up. You told me you were going to go over the proposal, when you didn't answer, I decided just to drive up and check on you."

"Lucky us. Have some wine."

I get up and get some wine for Sojourn and she sits on the couch next to Shannon.

"Shannon was smart enough to put my phone away so I could focus on work, uninterrupted. Where is my phone Shannon?"

She gets up walks over to her desk, unlocks her drawer, pulls out my phone and places it in my hand. I look down and see nine missed calls.

"Sojourn, this is the best secretary, best friend ever. Shannon has me caught up on everything now." I place my arm around Shannon's neck like we are childhood friends.

Sojourn gives Shannon a smile that looks like she just scratched her eyes out.

"Wow, Shannon. That was awfully nice of you."

"He pays me well to take care of him, I like my job." she answers wrapping her arm around my waist.

Shannon looks at Sojourn with a grimacing smile.

"Do I smell seafood Rick?"

"Yeah. We just had the absolute best steak and lobster dinner."

I look at Shannon as she is packing her things up. My approach intentionally interrupts her packing. I'm feeling a bit buzzed.

"Wow steak, lobster and candles this time of night, how did you manage that?"

"Shannon is magic Sojourn. I'm telling you the best. Thanks once again, Shannon. You were just what I needed." I give her a hug and a kiss on the cheek.

"Sojourn, let me walk Shannon out and I'll be right back up to go over the proposal with you."

Shannon doesn't even look back to say goodbye to Sojourn.

"I'm ready Rick. Let's go."

Chapter 9

Troy

I look at the puddle of wine forming on Tiffany's stomach and want to respond to her intimate invitation. Then I look into her eyes and see brokenness, a need to just be wanted and loved. Her eyes bleed with pain. I bleed with her. I don't want to bleed anymore.

"Not like this Tiffany." The words spill out of my mouth from my heart.

"Troy." Her words leave her mouth and land on me like a boulder. I know my rejection hurt her, it hurt me to say no. She covers herself back up with her robe.

"Come here Tiff." I grab her and envelope her in my arms. Her arms embrace me back and she digs her cheek into my chest, resting her head on me. I feel warm tears from her eyes land on my skin.

"We're going to get through this Tiffany, both of us."

"I cry every night Troy. Everyday my thoughts center on him. Some moments I miss him so much, then the next moment, I hate him. It's like I'm stuck. I'm trying to move on but the pain just won't go away."

"The pain doesn't go away Tiffany. I've never gotten over the remorse of losing my family to divorce. I've just had to learn to live with it. Forgive myself and press forward. Press forward with this painful thorn in my side."

Tiffany looks up to me and searches my eyes, as if I am the one that can deliver her from this pain. I can't.

"Tiffany, I can't get you out of this. We can walk side by side and go through this together. We can try to create situations in our lives and make decisions that won't lead to the creation of more painful endings. We can support each other."

She reaches up and softly kisses me on lips. I kiss her back.

"The one thing we can't do is assume that a moment of physical pleasure will heal years of hurt."

"Troy, I still love him. I feel so stupid. How can I still love a man that has treated me like this? A man that has obviously stopped loving me."

"You are lovely and worthy to be loved – even if he's not the one giving it to you. Don't think that love won't come back and find you, just be prepared it may have a different face."

Tiffany buries her head back in my chest.

"Tiff, I have to go. I need to run to The Coffee Bean office and the race to pick up my boys. It's our smoothie and movie night. We're going to pop some popcorn, watch movies and make smoothies."

"Troy, can I come? I could really use a break from this house and thinking about Richard with every corner I turn."

I don't normally bring women around my boys. I know she needs a break, but I'm not sure if it's a good idea to bring another woman around my children, even if it is a friend. I look back at her and her wounded heart moves me. It won't hurt. What harm could come out of it?

"Sure. It's still a bit early, so why don't you change and meet me at the park downtown. In about 2 hours. I'll let them run around a while in the park and then we'll have our movie and smoothies night."

"Thanks Troy. I am really looking forward to this."

"No problem Tiff."

"Troy?"

"Yeah?"

"I love you for this."

"Well I'm glad someone loves this raggedy old man."

I give Tiffany a hug and a kiss on the forehead. "See you later Tiff.

Chapter 10

Troy

I love the Coffee Bean, it's like a sanctuary to escape the pain and stress of regular life and just unwind. As soon as I walk through the doors, the office manager approaches me and gives me a short list of updates and communications to review.

As I sit with the list in my hand at the bar, I order a cup of coffee.

A pretty little thing sits next to me.

"Hi." I nod my head. "What's up?"

"Just trying to get all that is in my head to take off; even brain power needs a break every now and then."

I lightly smile and chuckle, "I agree."

"Troy!"

"Hey man!" I see an old buddy from school approach. Man, I

haven't seen him in years.

"Hey!" He passes me his card, "Stay in touch this time buddy! How are you and Sojourn?"

"Divorced, but good. And you?""Married, and well you know how that is.""Good?"

"Oh yeah, the best. Absolutely marvelous, the most wonderful thing, I've ever...."

"...she's here?" I interrupt him smiling.

"Yep, and when you see her tell her I said this is the best marriage in the whole wide world!"He laughs, "Then maybe I'll get some tonight!"

I laugh with him. We bump coffee mugs. "Here's to you keeping that magic man."

"Call me, Troy.""Yeah. Count on it."

I turn back and smile at the lady still sitting next to me.

"Old friend?"

"Yeah."

"My name is Shannon."

"Troy.""Yes. I heard"She smiles and downs a shot of alcohol.

"Want to fuck?"

Is she serious? I look at her trying to determine if she's serious.

She reaches in her purse and pulls out a condom and slides it to me, under a cocktail napkin.

I look at the cocktail napkin and grab her hand, "I have my own supply. Come with me to the back."

She doesn't answer. She takes the cocktail napkin and condom and places it back in her purse.

She follows me to the back. All that sexual energy toward Tiffany just found its release.

I know this is wrong. I know I'm supposed to be saving myself for Sojourn, but this isn't Tiffany. This isn't connected sex. It's not revenge sex. It doesn't really count. I don't know this woman; she doesn't really know me either. It's that surprise sex that just happens sometimes with no strings attached. The kind of sex that no one really knows about, so it doesn't really count; Sojourn will never know. My way of reliving stress, some people get a massage. This is good for me.

Chapter 11

Troy

"Alright boys, now that the movie is over, go and put your smoothie glasses in the kitchen sink, brush your teeth, put on your pajamas and head to bed. I'm coming to say prayers with you and tuck you in, in just a moment."

I look back at Tiffany, "Now you see the other part of my life when I'm not at the Coffee Bean or my telemarketing job."

"You have so many different sides to your life and personality Troy. How is it you were able to keep it together when I was putting the moves on you?"

I chuckle, "I didn't think I could resist. I just knew we were both fighting our pains and sex would have added to it."

I look up and reflect, "The other part of it is that a small part of me hoped that making better decisions would help me win my wife back."

"She's lucky she has your heart. To be the object of your affection must be a beautiful thing."

"Well I don't know. She doesn't seem to be responsive right now."

"I hope she never responds, she doesn't deserve you."

"Tiffany, I'm still weak. I didn't have sex with you because I would've been using you. I still slip up. Don't get it twisted. I like fucking."

I look at Tiffany in silence. "I better put the boys down, be right back." As I prepare to exit, I see a body approaching. "Sojourn?" I look at her with shock, then my eyes shift to Tiffany and can only imagine what is going through Sojourn's head. I know that there is no way I'm going to be able to explain my way out of this one. Sojourn looks at Tiffany as if she is an intruder.

"I used my key. What's going on Troy?"

"Sojourn. It's not what it looks like."

"Well what it looks like is that you and the kids had a movie date. Apparently, I'm the uninvited guest."

I hear the kids running around upstairs. "I need to check on my boys."

"I'll come with you and tuck them..."

"No Sojourn, wait here. I don't want them to see you, and become so excited that they won't go to sleep."

Now I hear crying, "I'll be right back. Sojourn, try not to jump to any conclusions."

I look back at Tiffany and all I see in her eyes is hate. Damn. This is why I should stick to my rules and not bring any woman around my children. Deacon was right; my situation is getting worse before it's getting better. I can't stop myself from this downward spiral. Have I fallen out of God's grasp? Whenever I try to do right, evil is right there with me.

I race up the stairs, put the kids in the bed, and pray with them.

"Boys, is there anything we need to talk to God about tonight?"

They look into my eyes, the youngest reads my heart, and the oldest reads my face.

"Daddy, you can do all the talking tonight, we'll just pray with you."

Children truly are a father's crown. I bend on my knees and kneel across the bed. My words get caught in my throat and my eyes well up in the darkness. My oldest says, "God we pray for the same thing Daddy is praying for. Amen."

The youngest says, "and we also want to tell Mary, your momma we love her too."

The oldest tells the youngest, "Tell God to come and get Daddy's prayer because it's stuck in his mouth."

"No, you tell Him."

"God, come and get Daddy's prayer because he's trying to say too much at one time and it's stuck in his mouth and we don't want him to choke and die. Amen."

The youngest says, "Amen."

The oldest looks at me, "Daddy, you can't say all the words at one time, because you will choke, just like when you're eating. Take your time and use one word at a time so your words don't get stuck."

The youngest chimes in, "and chew with your mouth closed."

I grab them both and hug them. "Thank you boys, I'll take my time next time."

I kiss them and tears run down my face. I'm trying so hard to restore this family. Lord I hope I'm doing the right thing. I know. I know. Shannon counted too. How do I stop myself?

As I go back down the stairs, I pause as I overhear Tiffany addressing Sojourn.

"Just so you know. Troy did me a favor, by giving me an opportunity to get out of my house. Nothing happened between us. But just so you're clear, it's not because I didn't try. I threw everything I had on him trying to seduce him. He resisted, mostly because he's hurting because of you. He loves you so damn much, it's sickening."

She looks at Sojourn with scorn.

"The part that is the most sickening of all is that you have your head so far up my husband's ass, you can't see what a treasure you have in Troy."

"You have no idea how I feel about Troy, or what we've been through. I'm not going to discuss any of this with you or defend myself to you, Tiffany."

"I'm sure you won't. You're a disrespectful bitch who stole my husband. Troy deserves better than you. How can he ever look at you and not see the moment when you kissed my husband and told him you loved him. My husband."

"Tiffany, I'm not the evil person you think I am. I've made mistakes. I've made them with Troy, and I've made them with Rick. You're not the only one in pain."

"I have no sympathy for you."

"Well you should, then maybe you would be woman enough to own up to the mistakes you made with Rick. I'm no more bitch than you are!"

"Don't blame me for what you did with a married man."

"Don't blame me for the unresolved problems you never fixed in your marriage. You drove your husband away."

"Sojourn, you know nothing about my marriage."

"I may not know about your marriage, but I do know that if any of us had a perfect marriage, neither one of us would be here now. We've both made mistakes and we're both paying for them now. You tried to seduce Troy and Rick is your husband, you should be seducing him, you're just as much of a bitch as I am."

"It's hard to seduce my husband Richard, when he has his bitch shoving her tongue down his throat."

"I've made mistakes Tiffany and am paying for them with my blood. Bitches bleed too."

"I have no respect for you, Sojourn. None. Yes, I made mistakes during my marriage; but I was still married to Rick, not you. You had no right kissing my husband. None. You're a blinded woman Sojourn and you don't deserve a man like Troy. You'll never be able to appreciate and see what a remarkable man he is. Even on Troy's worst, problem-filled day, he's more of a man than you are a woman!"

"I know Troy is a good man Tiffany. I don't need you telling me anything about him."

"Someone should tell him about you though, he's so blinded he can't see you for who you really are, but I see you. I see a woman he will never be able to trust. By the way, if you really are in love with my husband, you won't be able to trust him either. If he did it to me, he'll do it to you. Betrayal is in his blood now. You helped put it there."

That's enough. I step out from behind the wall. They both look at me with red eyes.

"Tiffany, let me walk you to your car."

Sojourn sits on the love seat and buries her head in her hands.

"Tiffany, you will always have my friendship, but I have to ask that you respect my house. Even if you don't respect Sojourn, she is the mother of my children and everyone in this house loves her, even in a state of imperfection."

Tiffany grabs her purse and swings it across her shoulder as if she is trying to slap Sojourn with it.

As we walk out of the door she asks me, "Troy, how long were you standing there?"

"Long enough. Tiffany, I know you're hurting, we all are..."

"Troy, I'm sorry."

"I know. It's ok. Forget about it. Keep moving toward that place of healing. I'm working on meeting you there. Just, don't be so quick to judge. I've made mistakes too. I'm no more man than Rick is or than Sojourn is woman. We all fall short Tiffany, all of us."

Suddenly, I'm hit with the realization I'm nobody to hate Rick. I'm guilty of my own sin; some of the same sins as Rick. Deacon Mitchell was right. Hating Rick, is hating myself, I'm no better than he is. What I hate, is not having my family together. I bring my attention back to Tiffany and give her a hug and she gets in her car. I look back at the house as Tiffany pulls off. I don't know if I want to go in there. I don't feel like fighting with Sojourn or trying to explain this situation. I'm tired. I drag myself down the sidewalk to the door and when I turn the doorknob, Sojourn looks up to me from the couch.

"Troy, I never should have come unannounced."

Her eyes are blood red and tear stained. Tiffany's words wounded her. I go to the couch and sit next to her. I wrap my arm around her and pull her into my chest, resting her head on my shoulder.

"Tiffany is right Troy. I don't deserve a man like you."

"Sojourn, we're both a work in progress. I'm broken and stumbling through this too. Be patient, but don't give up. I love you."

Chapter 12

Tiffany

Why did I act like that in Troy's house? Troy is fighting to restore his relationship. Jason fought to restore his with Jessica
and they're on a second vacation now. Maybe I should fight to keep
mine, maybe Richard is fighting too. I need to talk to him. I just
want to know if he loves me enough to give me some hope to fight
for this, or if I just need to walk away. If he can tell me he loves
me, I'll know. I'll have some type of confirmation, some reason to
hold on to the possibility that I can have my husband back. I just
need to hold on to something. I drive up to the apartment where
Richard is staying and park outside. I see his car; I know he's in
there. I'm terrified. I can't handle any more rejection through am-
bivalence from him. I can't just keep reliving this rejection over and

over. Please Rick, give me something to hold on to, are we worth this fight? I wipe my face clean and open the car door. I just need some sign that our relationship means something. I need to know that I mean something. I walk to Rick's door I feel my hand moving to knock and his door and then stop. What if....no, I can't keep second-guessing. I knock on his door. I don't hear anything, so I knock again. This time I hear the door unlock and he turns the knob cracking the door open and that's it. I push it open and see nothing but darkness.

"Lock the door, I'm in the bedroom."

I lock the door back and walk to the bedroom.

"What are you doing back Sojourn, you miss me already?"

He thinks I'm Sojourn. Bastard. "No Richard, it's your other bitch. The one you're married too."

"Tiffany."

I turn the lights on.

"Tiffany, I'm sorry. I thought she was coming back over to work on a project we haven't finished."

"Richard please, spare me with your lies. You don't work in the bedroom in the dark."

"I was going to get up, Tiffany."

"In your underwear?"

"Rick, just save it. I'd rather you just shut-up, than keep lying to me. Don't you have enough respect to just tell me the truth?"

"I do respect you Tiffany. I don't want to hurt you more than what you are already hurting."

"The lies hurt much more than the truth ever could."

We just sit on his bed in silence.

"Rick, I love you so much; but you sicken me. You're lies are like a disease that invade my heart and slowly kills me off. How could you be so selfish? How could you completely turn your back on me? I don't understand how your own needs could become more important than all that we have shared. You were the love of my life, and now you're this self-serving bastard."

"Tiffany, I served you for so long. I neglected to serve myself. Now, I'm taking care of me."

"Don't lie to yourself. Served me? You purchased me, bought things to make me smile. Smiles never were because of what you wanted to do for me, you did those things so I could run around and tell the world how wonderful you were. You loved all the adoration you received from everyone as my praises sailed off my lips. You did those things for selfish reasons also!"

"Tiffany that's not true."

"Isn't it though Richard? The minute you found another host to meet your needs, and sing you praise, you stopped needing me. And when you suck her dry and get everything that you need from her you'll move on again."

"Are you serious? Come on. Are you really serious?"

"You're like a hot air balloon, you survive on how much gas other people supply you to make you feel on top of the world. You lack your own supply."

"Tiffany you weren't there for me, I was always there for you."

"So you're making this my fault."

"You don't know how to be a good wife.

"You are just complete aren't you?"

"What?"

"Just complete. A complete jerk. A complete asshole. A complete every dirty word that exists. You fit the mold perfectly don't you? How dare you say I wasn't a good wife. You told another woman you loved her! I didn't do that. You were spitting in another woman's mouth. Not me. How are you going to blame me? I have been there for you Richard. I took care of you. You took care of me. We were in this together. I just don't understand why you abandoned me and started living all for yourself, with no regard to how your decisions would impact me. You act as if we weren't sharing our worlds."

I look in his eyes and see indifference. He doesn't care at all. Why am I even here, why am I trying to fight for something, for someone that obviously is not fighting back? I look and see this man that I am so in love with and want to slap myself for not being strong enough to get up and walk away.

"Tiffany, I love you. You're a strong woman; you'll navigate through this. I just need some time to figure all of this out." It's as if I can see each of his words flutter out of his mouth intertwined with lies and emptiness. I can't stand this.

"How about the rest of your life. Is that enough time?"

I look at him, still loving him, still wanting us to survive, but somehow my body walks to the door and exits. My heart lags behind, wallowing around in pain. My body throws a lasso around my heart and drags it outside the door, kicking and screaming.

"Goodbye Richard." The words struggle out of my mouth, as my heart doesn't want an ending to begin; yet my mouth won't allow for another painful journey to begin. So I press forward and close the door behind me and walk to my car. The door to the car feels so heavy, or my body is just so weak. I sit in the car and put the key in the ignition and look back to Richard's apartment door. How did we get here? How did I get here? I'm such a fool. Then they come. Tears. Tears fall down my face and I don't attempt to stop them. They feel so warm, falling down my cheek. Almost as if the painful reservoirs they emerge from are meant to comfort me as they soar out of my eyes and glide down my cheeks. I love you Richard. I love you, complete.

Chapter 13

Carlo

I look at the monitor of my baby on the screen during the ultrasound and my heart beats, with every heartbeat I see on that screen. Amazing. My child. I watch as the baby moves around in Sadie's womb and anxiousness begins to creep on me. I want to see my child. I didn't ask for fatherhood this way, but if this is how it is coming to me, I'll accept it. This has to be my child. Sadie looks up to me, "I can't believe all of this life is inside of me Carlo. Look at how fast the heart is beating and how active this baby is. We are going to have our hands full! The baby will be here any day now! Can you believe it?"

I nod my head acknowledging Sadie is speaking but my full attention is on that screen, watching my child. It's as if the baby is trying to get my attention.

"Would you like to know the sex?" The doctor asks.

"Carlo, do you want to know?" Sadie questions as she looks up to me.

"Yes. Is it a boy or girl, doctor? Tell us."

"Undeniably, you are having a boy. At the size he is now, it looks like he is going to be a big boy."

My heart leaps. A boy. My son. I look back to the screen and watch my son. Thank you Father.

The doctor begins to wipe the fluid off of Sadie's stomach and she begins to get dressed as the doctor exits.

"Bella."

"Yes Carlo. What is it?"

"I have to talk to Troy."

"Why? We won't know who the father is until the baby is born."

"I'm the father Sadie, I don't care what the DNA tests show."

I look at the black and white picture of the ultrasound in my hand. "I'm going to talk to him today."

"Well it looks like your mind is already made up."

"It is. Let's go."

As we get in the car, I call Troy on the phone.

"Hey Carlo, what's up man?"

"Troy, we need to talk. Can you meet me right now?"

"I'm at the Coffee Bean. I get off in about 20 minutes. It sounds important, what's going on Carlo?"

"It is. I'll see you in 20 minutes."

"Sadie, I'm going to drive to see Troy at the Coffee Bean. You can take the car back to the apartment. I'll call you later."

"What are you going to tell him, Carlo? Do I need to be there?"

"Bella. This is a difficult thing for all of us. Troy and I are like brothers, best friends. This whole pregnancy situation is a struggle for me in many ways. Unchangeable ways that I don't want to talk about again; but what I do have influence over, I'm going to take charge over and Troy needs to know where I stand."

"How do you think he's going to respond?"

"I don't know." I see The Coffee Bean in the near distance, "We'll soon find out."

I kiss Sadie good-bye and watch as she pulls out. I approach The Coffee Bean and can't help but to think this moment can change everything. I seat myself and the waitress gets Troy for me.

"What's up man?"

"We need to talk about this baby Sadie is carrying, Troy."

"Yeah. I know."

"Look at the point I'm at, I don't care what the DNA tests say, Troy. I'm going to be that baby's father."

"I understand that Carlo, and if the DNA tests confirm you're the father, you'll have my support in any way that you need it."

I look at him with a bit of anger. I know whatever he says next is not going to set well with me.

"But if that child is biologically mine Carlo, I'm going to be a father to that child, that child will be the sibling to my boys. I can't deny them of their sibling. It's not right. It's not fair to them or me."

"Troy what's not right is that child having two different fathers, to answer to. He doesn't need that confusion!"

"You said he. Is it a boy?"

I don't want to give him any information if it will cause a greater attachment. I watch as his interests peek.

"Is it a boy, Carlo?"

"Yes."

"If he belongs to me Carlo. I'm going to raise my son."

"He already belongs to me Troy, there are no other if's."

"Carlo, look I can appreciate where you're coming from, but we're saying the same thing. We want to raise this child. You have to understand where I'm coming from. How can I see my flesh and blood walking and pretend that my heritage, my blood and my life is not in him?"

I do understand where he's coming from, but it's not the answer I want.

"Carlo what you're asking is too much for a man like me, I can't turn my back on my own kid. I just can't do it."

I walk from the bar stool and sit on one of the couches in the coffee bar; we're definitely at an impasse.

"How about sharing a beer with a friend Troy?"

"Yeah, be right back."

Troy comes back with two beers.

"You know man, at first I was so distant. This whole pregnancy thing really hit me hard. Then the possibility that the child could be mine or yours was tough. You know I love and respect you brother, but I don't need a DNA test. That child is mine. If I ever have to fight you or Sadie to keep my son, I will." I take a sip of the beer, "I just have faith

Troy, unwavering. If Sadie insists on a DNA, I will respect her wishes, but I won't support them. I'm going to ask that she not have one."

"Carlo, I have to know. I can't have that question in my life un-answered."

"Well I hope you find your answer from up above like I have, but if I have anything to do with it, you won't find your answer from a DNA test on my child."

"How did you get there man, that place of unwavering faith?"

"I became a man that wasn't me." I finish off the beer and send for another.

"I started living out of an unsettled heart. I was acting and behaving and saying stuff that just wasn't me. I was letting my situation control me while trying to convince myself that I had everything under control and I didn't."

"I feel that, man."

"It's a horrible place to be to see your world as functional, only to realize that your eyes have been closed the whole time and in actuality the world you're in is lethal. Killing you softly, with lullabys of deception."

I take another sip of my beer, and then rest it on my leg. "Troy, that baby changed things. He gave me a reason to destroy this virus of depression and anger and fight to make things right. That's why I'm here. I'm taking control over those things that I can and I have control over how I'm going to raise this child." I look over to Troy, "Man I understand where you're coming from, but I'm going to raise my child. And I'm not getting permission to do it from a DNA test."

"I understand where ya coming from," he takes another sip of his beer. "How I feel about that baby has not changed, but I respect your position. When is the baby due?"

"Anytime now."

"Wow, it's been that long?" Troy puts his beer on the table; "I've been fighting to get Sojourn back for almost a year now? It's time."

"Time for what?"

"You know my heart is with your sister, I love her like I love no other, but Sojourn has been unresponsive and I need to start the process of letting go. I need to put my own controls in place."

"I hear you man."

"What time to you need to be at work Carlo?"

"I have about thirty minutes."

"Let's ride, we can keep talking about this. I'm going to close things up in the back and I'll be right back."

"I'm on call tonight, just drop me off at the apartment complex."

"That's cool, I'll be out in a minute."

Troy heads to the back and I sit back and enjoy he music. That's it. A small step, but my first step towards fatherhood. My first step for my son. "Daddy's going to take care of you boy. I hope you hear me. Daddy's got you. We'll be together soon."

Troy steps back out and two women step out into the main floor with him. They are both straightening up their clothes and fixing their hair.

"Carlo, you ready to hit the road brother?"

I just shake my head in disbelief, "Yeah, let's go."

Chapter 14

Shannon

"Good Morning Shannon, what's in store for me today?" He passes me his PDA and I begin to back up all his information and download his current schedule for today.

"Hey boss, I'll have it for you shortly." He walks past me into his office and I begin to brew his latte. I love that man. I wish he could see how having a woman like me is not only a benefit to him professionally, but could benefit him personally. I walk into his office with his coffee and put on his nature sounds CD and open the blinds to bring the sunlight in. I pass him his latte and he is at his computer reviewing his email.

"Something looks different with my email account Shannon."

"Yes sir." I lean over him while he is sitting at the desk and place my hand over the hand he has holding the mouse. I position so that the back of his head is resting right in the center of my cleavage. I begin to move the mouse and click on his mailbox to show him the new features. "You see, I've organized it for you. All incoming emails from the partners are red, so they stand out for you and I've changed your preview screen so could see more." My cheek almost touches his and I feel his head turn towards me. His lips scrape my cheek. "Thanks Shannon."

I know that's my cue to get up and let his hand go and retreat back to my office but I want so much more from him right now.

"No problem boss." I brush my cheek against his as I let go. He watches me as I walk out of the office.

"Shannon wait."

"Yes boss?"

"Show me again. I want emails from Sojourn in green."

I walk back glowing, yet a bit perturbed about the mention of Sojourn's name. I think I finally got him to notice me. I lean back over him, placing my hand on his, pressing my breasts on the back of his head, then maneuver the mouse to make the setting adjustments. I know the scent of the perfume I sprayed on my chest is flirting with his nostrils. I rise just a bit so that his head is no longer receiving the warmth of my breasts and place my cheek right next to his. "Anything else I can do for you boss?" I release my words as gentle breaths that land on his cheek. I feel him searching for air, I got him. But not yet, I'm not going to make it easy on him. I walk around to the front of his desk and give him a sneak peak of my cleavage as I lean over and organize his desk. He doesn't say anything

"If you need anything else boss, let me know." I make sure as I exit I give him a nice shot of me from behind and I cascade toward the door. I almost trip as I bump into Sojourn who is entering at the same time I'm leaving. As we cross paths she looks at me with cat eyes and my eyes return a scowling look. She is always coming in for the kill, right after I set Rick up. I despise that woman.

Chapter 15

Richard

I look up from my computer and see Shannon walk into my office. I know I'm not going crazy, my email system looks totally different. "Something looks different with my email account Shannon." Shannon looks different today. I try not to stare, but she is certainly looking considerably bustier lately. I try to focus on her face, but the center of my attention keeps gravitating to her cleavage. She leans behind me and I feel the back of my head centered on her bust and her hand is caressing my hand over the mouse. This woman is feeling good and smelling good too. Why have I never noticed her before? She maneuvers the mouse and shows me a couple of things on the computer screen and then releases her embrace and walks toward the door, I want to feel her touch again. "Show me again. I want emails from Sojourn in green."

She turns around and smiles. She gets even closer to me and I begin fighting urges to feel her lips touch my skin. I feel my body responding to her gentle touch. Her words escape as soft whispers that compassionately tend to my every need. My breaths grow shallow as I fight the urge to touch her.

"If you need anything else boss, let me know." She leaves and my eyes watch as my stare attempts to reel her back in. Then my glance is intercepted by Sojourn.

"Sojourn."

"Hey Rick."

Out the pot and into the kettle. I have to get out of here, my erotic senses are off the chart. How am I supposed to work like this?

"So Rick, I have to ask, did I interrupt something?"

"No..." My words are interrupted as another visitor comes in my office.

"Well how about me, Richard, did I interrupt something?"

"Tiffany."

"Why not call me by my title, wife!"

Well, erotic senses are definitely at a negative five right now, and my 'It's about to be some drama' senses are screaming.

"Do you think you can ask your piece of rancid meat on the side to leave, so we can talk?"

I open my mouth to respond and Sojourn's words steal my opportunity to speak, "Look, Tiffany you're at my place of business, and

I will not have you disrespecting me here. Don't you think you did enough damage at Troy's?"

"Troy's? What were you two doing at Troy's?" I ask in surprise.

"Why don't you ask Mrs. Wife in heat over there, what she was doing at Troy's?"

"What were you doing at Troy's house Tiffany?"

Sojourn's words overpower anyone's thoughts or response attempts. "What? A loss for words? Well let me fill in the blank for you Mrs. Wife, that is your title isn't it?"

Sojourn looks to me, "She did all she can to throw all of her precious woman gifts on Troy to seduce him into loving her, but it didn't work did it?"

Sojourn walks up to Tiffany and stares at her like she is a woman down, "It didn't work because he still loves me." She looks back to me and then her eyes land on Tiffany as if she is going in for the kill, "and he's not the only one." her words stay in the room and stab Tiffany in the heart as she crudely walks out of my office. That was low, even for Sojourn. Tiffany looks to me as if she wants to run to my arms for comfort. My eyes embrace her, but instead, she turns away and runs out of my office. And I'm supposed to work after this? And Tiffany believes I'm the insensitive one.

I look up and see Shannon walk in my room and close the door. I hear her turn the lock as she approaches me. Now what?

"Rough day at work boss?"

"It's rough on all sides Shannon. Why stop at work? My personal life is running neck and neck with a terrible day at work, it's just bad, bad, bad."

"Well, I closed the door and locked it. No more visitors for a while. You're still at work and I want to keep my job so I need to help you keep yours. Take your mind off of everything. All except the work piling up in that inbox. Focus, I'll take care of the rest boss."

She turns me around to my computer, puts my hand on the mouse and begins to massage my neck and back.

"You got me for thirty minutes boss, and then you can get out of the office, go on your site visits and get some fresh air. I'll hold everything down here."

Shannon's words are just as comforting as her touch.

"Thank you Shannon."

Shannon is someone who can appreciate me and she respects the fact that I have a job to do.

"Thank me with my next paycheck." She says with a smile. The massage is helping; she always knows just what to do.

Chapter 16

Tiffany

I race out of Rick's office and walk into the parking garage of his building. Then I stop, I want to turn around to see if he is coming behind to check on me, to comfort me or just be there for me, but my neck won't move. I just stand still in the parking garage hoping that he will be there, but I just can't shoulder anymore painful disappointments by looking into nothing or the eyes of nothing. My heart is trying to tell my neck to move, but my body won't release its grasp. Instead, my feet keep walking. Then I see it, Sojourn's car. I recognize it from the night we were both at Troy's. I approach her car and circle around it as if I am preparing for an attack, and I am. I reach in my purse, pull out my compact and my tube of red lipstick. I apply a fresh coating of lipstick, filling out every curve of my lips to perfection.

"Well big red, it's been real, but you have a much greater purpose now than making me look good." Then as boldly as I can I write the word BITCH on her front windshield. Now she can be known by her title. I put my purse back on my shoulder and each step I take to my car is a little lighter, and I lavish in these softer, less painful steps. My walk isn't always this easy, but right now, in this moment my whole body is walking to the beat of a little bit of contentment. I'll take it where I can get it. I put on my sunshades and call Troy.

"Hello?"

"Hey Troy."

"What's up Tiff?"

"Troy, I need an attorney. Who did you use when you and Sojourn divorced?"

"Tiff, Sojourn and I are divorced. But right now I'm fighting like mad trying to put my family back together, are you sure you want this?"

"Troy, Sojourn is playing you. I just left Rick's office, she was there."

"That's not unusual Tiffany, they work together."

"Troy, when you hang up with me, call Sojourn and ask her where she had just come from the night she came over when we were together. You need to hear this from her mouth and not mine."

"Tiffany, why are you doing this?"

"Because Sojourn is a bitch Troy, and she doesn't deserve you."

"I suppose you do?"

"I don't know Troy, but I do know that she doesn't appreciate the man that you are and I do."

"Tiffany, I'm not the man you think I am either. I've made my share of life mistakes, some of which are the same ones Rick has made. You give me too much credit."

"Well, she doesn't give you enough."

"Sadie may be carrying my child, I have two boys already and I still love that woman. So even if you would be good for me Tiffany, I'm in no place to start a relationship right now. I want you to be clear on that; I've got some real soul searching to do. I need to know where I stand with God right now. I'm a fallen solider, no better than Lucifer. Whatever happens with us or between us, don't get attached or emotionally involved or whatever we do have we'll lose."

"Does that mean you want to give us a chance?"

"No. It means, I'm open. That's all; this is not a relationship of chance or one of hope that it may become more. That option is closed, Tiffany. Don't fool yourself into thinking you can open it. It's sealed shut. God is the only one that can open that, and right now we're not even on speaking terms."

I listen in silence as Troy speaks; it's hard to separate what I want from what I need.

"Think carefully, how you want to handle things with me Tiff. I don't want to add to your list of disappointments."

"Troy, being with you helps my pain go away and I love that. I want to spend time with you."

"It would be more beneficial if you spent that time with yourself to move past this, instead of thinking that I have anything to do with your recovery. It has to be all you. Don't jump from one disappointment into another. It's just not worth it. Taking a journey of chance to get into a relationship with me has only one destination and that's disappointment Tiff, ask Sadie."

"Ok. Ok Troy. I get it. I know I need to recover from Rick without being co-dependent on you, but you are a support for me, I need to keep that in my life."

"You need more than a man Tiffany, you need God. Lean on Him."

"I hear you Troy. I do. Thanks for being there. Can I see you today?"

"No. Not today. I'm working the telemarketing gig tonight. Working two jobs is wearing me down. I'm going to resign from my telemarketing gig and focus on me a bit more. Carlo and I are going to finish this last round of beer and I'm going to drop him off and then get ready for the second job."

"Ok. Bye."

"Alright Tiff. Later."

When I hang up with Troy, I feel sad again. Richard apparently loves Sojourn, Troy loves Sojourn and that leaves me rejected and dejected. How did she twist both men around her finger and keep them there? Troy I can understand, but Richard was mine. She had no right. He didn't either. How is it that I still love that monster? What is wrong with me? I pull up to my driveway, drag in the house and now, my walk hurts again, it seems it hurts more than it did before. I go to the bathroom and look at myself. What is wrong with me? Why am I not loved, respected and appreciated. I look at my perfectly made up face, my body, my long bonded locks and wonder what I look like if I were to just be me. Not Richard's trophy wife, not pretending to fit in the elitist social scene, not wearing the latest designer fashion trends. What would I look like if I were just me. I look at the shower stall, "Do it Tiffany. Just do you." I walk to the shower and run the water, while it's warming up, I undress, grab a bottle of shampoo and go back and hop in the shower. I just stand directly under the showerhead and allow the stream of water to cover me. As each bead of water hits me, it cleanses me. It hits my body and as it makes contact with my skin and rolls down it each drop eventually falls off me and races down the drain. Each droplet of water takes a piece of that woman I saw in the mirror and shove her down the drain as well. I let the water soak my hair and as I grab the shampoo to cleanse my head, the water and the shampoo loosen my tracks and I begin to completely free these fake attachments and extensions from my head. As each track of hair hits the shower floor, I feel more of that woman in the mirror disappearing and Tiffany emerging. When I free the last track of extensions from my head. I run my fingers through my natural hair and it feels so good. It feels so, so, so good. I stay in the stream of water and feel like the water has stopped cleansing me and is now rejuvenating me, restoring me. I feel a certain indescribable freedom. The make up runs off my face as the soap and water chase it away. My mind runs to Richard and the water pounds my body so hard that my mind releases him. I think of Sojourn and how she has captured and enslaved my husband's heart and the beads of water incessantly pound me and settle on my skin, grasping me in an embrace and I am soothed. My feet wade in the water as each bead takes its turn going down the drain.

"It's over." the words escape my mouth as whispers but emerge loud and clear under the penetrating beads of water. I lightly chuckle, "It's over." My heart feels as if it has been rescued. "Oh Father, thank God, it's over," travels from the depths of my heartbreaks through my mouth and runs to the Heavens as a tearful praise. "It's finally over." My lungs release the last breath of pain and my hands reach up to the crystal shower knobs and I turn the water off. The water drips off my body and I feel free. I step out of the shower-soaking wet as each foot leaves an imprint, evidence of my wet journey. I look in the mirror and see me. Naked. I'm not clothed in pain, or some false identity trying to be accepted or someone I'm not. I'm not clothed in Richard or work, dependency or depression. No expensive jewelry trying to cover up the person I see standing before me. I'm naked and what I see is Ok with me, a tear leaps from my eye in joy and dances all the way down my face. I stare at that woman and my words search her, "Tiffany, why have you been hiding? You're beautiful to me." More tears emerge in concert and they all frolic around my face in celebration. "I'm free."

I throw on my shower robe and go get the phone. I dial the number to my hairdresser.

"721 Hair, may I help you?"

"Hey Lou Lou, It would mean the world to me if you could take me right now. I just took all these tracks out my head and..."

Interrupting me she says, "Do you already have the hair that you want me to put in?"

"No. No. I don't want more in. I want you to cut my hair down to my new growth and shape me. I'm going natural."

"You sure you want that girl?"

"Yes. Can you take me?"

"Yeah, come on in. I got you."

"Thanks, I'll be there in the next thirty minutes."

"Ok girl, come on."

I look back in the mirror at the beautiful piece of me staring back, "Welcome back girl."

Chapter 17

Troy

Tiffany's words stay with me. I want Sojourn to tell me where she
was the night she came over. I dial her number.

"Hello?"

"Hey babe."

"Hey Troy. What's up?"

"Just reminding you I have to work tonight, so you need to get
the kids."

"Yeah, I know. I'll get them. I'm packing up now."

"Sojourn, I talked with Tiffany today."

"Oh please, don't mention that woman to me, she came up here
causing a scene today. I had to put her in her place Troy. She takes
things too far."

"Sojourn."

"Yes, what is it Troy?"

"Where were you just before you came over to see me that night Tiffany was here?"

There's silence. "Why Troy?"

"Were you with Rick?"

"What did Tiffany tell you? I can't stand that…"

"Sojourn! Answer the damn question!"

"Yes, but it's not…."

I hang up the phone. I don't even want to hear what it's not. I know what it is. That's enough. I've worked too hard on putting this family together. I've sacrificed so much, I'm done. I see Sojourn's number pop up, but I refuse to answer it. I don't want to hear any excuses from her.

I look back at Carlo sitting on the couch and consider how we are going to navigate through Sadie's situation. There's nothing more I can do. I have to know. I continue to walk to the back of the office when I turn I see two girls I met the other day waiting for me behind my desk.

"What are you doing here?"

"We told Trudy, you were expecting us and needed to talk to us privately." I need to give Trudy security training. They start peeling their clothes off. "Would you prefer we leave?"

"Finish what you came for." Races out of my mouth with a smile, I'm taking it.

What am I doing? I can't stop myself. What am I doing? It seems sex is the only thing that de-stresses me in life. Damn.

Chapter 18

Troy

"Carlo, you ready to hit the road brother?"

"Yeah, let's go."

"Carlo, man no matter what happens with Sadie and this baby, I'm always going to deal with you as my brother."

"I feel that man. I got you too. I just don't know how we both can come out on top with this."

"We'll make it through, I don't know how, but what I do know is no matter what, that baby is going to be loved and supported."

"Yeah, I feel that man."

"So are you and Sadie going to make this relationship official?"

"I'm not rushing into anything until I know I can be the man she and my son will need for as long as the commitment I make to her lasts. Even after that, I still have a son to raise."

"Fatherhood is a beautiful thing."

"I'm looking forward to it Troy. Sadie and I still are learning about each other, growing. We'll see what happens. What's up with you and Sojourn?"

Just the mention of her name shoots through me like a hot bullet penetrating my skin and burning on impact.

"I don't know Carlo. She's playing both sides of the fence. I love that woman with all my heart, but I can't support what she's doing. I don't believe in it. I'm angry with her, it's time I make a decision."

"You're playing both sides too brother. You're not angry with her, you're angry with yourself."

I don't answer. He's right. My phone rings again, its Sojourn. When I look back up all I see is red. A big red truck running the stoplight heading right toward us. Carlo and I both see it and realize there is no stopping it or steering around. My body immediately tenses up bracing for impact. I slam on my brakes, the truck slams on its brakes and all the screeching sounds from both sets of brakes almost sound melodic and then nothing. The truck hits us and sends our car into a tailspin. The airbag deploys and our bodies are dancing around to the rhythm of screeching brakes and smashing metal. I feel the car drop and my body moves with every movement of the car. We hit another car and slide right under it. Pain is everywhere, every part of my body hurts. I feel pressure from all around. I want to look over to Carlo, but my body won't move. My voice tries to call his name, but the words sit on the back of my throat, refusing to topple out. The crashing harmony is silent. Complete silence is slowly dancing around in the car, and then I hear a faint sound in the background, fighting through and breaking up the dance of silence. My phone is ringing. Sojourn.

Chapter 19

Richard

"Hello?"

I hear a lot of breathing and then I recognize it as Sojourn's voice. Immediately I know something is wrong. The panic in her voice has reached through the phone and has my complete attention in a chokehold, "Rick, please meet me in the parking garage. I need you now."

I don't even question what it is about, "I'm on my way."

I look at Shannon as I exit out, "That's it for me today Shannon. Work just isn't happening today. Call me on my cell if you need to."

"Sure boss, that goes both ways. Call me if you need anything. Anything at all."

I rush out and head to the parking garage; my mind is completely consumed with Sojourn and the panic in her voice.

As I approach her, I see her leaning on the hood of her car and the writing on the windshield.

"Sojourn, if Tiffany did this, I'm sorry."

She looks through me as if no words came out of my mouth at all. "Rick, take me to the hospital downtown. I don't think I can drive, something has happened to Troy."

We begin to walk to my car, "Sojourn what's wrong."

"I don't know Rick, I'm scared. I tried calling him and he wasn't picking up. Then I tried once more and a stranger picked up the phone and asked who I was and how I knew the person I was calling. When I told him, he told me to get to the hospital immediately. That there had been an accident." Tears begin to stream down her face. "I'm so scared Rick. I'm so scared." She cups her head in her hands and cries inconsolably.

"Sojourn, don't think worst case scenario right now, let's wait and see what's up when we get there." I begin to think in my mind that I am the very, very last person Troy would want to see with Sojourn at a time like this. Maybe I should just drop her off and leave, but that wouldn't be right by Sojourn. No other words are exchanged while we make the short trip to the hospital. What a day. I can only hope that Tiffany is not there. With all of this intense emotion and drama in the air, if all of our paths cross at the same time we're either going to need a doctor or an officer.

We arrive at the hospital and go to the ER. I sit in the lobby as Sojourn inquires about Troy's whereabouts. Sojourn looks back to me and motions for me to come with her to the back. I get up and begin to follow her, but think that Troy seeing me is a very bad idea. As we walk she asks the nurse what happened, "I'm not sure ma'am, all I know was that there was a major accident. They just arrived, so we are working on him right now. I'll try to get you a status report." As we walk with the nurse they rush another person by on a gurney and when Sojourn looks down, she nearly collapses. I follow her gaze and see Carlo being whisked away.

"Ma'am?" The nurse asks. "Do you also know the friend that was accompanying him?"

I respond for Sojourn, "Yes, that's her brother."

The nurse motions us to sit down, "I'll be right back with that status report."

When we sit down and watch the nurse disappear in the hall and Sojourn sinks into my chest. I don't have any words that can comfort her. What she needs is answers and the only one who can give her that is the doctor or nurse. So I just sit and hold her. I can't help tossing around in my mind what Troy's reaction is going to be if he sees me with her. I look up and see the nurse talking to the doctor and point-ing in our direction. I tap Sojourn and stand her up, the doctor ap-proaches us and before he can get a word out, Sojourn speaks.

"Doctor, please tell me what's happening with my husband." I look at Sojourn with a bit of shock and surprise, she called him 'husband.'

"Mrs. Hanson, Troy should recover fine. He has a few broken bones that we mended and set in place, we'll order physical therapy for him on an outpatient basis for about three to four months. He also has a mild concussion, so we are going to keep him here over-night to continue to monitor him. He should be clear to go home by tomorrow. He needs to get a lot of rest and take in plenty of fluids."

"So he's ok?"

"I'm sure he'll be fine."

Those words landed on a Sojourn like the hook of a forklift, tak-ing a huge weight off her chest.

"What about my brother Carlo Ricci"

"I'll have the nurse get an update for you on Mr. Ricci."

"Did something terrible happen to him?"

"I'll get you an update; however I can tell you that his injuries were a bit more severe than Mr. Hanson's. The initial impact from the accident hit the passenger side where he was sitting. I know he's in surgery now, but I don't know anything else."

Sojourn's face falls; tears quietly roll down her face and fall to the ground. She looks at the doctor almost begging him to tell her a different story, but he doesn't.

"The nurse should have taken your husband to his room by now. You can go see him. The police will need to come to the room and finish their traffic incident report, so be prepared for that. I'll get you that update on your brother."

He nods his head and walks away; the nurse approaches us and guides us to Troy's room. I peek in and see Troy sleeping, so I cau-tiously step in. I just don't want any more drama. Sojourn goes to his bedside and grabs his hand. He opens his eyes and looks to Sojourn with a smile. He looks over to me. Here we go, drama round three.

"Troy, when I got the news that you had been in an accident, I asked Rick to drive me here. I couldn't make this drive by myself." Troy looks at me, with tired eyes, "Thanks for driving Sojourn here safely."

"No problem." I watch as the police enter the room, "Sojourn, why don't I go and check on Carlo."

"Oh my goodness, I need to call Sadie. She needs to know what is going on, please go and see what you can find out."

I leave and go down the hall and search for the nurse. I'm really surprised he didn't go off, perhaps he's to broken up to be pissed. I almost run into the nurse as I get off the elevator.

"Nurse, I was just on my way to find you to get the status report on Carlo Ricci."

"Yes sir. I have an update. He is out of surgery and is in recovery right now. His situation is still critical. He's in a coma, so we're not completely sure of the damage caused by the head injury. The doctor can give you a better report. I'll send him to Mr. Hanson's room."

"Do you think he's going to make it?"

"Well we're in the business of saving lives, so we'll do everything we can for him."

"Thank you."

"Yes sir, the doctor should be there shortly."

I look back towards the elevator and can't even bear to go and deliver that kind of news to Sojourn. Instead, I look to a vending machine and grab a cup of coffee. I need to call Shannon.

"Hello Boss, what can I do for you?"

"Well I need you to do something for Sojourn."

"Ok, what is it?"

"Can you call her people and let them know that she is going to take the rest of this week and next week off."

"Sure, no problem."

"Thanks Shannon."

"Sure thing, we miss you around here, so don't even think about taking a week off also!"

I chuckle, "We'll see how much you love me when I get back."

I hang up the phone and take the elevator back up the stairs to Troy's room. When I get there Tiffany and Sadie have already arrived and are frantic and out of air. I almost don't recognize Tiffany because she has cut all of her hair off. They must have walked in the door right before me.

"Troy, I don't want that woman in this room. I don't want her here."

"She didn't come to see you Sojourn, she came to see me." Troy says in an admonishing tone.

"How are you Troy?" She asks.

"I'll survive."

"Somebody better tell me about Carlo." Sadie demands grabbing her stomach, with a look of pain in her eyes, Sojourn looks to me.

"The nurse said that he is out of surgery, but his condition is critical. The doctor should be in here soon."

"What? What does that mean, what does critical mean?" Sadie asks.

"I don't know. He's in a coma."

"Oh dear Lord." Sojourn says covering her mouth.

"What else did she say?"

"That's it Sojourn, that's all she told me. That's all I know." I look back to Tiffany and am still stunned by her hair. Sadie starts panicking, her breaths leap out of her mouth and she gasps to take more in while holding her stomach with both hands.

"Sadie!" Troy says, "You need to calm down before you go into labor."

"Sojourn, go tell a nurse to get me a wheelchair so I can go see him." Troy demands

Just as Sojourn approaches the door the doctor walks in.

Chapter 20

Troy

The doctor walks into my room and I'm tired and my body is sore. The nurse comes in with him to take my vitals; I hope she has a pain pill with her. I'm anxious to hear about Carlo.

"Well, I have some information on Carlo Ricci for you."

"Doctor, please is he ok?" Sadie asks.

"He's a fighter. The surgery went fine, but only time will tell now. He's in a coma, and is in a room. You can go and see him."

"What does that mean doctor, how long will he be in the coma?" Sojourn asks.

"We can hope for the best, but we have no way of knowing. We're keeping him on the intensive care unit so we can monitor him closely."

Sadie begins to let her anxiety take over her.

"Would you like me to take you to his room?" the nurse asks.

"Yes, please." As they exit the room, I call back, "Please bring me back a wheelchair. I need to see him. Doctor wait, one more thing. "The doctor turns around and comes back in the room alone.

"Doctor, please before you leave what is the outlook? What are Carlo's chances for survival?"

"I see you wear a cross on your neck are you a believer?"

"Yes sir I am." My heart sinks as my relationship with God is strained.

"So, would it be a safe assumption to assume that the book you study is the Bible."

"Yes. That's a safe assumption. But please tell me is Carlo going to make it?"

"Troy, I'm a doctor and a very good one. The books I study for my profession are various medical journals and scientific reports. I can tell you that the best textbook analysis would say Carlo's chances for survival are slim. I would have to say based on my experiences in cases like this what has proven to be scientifically true, as it is documented and supported by evidence would also forecast a dismal prognosis."

He looks at me and no other words escape his mouth or air enters mine.

"Troy, that's what the books I study say. What does the book you study say?"

I look at him with silence, but I feel an unsettlement in my heart. God's word soars from my spirit and races out of my mouth, "Doctor, my book says all things are possible to him that believes."

He looks at me with a twinkle in his eye, "Well you need to decide if you trust the words in your book or the words in mine. As his physician, I will do everything I know how to do to save him. What will you do to save him?"

He looks at me, and I look back at him. Our eyes acknowledge a goodbye and he exits the room in silence. The nurse comes back in with a wheelchair.

"I'm doing this for you Mr. Hanson, but don't you forget you were in this accident too. You need some rest, after you see him. I want you to get some rest. It's an important part of your recovery. You have a concussion."

"Yes. That's fine, but I need to see him. I'll rest afterwards and behave myself."

The nurse helps me in the chair and wheels me out, "Ok buddy, let's go."

When we get to Carlo's room, Sadie is in hysterics. Sojourn can't do anything because she is just as upset as Sadie. Tiffany is trying to relax Sadie, and Rick is trying to relax Sojourn.

"Uh. Oh." Sadie's words sting me.

"What is it Sadie?"

"My water just broke."

"Tiffany, Sojourn you need to get her checked in. Carlo's not going anywhere, but this baby is. Go get Sadie taken care of, I can't do it."

"I'll go with you all." Rick says and he holds the door open and usher Sojourn and Tiffany out of the room as they support Sadie one each side.

I'm left with Carlo alone.

"Carlo, look man, you're going to have to pull out of this. Sadie's about to have this baby and that boy needs you. Come out of this man."

Now I know why Carlo could say with confidence that the boy Sadie's carrying was his. Because it doesn't matter what science says, what matters is what God says. I look back to Carlo. "I better understand your point of view now Carlo. I know why you didn't want the DNA test." Then my words stop, is God speaking to me? How would I have arrived to this place without the voice and comfort of God? You hear me don't you Lord? You hear me. Father, I need you to restore this fallen solider. Am I in your reach? I want to return to your army, but I just can't break free of this sinful lifestyle. Hear my prayer. All this time, it wasn't you not speaking to me. It was me not speaking to you. You were speaking to me in so many different ways, I just didn't see it. I wouldn't hear it. I was loving sin, more than I was loving you, that's why I couldn't speak Father. I wasn't ready to let go of my sinful behaviors. Lord, I can't say that I'm ready now. My spirit is willing, but my body is weak. If you still have love for a fallen angel Lord restore me, in spite of me. Father, I humbly ask that while you restore my spirit, heal Carlo. Father send an army of 10,000 angels to come in this room and protect him from the arrows of the enemy. Father if the enemy is using me to attack him or anyone else, send 10,000 more angels to protect me. Father, I know you're able. I pray that you are willing. In the name of Jesus, I petition my request to you. My soul won't stop requesting you go until you bless me. Amen. I look back to Carlo, "Carlo, you have to give me some sign." I grab his hand, "Just squeeze it Carlo. Just squeeze my hand. Let me know you're fighting to come out of this." I feel a squeeze. "Carlo, the police told me that during the collision, I slammed on my brakes so hard that it put all the tires on flat. That's the reason we slid under the last car. He told me had we not had flat tires, we would not have slid under the car and the engine would have exploded on impact. He said our survival was pure luck, but I know that wasn't luck that saved us, and it's not by luck that you're alive and I'm alive. You're alive I'm sure for many different reasons, but one of them is to raise that boy. The fact that we can still breathe air isn't by accident; it is will and purpose of God. Squeeze my hand again if you hear me. He squeezes, his eyes remained closed. "One last time Carlo, squeeze my hand, give me hope." He squeezes. "Thank you Father. Rest Carlo, I'll be back to give you an update on baby boy. Three squeezes is confirmation enough for me."

The nurse comes back in grabbing my chair, ready to take me back to my room. Tiffany walks in behind her.

"Ready to go back to your room and rest Mr. Hanson?"

"Not quite yet. Can you get the doctor? I think Carlo is coming out of this coma. If he is, I want to be here when he does."

She walks over to him, examines him with her eyes, and looks at me, "Alright, I'll ask the doctor to come in, it'll be a few minutes but after that, you have to get some rest."

"One step at a time." I say smiling. She walks out and Tiffany looks to me.

"How you doing solider?"

I look at her, "Why do you call me solider?"

"It takes some bravery to continue to stand for what you believe with all you've been through. You even picked me up with your friendship and carried me through the battlefield."

"Thanks Tiff." I look to her smiling, "God and I are on speaking terms again." I watch as her eyes light up and dance around in my excitement.

"So what does that mean?"

I don't answer her question, because I don't have an answer, instead I divert her line of thinking.

"I like what you've done to your hair."

"Well thank you sir."

"Now, when you get tired of your afro, we'll lock it up like mines."

She smiles, "Sisterlocks may very well be my next style."

"I'm feeling your Dashiki also. You're new look becomes you Tiffany."

"I'm working on becoming me."

She sits in a chair next to me, "I'm free Troy. It still hurts a lot, but I'm free. I'm not going to try and conform or transform my life to anyone else's expectation of who I am or what I should be. I'm just going to live as me. I'm not even going to throw all my women gifts around anymore."

She gives me a sly smile, "You were right to hold steady. Seeing Richard was easier today, not easy, but easier. I'm ready to forget about former things and dwelling in the past, God is doing a new thing. I feel it springing up in my life. He's making a way for me to get out of this wasteland of pity. I feel it Troy. I'm still in this desert of hurt, but

I'm sailing out on a stream of hope. Hope has become my escape. God has provided me a way, and I'm taking it."

"What's the update on Sadie?"

"Well she's definitely in labor and dilating."

"How much longer until the baby comes?"

"It's on its way now."

"What about him? Do you think he's about to break out of this coma?"

I look up and see the doctor come in.

"Well we'll soon see."

"Doc. Carlo is responsive. He squeezed my hand in response to me on three different occasions."

The doctor walks over to Carlo as he talks to me, "Many times, comatose patient's bodies will experiences uncontrolled reflexes, so I don't want you to get your hopes up."

I smile at the doctor, "That's what your book says."

He smiles back as cynical laughter escapes, "Ok, let's see what's going on with Mr. Ricci." He does a series of tests and Carlo responds to all of them.

He takes off his glasses and looks at him, and then at me, "I can't explain it, but it looks like you're right. He may be beating this thing, I don't know how. There is definite brain activity and he is responding to my voice command."

Sojourn and Rick walk back in the door.

"Sadie is out of delivery Troy. Something strange happened though."

I look at her confused, "What is it?"

"She had twins."

"Twins?"

"Yes. Twin boys."

"How is that?"

"The doctor somehow missed it. It went undetected the entire time. There were some visits where the baby was so active; it was hard to detect the heartbeat. So on those visits, they didn't even do the ultrasound because they could see all the activity in the womb. It's possible one baby was hiding under the other. It's not entirely impossible for these things to occur, but it is unusual. Nonetheless, there are two boys."

The doctor looks at Sojourn, "Well that's not the only unusual thing occurring today. Mr. Ricci is coming around. Have a nurse buzz me if he wakes up, I'll be back to examine him them."

He walks out.

"Three miracles in one day?" I softly say.

Sojourn walks over to me, and sits on the edge of the bed next to Carlo, "You and Carlo both survive this accident, Sadie has twins and Carlo comes out of this coma. I couldn't ask for a better day."

The nurse wheels in Sadie, "She insisted on coming to see Mr. Ricci."

"Please, just this once. Can you make an exception and bring the twins to see their father?"

The nurses calls as she exits the door, "I'll see what I can do."

"How is he, Troy?" Sadie asks.

"He's coming out of this coma. He's pretty responsive. He seems as if he is trying to wake up."

"Thank God." Sadie says in tears.

"You got that right." I answer.

Carlo begins to move. His eyes open. He looks around and seems to be a bit dazed. "Tiffany, get the doctor!"

Tiffany runs out of the room, "I knew it! Welcome back brother." I say.

Carlo looks over at me, Sojourn and Sadie.

"Where are my boys?"

"Wait, how did you know there were two?"

"I saw them. I was watching as they were being delivered." I try to hide the concern on my face, but my eyes are flashing with worry because I know what he is saying is impossible, there is no way he could have seen this.

"Carlo, we were in an accident, you hit your head pretty hard man, you're right. You have twins, but you've been here the whole time, in a coma. There is no way you could have seen the birth." The doctor walks in, begins to ask him a series of questions and perform a series of examinations.

"Mr. Ricci, your body seems to respond as if you were never comatose, I can't explain this. This is really one of those medical miracles. Maybe that airbag did a bit of good."

Carlo looks at the doctor, "Where are my boys? Bring them to me."

Sadie speaks up, "Carlo, the nurse is working on it. How are you feeling?"

"I'll be fine Bella."

"Carlo. I love you so much. You gave me quite a scare." Sojourn says.

"Don't be scared of death, it is a natural part of life. I'm here. I want to see my boy's dear sorella."

The door cracks open and the nurse wheels in the twins. The doctor is still looking Carlo over, and looking at all his charts.

Sojourn and Tiffany both place a baby in each of his arms and Carlo kisses them on the head.

"My boys! Gianni, the oldest because God is gracious and Valentino because God's grace has given me boys of strength and good health."

Chapter 21

Carlo

T he red truck hits us and I feel as if my body is being ripped to shreds as it is bounced around the cabin of the car. Then nothing. I feel my body still moving but I don't see, or hear anything else. Then the motion of my body begins to vanish and I feel nothing at all. I open my eyes and look around me and I see blood, I feel blood and I feel a presence. I get out of the car and walk around the vehicle looking at all the damage. I look down at my hands and they look clear, as if I can see right through them. I look back at the car and see my body, still and motionless. I stare at it, as if I'm in a museum gallery trying to interpret and connect with what I see. I watch Troy lay still next to me. I sit on the sidewalk and just watch. Watch all the commotion around us, good Samaritans trying to help. I watch the jaws of life pry our bodies out of the car and put us on a stretcher for an ambulance to whisk us away. "Come, I want you to see something." I hear the words with my heart and not my ears, and I'm not afraid. So I follow the words and see two small babies, clear like me. Smiling and playing with each other and I pick them up and they play with me. The oldest softly kicks me and the kicks land on me like laughter. They grasp my finger and don't let go; the smaller one has quite a grip. He's strong and of good health. I don't want to him to let go. I continue to play with the babies, but my ears hear something. It's Troy, talking to me asking me to squeeze his hand. I look and see he is in the hospital leaning over my body grabbing my hand. I squeeze almost irritated that he has interrupted my play and continue to play with the babies. I don't use words with them, and they don't use words with me, but how we feel and what we are experiencing feels like a tango with our hearts. I hear Troy again, asking me to squeeze and I squeeze his hand, and the babies begin to squirm and become upset. They must sense my frustration. Troy asks me to squeeze again and I squeeze. Troy! Enough already. I feel the babies scream, they're leaving me. "It's time for them to go. Do you want to go with them?"

My heart screams "Yes. Please. I want more time with them."

"So it will be. Come."

The boys and I return together to the hospital. I see Sadie pushing, in labor. One of the babies, leaves and Sadie gives birth. I see his flesh. My son. I look to the boy left with me he jumps in my arms and embraces me. I don't want him to leave. Slowly his grasp loosens, I cry as I see him struggle to hold on to me. He doesn't want to leave. I try to hold on and loose my grasp. No. My son. I feel as if I lost him. Then I look down and watch as he is delivered from Sadie's womb. The doctor is startled to see movement in Sadie's womb. He reaches in her womb and the room is in a stir. The second is fighting to get out, but he's caught. Tangled in the umbilical cord, his heart rate stops. No. Son, I tried to hold on, fight, fight, you can do this. The room races at lightening speed the doctor performs a C-section and takes the second one out and he lets out a scream that fills the room. He made it. God is gracious.

"He's a strong little fellow." The doctor says.

"It's your turn to go back now." I hear my heart whisper and I obey.

I go to my room and see Troy and I feel myself being absorbed back into my body. Darkness and pain, it is as if the lights are turned off. I struggle and fight to open my eyes. I want to see my boys. My spirit moves faster than my body will respond. If I could just get my eyes to open. I hear Sadie's voice.

"How is he Troy?"

"He's coming out of this coma. He's pretty responsive. He seems as if he is trying to wake up."

"Thank God." Sadie says in tears.

"You got that right." I answer.

Finally my eyes open.

"Tiffany, get the doctor!" Troy's excitement sends Tiffany out the door running.

"I knew it! Welcome back brother."

"Where are my boys?" I whisper looking at Troy.

"Sadie gave birth about 4 hours ago. Wait, how did you know there were two?" I see fear in his eyes.

"I saw them. I was watching as they were being delivered."

"Carlo, we were in an accident, you hit your head pretty hard man. You're right. You have twins, but you've been here the whole time, in a coma. There is no way you could have seen the birth."

Troy and the doctor continue to talk to me, but I can't focus on anything but my boys. I look at the doctor, "Where are my boys? Bring them to me."

Sadie speaks up, "Carlo, the nurse is working on it. How are you feeling?"

"I'll be fine Bella."

"Carlo. I love you so much. You gave me quite a scare." Sojourn speaks to me with a mouth full of tears.

"Don't be scared of death, it is a natural part of life. I'm here. I want to see my boys dear sorella."

Tiffany and Sojourn place the babies in my hands. I kiss them with pride, with love and with thanks to God.

"My boys! Gianni, the oldest because God is gracious and Valentino because God's grace has given me boys of strength and good health."

Another nurse comes in, "Mr. Hanson, I'm sorry, you have to go. Doctor's orders, you need your rest, so you can be released tomorrow."

"Carlo," Troy calls to me as he is being wheeled out of my room, "We'll talk. The boys are beautiful. Congratulations." He calls back to the doctor, "I trust my book, Doc."

Sojourn looks to Rick, "Thanks for the ride, I'm going to stay the night here with Troy and my brother."

"Ok. Oh, Sojourn, I called the office and told them you would be out the rest of this week and next week as well."

"Thanks Rick. See you later."

"Bye Sojourn."

"Ladies, I'm still a bit perplexed and concerned about his condition. I don't know how stable it is and Iwant him to get some rest. I'm going to ask that he only have one visitor at a time."

"Sojourn, Tiffany if you don't mind, I would really like a moment with Carlo before I have to go back to my room. Can you wheel, Gianni and Valentino back to the nursery for me?"

"Sure." They both answer. They take the babies from my arms and cart them back to the nursery.

Sadie looks to me, "Carlo. How are you?"

"I'm tired Sadie. My body hurts, but my spirit is celebrating the birth of my boys."

"How did you know I birthed twins?"

"I was with them Sadie. Somewhere between life and death my boys were with me and I was with them."

"I don't understand Carlo."

"Bella, my body is tired. Stay with me while I rest. I'm glad you're here."

"I love you Carlo."

"Thank you Bella. I'm tired." My eyes grow heavy, and excitement floods my heart, but my body is weak. I close my eyes and allow rest to consume me.

Chapter 22

Tiffany

Sojourn and I wheel the twins back to the nursery.

"You're still a bitch Sojourn." I say with a smile.

"I know, you wrote it all over my car."

"Yeah, I guess I'm a bitch too." The words quietly run out of my mouth.

"What I should have written was that I'm so angry that I couldn't fix the problems in my marriage. I'm angry with myself, I'm angry with Richard. I'm angry that there was so much distance between us that there was enough room for him to fall in love with another woman." I look at her with a sad smile and heavy eyes, "There wasn't enough room on your window for all of that so I settled on the word Bitch." I end with laughter.

"Sojourn, I'm so sad that he has chosen to love you instead of me. I still love him, I never stopped. I've been trying and trying every night to stop loving him, but every night when my tears flush him out, by morning the love I have for him forces its way back in, without my permission might I add."

We sit in some chairs right outside the window to the nursery.

"It's easy to love a guy like Rick." She says with an empty glazed-over stare.

"Don't I know? It's easy to love a guy like Troy!"

She looks at me with a catty stare and the lightly laughs, "Yeah, I guess it is."

"I look at you and wonder, what do you have over me? Was it the sex? Did you communicate better than me? I don't know. I don't know how you got my man to make you the center of his affection. You certainly don't look better than me. How could he fall in love with a woman like you, when he had a damn good woman like me?"

"Be careful Tiffany, I'm almost ready to take offense."

"Well don't. You know Sojourn, it's not what was wrong with me, or what was right about you, it's what's wrong with him."

"You'll fall in love with him. Then, that one little thing in the relationship that's missing will soon become everything that's wrong, and then he'll set sail looking for someone who can fill that one little need, like cooking. Then after that, he'll find someone else who fills the need you can't meet. And when that happens re-member my words it's not you, it's him. It's what's missing in his life, not what's wrong in yours or mine. It's not the cooking. Until he can decide to fix what's wrong with him, he'll blame or convince every woman he has a relationship with that it's something wrong with them, because he's too stubborn and prideful to examine his own weaknesses. So instead, he'll boast in yours. All the while denying his own."

Sojourn doesn't say anything.

"I know I said some pretty horrible things to you, but you're no different from me. And what differences we do have, time will soon fade. I meant what I said when I told you betrayal is in his blood now. You're no different from me. He had such a lovely dance with betrayal the first time, he'll believe he can do it, over and over and over again."

I look at her, "You know why? Because he won. He got what he wanted."

"You cut your hair."

I rub my fingers through it, "Yeah. I'm loving it too, this freedom."

"Why did you do it?"

"I loved Richard so much, I tried to become an object that he would love and appreciate forever. There wasn't anything I wouldn't do for that man. Nothing. I would have died for him." I release a painful chuckle, "What a waste that would have been." I look off into the walls and my eyes get lost in the serene colors of the nursery, "I cried Sojourn. I cried night after night. I prayed night after night. When none of that chased my pain away, I tried to feel better by having sex with Troy, that didn't work either. I tried attacking you, but the pain was still there. Nothing I did would chase my pain away. I couldn't run anymore, even walking hurt, girl. Crawling hurt, it got to the point that even moving hurt. So I stood still and looked at myself in the mirror. I saw what I had become by trying to satisfy and please my man. Trying to get him back, to make him want to love me again and it didn't work. So I showered and shed that woman in the mirror, and I was left was just me." I look at her with a tear in my eye. Tears that don't cry for me, tears that slide down my face and rejoice with me. "I liked me. I liked me a whole lot Sojourn. Now, I'm ready to celebrate my return. My freedom from the captivity of trying to be what he wanted, and not what I needed."

"That's quite a journey Tiffany."

"My journey may soon be yours."

"No. No. I've had one. Definitely don't want another."

She looks at me with a solemn stare, "Remember? I'm one divorce ahead of you?"

"I said some pretty awful things to you, Tiffany."

"Why do we as women do this? Why do we fight each other over the wrongs men do to us? Why do we find all the wrong in ourselves? Then find all the wrong in the other woman and tear her down as if tearing her down is not dismantling ourselves in the process. And all the time running back to the man ready to forgive him, without forgiving ourselves and each other?" I ask her.

"You fucked my husband Sojourn. You were wrong."

My eyes embrace her and not attack, "It still hurts, the loss of that relationship. But I forgive you. Not because of who you are, but because of who I am."

She looks at me, "Bitches bleed too."

I shake my head in agreement. She's human just like me trying to build a future, filled with fantastical hopes and dreams protected by an army of fear and insecurity. Carrying pain in captivity and imprisoning who she really is. Not living free, but living encapsulated in a wall of insecurities. When threatened, attack. Attack not with love, but with hate; attacks that are launched with the intent to destroy, in order to protect our hidden insecurities from becoming a reality. Hating the fact that we lack the courage to release our authentic self and accept the gains and losses of love – in freedom; which is so much better than accepting gains and losses of love in captivity. So she bleeds just like me. The only difference is, I opened my cell and shed my prison garments of fear and insecurity. I'm walking out of my penitentiary. I may still be on the prison ground, but I'm making my way to the exit.

"Yea, we do." I look at her as I stand up, "I'm sure Troy would love it if you were to go spend some time with him; I'm going to stay with Sadie. She's alone right now, and is going to need some help with this whole motherhood thing."

She stands up, "Ok. See you when I see you."

"Good bye." I nod my head and walk towards Sadie's room and my phone rings; it's Jessica our co-worker.

"Hey Jess"

"Hey Tiffany. How's Sadie?"

"I'm heading that way to check on her now. When are you coming back girl? We miss you."

"I'm packing my bags now. I've so much to update you all on. I found out who Jason's little fling was with and it opened up all those old wounds."

"Jessica, don't go back to where you were before. Keep moving forward."

"I know Tiffany, I just want that woman to feel my pain, and I want her to know how she hurt me."

I chuckle, "Don't I know it, but she didn't do it alone. Just resist. My new mantra is, 'Forget the former things; do not dwell on the past. I am doing a new thing! Keep pressing forward.' So press with me girl. Keep pressing forward."

"I wrote a poem while I was out here. One for you and one for Sadie. Tell Sadie, I'll be back before she gets out of the hospital and will take her home."

"I will Jessie. I will."

"Ok then, press on."

"Yes, press on."

Chapter 23

Richard

I walk into my office to work and anticipate that I'll actually be able to focus now that Sojourn is out and Tiffany is with Sadie. I have no other distractions.

"Good morning Shannon."

"Good morning Rick." Like routine I pass her my PDA to program it with today's schedule and walk to my office looking forward to my latte. When I get to my chair, I see she has left a card in my seat. She always knows how to make me smile. I look up and hear my cell phone ring.

"Hello?"

"Hey Rick, I just want to thank you for all you did for me yesterday."

"No problem Sojourn. How is everyone doing?"

I look up and see Shannon bringing in my latte. I grab her hand before she leaves. "Thank you," I silently mouth the words. I hear Sojourn talking to me, but Shannon distracts my mind. I don't know if I am just now noticing her, or she has always shown this much cleavage.

"Troy is going home today. He's fine. Carlo is recovering, and has good memory and recall. Carlo seems to be a genuine medical miracle."

"That's great!"

"So tell me what are you doing? Are you working things out with Troy?"

"Well, we've already worked it out, we're divorced remember?"

"You know what I mean Sojourn. You know he wants to reconcile."

"I talked with Tiffany last night Rick. It was decent, for a change."

Sojourn abruptly changes subjects on me, avoiding my question. "No blood?"

"Well, not the kind of blood you can see, but I believe we're both bleeding right now."

Shannon walks back in, and passes me my PDA, "All of your information has been updated."

"Sojourn, I need to talk with Shannon. Am I going to see you later today?"

"I don't know. We'll see what happens."

"Alright, I'll talk with you later then." I hang up with Sojourn and call Shannon in my office. "Shannon, I need you to quickly give me an update on all of these messages from yesterday. I need to get caught up."

"Sure boss." Shannon looks at me closes the door and locks it. Why did she do that? Reading my face, she answers, "I locked the door so we won't have any interruptions."

She leans over and grabs the messages from my hand. "Let me show you something boss," she picks up my hand, places it on the mouse and puts her hand on top of mines. She opens my mailbox and goes to the notes section. "I have logged all of your messages on the computer where you check your email. You'll find detailed notes with each message and the necessary action that you need to take. I gave you paper messages as a back up."

She looks at me with a smile. "You see, I take good care of you." She kisses me on the forehead.

My eyes are drunk with sexual energy. "Do that again."

"What? This?" and she kisses me again.

"Yea. Do that again." She kisses me again on my lips, and again on the corner of my lips, and back to the center of my lips. "Don't stop me boss."

She slips off her shoes and allows her dress to fall to the floor.

"Can I kiss you with my other pair of lips?" I don't know what to say. Before I answer, she has unbuttoned my pants and has slipped on top of me. She grabs my face with both of her hands and lifts her body up and down on top of me. She kisses me, while her inner muscular walls grip me from all sides. I feel her wet body easily glide with each movement of her hips. She loosens her bra and I watch as her breasts bounce free and she presses them against me and they settle on each side of my neck. I grab one of her breasts with my tongue and suck on her nipple as she continues to glide up and down on top of me. Her body feels so good, wet, soft. She kisses me on my neck and whispers, "No strings attached. Just sex. Take it! I want you to smile. I want to be the one give it to you."

She grabs me with the wet walls of her inner muscular body, "You've got to be able to handle this, boss. Take it." She wraps her hands around my neck with her fingers stroking my hairline and her thumbs lodged into my neck. "Take it boss!" She gets up leans over my desk and turns her head looking back to me. "Come visit me through the back door."

Shannon smiles at me and I respond to her invitation to visit her body through the back door, pulling out as I'm exploding with pleasure.

"Shannon that was amazing. I loved it, but we can never cross that line again. Never. I don't want to lose my incredibly helpful and sexy assistant over emotional garbage."

"I can always quit."

"Shannon, I need my workplace to stay consistent. You help with this. I need you more in this role than in any other role in my life right now."

"I want to keep a smile on your face. I've found another way."

"Let me worry about those smiles. If you really want me happy stay in the role as my executive assistant."

"No problem boss." She answers, as she gets dressed. "You have a message from the Vice President of operations from our competing company, Rayford Robinson. He's called for you twice already. Please make sure you call him back."

"Shannon, do we have an understanding?"

"Sure, but I don't see why Sojourn gets to have all the fun. If you change your mind, or she drops out of the picture, you will always, always have me. Till death do us part."

What? Till death do us part? Is she crazy? "Ok Shannon. Get Rayford on the phone for me."

I have one of those nauseous feelings, bubbling in the pit of my stomach. Why do I feel like I just made the biggest mistake of my life? I look at Shannon as she exits out of my door. My eyes are punching me in the gut, why Rick, why did you do it? You need to learn to just say no.

Shannon's voice interrupts my thoughts and her words feel as if they are suffocating me, "Rayford Robinson is on the phone."

I've royally screwed up, "Send the call through."

"Rayford! How you doing?"

"Rick. I don't have much time so I'll be brief and we can talk at length later."

"Sure what's up buddy?"

"I really enjoyed our discussions during our last golf game. Your name came up, again at a board meeting and again at a partner's meeting. The work you're doing is coming to the attention of some very influential people in my organization. Once it looped around to me, in a circle of three that was confirmation enough for me."

"That's great Rayford, but what does your confirmation mean for me?"

"We want you on our team Rick, and we'll double your salary to get you here."

Wow.

"Rick?"

"Yeah."

"Think about it. We remove the offer from the table by 5:00 pm tomorrow."

"Rayford, thanks for the offer. You'll hear from me before then."

"Alright Rick, talk to you soon. Bye now."

"Bye."

Wow. Double my salary, and a fresh start. I could use a second chance in creating a work environment free from women that I've blurred lines with. This is a no brainer for me. I'll take it.

Chapter 24

Shannon

Rick is going to love me. I can make him fall in love with me, even if he doesn't realize it now. I won't stop until I get my man. I just need to get Sojourn out of my way. Once I take care of that major distraction, I'm home free. He thinks she's this exceptional friend, colleague and lover – all I have to do is show him she isn't. When she finds out that I slept with Troy and can position myself to take him, she'll buckle from the strength jealousy has on a woman's heart. She'd crumble if she knew another woman could take him away from her forever. Once Rick sees this obsession she has with Troy. He'll be all mine. Once I accidentally forget to take my birth control, he'll be in my life forever. That's the thing about accidentally forgetting to take birth control; no one can prove it wasn't by accident. Unless of course

I confess, and that will never happen. Rick is not the kind of man that can bring a baby into this world and have it not affect him in a deeply emotional, bonding way. Not even Sojourn can compete with a newborn. I feel guilt trying to sneak up on me, and thwart my plans. It's like a thief trying to steal my joy. Look guilty conscience, I'm not a bad girl, just an ambitious one. Many people do worse trying to climb to the top of the corporate ladder, all I'm trying to do is climb to the top of my man's heart. I'm not wrong for wanting to give him love, good love at that. I'm just painting a landscape and preparing a future that we will both enjoy. He can love me. Why wouldn't he? I'm beautiful, smart, successful, talented and just overall a good person from a good family. He just can't see the potential and possibility in us right now, but he will – and when he does, I'll have our future ready for us to enjoy. I'm preparing now, so when the moment comes when our paths cross, we will be forever intertwined. Why should I feel guilty about taking my destiny and fate into my own hands? I'm only showing Rick the truth about Sojourn the mud princess and the truth about the love I have for him and what that love can mean. No harm in that. Rick is my man. I'm not going to allow guilt to overcome my conscience for going for something that is important to me. I'm going to get my man.

Chapter 25

Troy

As I lay in my hospital bed, I lay in shock. A car accident, twins and Sojourn at my bedside. I look over to Sojourn and search her eyes. Not even sure what I'm looking for anymore. "Sojourn, you know I love you, but I'm not keeping my heart on hold for you anymore."

"What do you mean Troy, are you seeing someone?" She asks with me with innocence, but I know there is no naïveté in that question.

"No. I'm not seeing anyone, but I may start."

"Start with who?"

"Actually, the only one who has expressed interest in me right now is...."

My sentence in interrupted by the creak of the door opening. I see Tiffany pop her head in the door, with her new sassy cut. My eyes smile. Sojourn watches as my facial expression changes and then looks to the door to see who is coming to visit me. When her eyes catch that it's Tiffany peering through the door, she cuts her eyes back to me in an attempt to obliterate any intentions I may have.

She forcefully whispers "Over my dead body." Her eyes dead-locked on me. I know she means every word. Her eyes roll with attitude as they take aim on Tiffany.

"Hey Troy. How are you?" Tiffany asks unknowing that Sojourn is ready to take aim and fire.

"Tiffany. What are you doing here?"

"Well as soon as I could get off work, I came over here to check on you. You should be going home today. Am I right?"

"Yes, my lady you are."

"Do you need a ride?"

"No. Sojourn has it covered."

I see the look of disappointment slowly glaze over her face. She turn's to Sojourn, to seek some approval, in the guise of support, "If you want to stay here with Carlo, I can take Troy home Sojourn."

I attempt to speak before Sojourn has an opportunity to dis-charge her weapon–her mouth, but it's to late, Sojourn's body begins to respond and silences me. I feel her tensing up. She doesn't move one part of her body, only her eyes. Her lids slowly close and as they open you see her eyes taking aim, "He just told you I have it covered." Damn, that had to have landed hard.

Tiffany searches Sojourn's face, her glare stung Tiffany with a subtle force unable to be ignored. She tries to find where Sojourn's vile attitude is coming from. It's the look of a woman marking her territory. I watch as Tiffany's face changes from an inquisitive one to, an 'oh you bitch'. Obviously, she has recognized Sojourn's source of contempt. Please back down Tiffany, I don't feel like being in the middle of a fight. Not again.

"Tiffany, that was very nice of you to offer, but..." her words abruptly cut me off, she fires back at Sojourn with bullets pretending to be words.

"You're jealous. You're jealous of the friendship I have with Troy."

"Why would I be jealous of you Tiffany?"

Here we go, frustration races across my body, suffocating any air I attempt to breathe. I watch as Tiffany stands up and prepares to walk toward the door.

"Troy, I'll catch up with you later. I'm going to check on Sadie and the twins. Your hold on Richard is temporary, Sojourn; but it matters not. I'm finished with him. I guess if I were you, I'd be jealous of my friendship with Troy too. It truly is something special."

She pushes the door open, doesn't look back and exits as quickly as she came in. I turn to Sojourn.

"I detest that woman Troy."

"Sojourn, be easy. She hasn't done anything at all to you, but you have done plenty to her and it doesn't change where we are. You'll need to find a new person to blame."

I watch as a tear forms in her eye.

"How did we get here Troy? How did we manage to screw life up so bad? We had a really good thing going. When I thought I was going to lose you, it was just too much for me to bear. The thought of losing your heart hurts just as much as the thought of you losing your life."

I grab her hand and kiss it.

"Troy, are they yours? The twins, when are you going to find out?"

"I can't find out now Sojourn. Those twins are Carlo's reason for living, for breaking through the coma. I can't take that away because I want a DNA test."

"We have to know Troy. We need to know if those babies are siblings to our own. The kids deserve to know."

"He has already told Sadie not to go through with any type of paternity test."

"Well are you going to do something about it?"

"Yes. I'm going to leave it alone; and you should do the same."

"I can't Troy."

She gets up and heads toward the door.

"Where are you going Sojourn?"

"I'm going to talk to Carlo."

Sojourn exits without looking back as a nurse enters. She looks at me as if I'm a familiar face and tosses me a sheepish smile.

She reaches takes my vitals, records them and puts the chart down. She reaches toward my blanket and pillows.

"So you went through all of this just to play doctor again?" She says as she reaches under my blanket and grabs me. My body responds and hardens in response to her touch. What?

"You remember now don't you? You remember by touch. Feel familiar?"

I try to look at her in shock, but pleasure shoots through my feeble attempt. She begins to stroke me.

Stop, stop, stop. Screams in receptive whispers inside of my head. *No I don't remember, but I like the touch.* All my frustrations begin to release their grip on me and life feels good. I feel euphoria. Sex gives me a high that I don't want to come off of.

"This time, I'm the doctor and you're the patient." She whispers as she continues to stroke me. Pleasure pumps with a steady beat throughout my body. As if pleasure is giving me a massage from the inside out. Pounding. I don't want her to stop. My eyes embrace her.

"Next time, I visit the Coffee Bean, I'll bring my uniform and meet you in the back office. Right now, lay back and relax."

"What I'm doing should stimulate a knee jerk reaction. I grab you and you grab me. If you don't, I'll have to assume something is wrong with you." She takes one hand and unbuttons her shirt and sends one breast into freedom.

"I stroke, you grab."

I grab her breast and she strokes more aggressively. Physical, mental and emotional pain runs away into hiding.

"I'm looking for a healthy response from your body. I know you want to release. I'll give it to you. With instructions to follow when you get home."

Why can't I stop myself? Stop. Stop, Damn it! My body completely ignores my mind. Oh well. I can't say I'm sorry it did. I give up. This feels to good. I grab her hips with my other arm and move her closer to the bed. She lifts up her dress and climbs on the table and straddles me. She begins to stroke me with two hands.

"You remember now, don't you Troy?

Hell no, I don't remember, but why let that get in the way?

"I need a taste before I can completely allow you to be released."

This woman is about to send me over the edge.

"It's time for me to release you. You ready to go home?"

"Yeah."

I release completely, my mind, body everything explodes. I want more.

"I'll clean you up and will be back later to check on you. Be a good patient until I return." She gives me a quick sponge bath, kisses me on the cheek and leaves. I think I have a problem.

Chapter 26

Carlo

"Mr. Ricci, you are recovering beautifully." The nurse looks at me with caring eyes.

"My body is still sore."

"It will be for a while. The pain medication will help with that."

The door to my room swings open and in comes Sojourn.

"Hello beautiful brother!"

"Sojourn."

"Nurse, how is he?"

"He's a fighter." She says with a grin, "I'll leave you two alone."

I look at Sojourn, and can't help but recall all the memories we have together. I've known her most of my life. She's been the one person in life that has never left my side.

"Carlo, I have to know if those kids belong to you or Troy. Will you have the DNA test?"

"No."

"Why, Carlo?"

"I don't need a test to prove paternity."

We sit in silence. She finally is realizing that there is nothing she can do to change my position on this.

"Well then tell me, how's my brother?"

"I'm doing well, but as for your brother, I've never met him."

"What are you talking about, Carlo."?

"Sojourn, we've known each other all our lives, and have shared many, many life experiences, secrets and memories, but the one thing we don't share is a blood line."

"Carlo, I know that, but I love you like I would if you were mine. I don't need a bloodline"

I look at her and don't say a word. Finally the words make their way out of my mouth, "and neither do I. I don't need a bloodline to know that these boys belong to me. They will be raised as if they are mine, even if they aren't."

Her body backs down, at least for now. I know she'll come back to this when she feels I can be more influenced.

"You don't want to be my brother anymore? Why do you want to end our relationship now?"

"I'm not."

"Well what are you to me, if not my brother Carlo? You are the one man in my life that has always been there. Always. You have always loved me regardless of the mistakes I've made, or how ugly I look when I first wake up in the morning. How can you claim we don't share a relationship deeper than a bloodline?"

"I've always been whatever you needed me to be Sojourn. What do you really need me to be in your life now? You don't need a playful brother."

I turn my head to her so that I have her full attention, "I'm not your brother. It's deeper than that."

She sinks her cheek in the palm of my hand. "I know Carlo. When my family moved to Italy and we met you and your family, we spent every day together, every day until my father was transferred back to the states. When your father died and your mom moved back to the States, you all moved right down the street from us. You've been the best friend, the only true friend I've had my entire life. I wanted you to be my brother so bad because bloodlines can't be broken. I never wanted you out of my life."

"We've been there for each other." The words escape my mouth as gentle kisses.

"Sojourn, what's going on with you and your love triangle? I've already told you I don't approve of you playing two sides of the fence."

"I know brother. I know. I'm lost. I love them both, but neither of the relationships feels right. I don't want to lose Rick and I definitely don't want to lose Troy."

Again, she calls me brother.

"Make a decision Sojourn."

"Enough about me. What's up with you and Sadie?"

"Well we're about to raise two boys together."

"Are you getting married?"

"I don't know. We've had some hills to climb. We're still getting to know each other. I'm taking my time. She should also."

"I love you, Carlo."

She grabs my hand and holds it.

"If I had a marriage as solid as our friendship, I'd be in good shape, brother."

She still calls me brother. She leans over and kisses me on the cheek, "What would I do without you?"

"It's over with you and Troy for now Sojourn, he's not waiting around for you and why should he? As for Rick, leave that man alone until his divorce is final, if he divorces at all. He's still married and he's not married to you, so stay out of it!" I look at her with my eyebrows raised and stare at her with my eyes focused from the corner of my socket, "That's it Sojourn, leave them both alone."

"Brother..."

Enough! "Come here baby girl."

"What?"

I grab her neck and it takes all of the strength out of me. I pull her near me and kiss her as long and as hard as I can, until my strength leaves me and when it does my hand falls off from her neck and she slowly releases her lips from my embrace.

"We both know brothers and sisters don't kiss like that so you'll need to give me another title."

I look at her and no words leave her mouth.

Her eyes peer into me as if she is trying to connect with my mind and heart to understand me.

"I love you too Sojourn." Leaves my mouth in a whisper meant to clear her confusion. She shakes her head up and down in a yes movement as if affirming that she already knows how I feel.

"Sojourn, go on and go. I need some rest and have some thinking to do of my own."

"Carlo, you know we can't." Her voice begins to trail off, " Troy, Sadie…"

I interrupt her before she has a chance to finish. "I know." It always seems the heart of a man has a fine way of making a mess out of life.

"Don't force me to be your brother anymore, I'm not going to play that game. We've been playing that game since grade school."

She laughs cutting through the tension. "It worked for a while because both our moms were African-American, but no one believed I was your Italian dad's daughter."

I laugh with her, "That's ok, they didn't believe I was his son."

The ignorance of some people sometimes is so ridiculous it's funny.

"Listen Sojourn, I can't tell you when my feelings about you changed, but they have. Troy is one of my best friends, I know how he feels about you, and I'd never betray that. Sadie is a good woman; I wouldn't want to hurt her. Unless our lives becomes un-messy, consider that the first and the last."

"So you're back to being my brother?"

"Hell no." I softly chuckle, "I'm sure you'll come up with a new tag line for me."

"It was the accident wasn't it? It changed you."

"Yeah."

"What happened?"

"Coming so close to death, brought me closer to life." I turn and look at her trying to determine if she can handle what I'm about to say. My spirit searches her.

"Sojourn, I saw my boys while I was on other side of life. I was dead and alive at the same time. I don't even know if I can explain it. I don't know how death and life can occupy the same space at the same time, but it did. My body was gone, but my life wasn't."

"Did you see Him? God?"

"I didn't see anyone, but there was a presence there with me, that didn't give a name, and I didn't ask."

I see Sojourn's face dancing with both a search for understanding and surface curiosity.

"I made a choice to come back to be with my boys. I don't need a DNA test."

"Your feelings for me, did they change while you were on the other side?"

"No. I've always loved you. That hasn't changed. What has changed is that I have a clearer understanding that life is about choices. I'm choosing not to pretend anymore. I'm choosing to live as authentic as I can."

"That's a brave stance to take Carlo. Authenticity doesn't always feel good to those around you."

"Deception is much worse; the people around me deserve to deal with the truth."

"I don't know how I feel, or who I should allow to handle my heart."

"Sojourn I don't have answers for your life. But as for me, I search for my own truths and live my life by them. In that way, I deceive no one – friend or foe."

Sojourn leans over and rests her head on my shoulder.

"So now you know how I feel. I'm not your brother." She lifts her head back up and her eyes lock with mine.

"You can deal with me, handle me in the way you choose, but at least you're dealing in truth, knowing how I feel about you in honesty. The people that are close to me, and even those that aren't, deserve to know the truth. And I'm choosing to live that way."

"L'amore della mia vita." She whispers to me with one tear escaping her eye.

I smile at Sojourn; she's speaking my language. I often forget her fluency in Italian, but when it lands on me, it's as sweet at sugar.

"Love of your life, huh?" I look at her with compassion. "We still have a lot of living to do amore mio."

She grabs my hand, "Sojourn, regardless of what happens, I will not betray Troy or Sadie, more than I already have. I need to tell them the truth. Once I discover what it is for me."

"I know." She says solemnly.

"Lies are so much easier to live. It's much easier just playing the role of your brother."

Her eyes seem to have cleared a path to better understand me.

"I mean it when I tell you to leave them both alone for awhile. You need to determine what you really want and not allow any distractions to get in your way, including me."

"Ok." Is all she says. She kisses me on the back of my hand and walks out the door.

Chapter 27

Richard

"Rayford, when do I start?"

"Glad you accepted Richard. We're glad to have you. Go to HR for all of your paperwork and we have a board meeting at 1:00pm tomorrow, we will introduce you to the board at that time."

"You all move fast don't you?"

"Just trying to keep pace with the money!"

I laugh. I'm either going to love working here or hate it.

"When will be my official start date?"

"You can officially start at the beginning of the month. That will give you enough time to transition to us without burning any bridges and give yourself a little R&R."

"Perfect."

"Head to HR now, so you can begin the paperwork process."

"Will do."

As Rayford and I part ways, I can't help but have a bit of a rush. It's almost like a second chance, a fresh start. It's exactly what I needed. I'll miss Shannon's work ethic. She kept things together for me, but all good things must come to an end. As I open the door to HR, I'm greeted warmly.

"Hello Mr. Young, Mr. Robinson told us to expect you."

Wow, they are really on top of things here.

"Have a seat Mr. Young and I will bring your contract and other paperwork. You can take all of this with you. You will need to set up a physical for the insurance policy. I can schedule the appointment for you if you'd like."

"That would be great, even better if I can go in this afternoon and get it over with."

"Sure. No problem."

She courteously walks off and I begin to review the contract and complete the new hire paperwork.

"Mr. Young, you can go in after your finish your paperwork, they are booked, but they are going to work you in."

"Marvelous. Thanks."

I finish the paperwork, sign the contract and return it.

"I appreciate the help, I'm going to get the physical, can you let them know I'm on my way?"

"Absolutely. Oh and welcome aboard, we're glad to have you."

The address to the doctor's office is in the same hospital where Troy and Carlo are.

I'll be on a different floor, so I doubt I'll run into them. A quick physical examination and lab work and I'm out. I need to prepare my office and company for my departure. It feels so good to have a fresh start a second chance at life. I know I've screwed up in so many areas. Thank you Father for restoring a fallen man like me, this job is just what I need. God is so good.

Chapter 28

Shannon

So Tiffany is at the hospital. Secretaries always have the dirt on everyone, it's like a code we share. We all know that we, the administrative assistants, secretaries or whatever title we are given, hold the keys to all the gossip, information and are always in the know about everything. I knew just who to call. I think I'll ask for my gynecologist to work me in today so that I have a legitimate reason for accidentally bumping into Tiffany at the hospital. I will get the inside information on what's going on with Sojourn and Rick. I send Richard a quick text letting him know that I will be out of the office for the rest of the day for a doctor's appointment and go on my hunt for the dirt I need to show Rick that Sojourn is not his soul mate, I am.

As I pack up my things and head out the door, my cell phone buzzes and it's Rick responding to my text.

Ok Shannon. See you later.

Later indeed. I head to my car and drive to the hospital for my bogus MD appointment in hopes of running into a Tiffany. I check in at the front desk and anxiously wait for them to call me to the back so I can get this over with.

When the nurse calls me into the room, she asks me what brings me in today.

"I need a pap smear and other general testing run."

"Are you experiencing any symptoms? What kind of testing do you want run."

"Well, I've had to go to the bathroom more frequently than normal. Perhaps run a test to see if I have a bladder infection."

"Are you sexually active?"

"Yes."

"Are you using birth control?"

"Infrequently."

"Do you want us to do STD testing and a pregnancy test?"

"I don't think that it's necessary."

"The doctor is going to strongly recommend it."

"Ok. That's fine then."

"Ok, go to the lab so they can collect a urine sample and blood work. When you come from the lab come to this room, get undressed, put on this gown with the opening facing the front. The doctor will be in shortly after that."

After I deposit my urine sample I go back to the room and get undressed, my mind can't help but to daydream of a future with Rick and a child. We would make a perfect family. I only need to put a few more pieces in place before he is mine. The doctor walks in and my daydream fades away.

"Hello Shannon." She speaks as she reads over my chart and the notes the nurse has made in the computer on my chart.

"Hello, Dr. Cartman."

"So we're going to do a pap smear, a wet mount to check for STD's and a pregnancy test?"

"Yes."

"Ok. Nurse Lynn is getting the results of your pregnancy test now."

Her questions don't stop as she examines me. "What kind of symptoms are you having?"

"Frequent urination, I think I may have a bladder infection."

"We'll find out soon enough. Once we run all of the tests, we'll be able to see what the cause of these symptoms is."

As she finishes the pap smear, the nurse walks in and passes her a sheet of paper.

"Well Shannon it looks like your pregnancy test came back positive."

"What?" I ask in both surprise and excitement.

"Yes. You're expecting."

"Wow. I can't believe it. I wanted it to happen, in fact I was going to plan for it to happen, but I didn't know it occurred already!" We had sex for the first time just a couple of weeks ago.

"We'll need to make another appointment for you before you leave."

"Doctor Cartman, this is great news. Thanks. My dreams are coming true."

I bustle out of the doctor's office and run into Rick. I totally forgot my mission and that was to run into Tiffany, but this is even better. I can't wait to share the good news with him.

"Shannon," he pauses, "Hey."

"Hi Rick."

"Your appointment with the doctor was here?"

"Yea, what are you doing here?"

"I just had a physical."

In the corner of my eye, I see Tiffany walking up behind Rick. He doesn't see her approach.

"Rick, I just left my doctor and she said I'm pregnant." I make sure Tiffany is in earshot to hear me before Rick detects her presence.

I hope to see excitement race across his face, but I see panic steal the joy from him.

"What?" He exclaims in a loud whisper. Tiffany was in earshot to hear me and beams.

"Well, congratulations Shannon! Glad to hear that someone has good news around here." Tiffany's words gallop around me with joy.

I smile, perhaps if Rick sees Tiffany's excitement. Some form of relief will allow him to enjoy this moment with me. Rick, looks to Tiffany pale-faced.

"Well who's the proud papa Shannon?" Tiffany asks. Rick's glance attempts to strangle the life out of my response.

"In due time, but I'll say this. He'll be the perfect compliment as a life partner and a great father. It'll be our first bundle of shared joy."

"Wow, so is a marriage in the horizon?"

"I hope so. We'll see. We already make a great team, but you know how men are – they don't respond well to pressure, but I'm confident he'll come around in due time."

Tiffany gives me a pity smile, as if she feels sorry for me. Bitch. If she only knew, this was my biggest break and I'm on cloud nine! Rick doesn't say a word, but his eyes are bloodshot red. When he calms down and this settles in, he'll reflect on how well we work together and he'll bond with this pregnancy and bond with me. I love him so. He'll come around.

"Tiffany, I need to talk with Shannon about some work issues, can you excuse us for just a moment?" Rick speaks to Tiffany trying to steady his voice.

"No problem Richard, I was just on my way out. I've already checked on Troy and Sadie, so I'm headed home; nice to bump into you Shannon. Richard."

I better act now, if I don't talk to Tiffany now, I may not get the chance again.

"Rick no problem, I can talk to you. I just need to run to my car really fast, I left my cell phone and don't want to miss a very important call. I'll be right back. Tiffany, I'll walk out with you."

Tiffany glances back with that 'I feel so sorry for you' pitiful smile and nods her head 'Ok'. So we walk out together. Rick's eyes follow me in fury. I feel the heat from his glare burning on the back of my neck. I know he wants to ask me if this is possibly his child and the fact that I'm putting him off is not sitting well with him.

"So Shannon, when will you debut your beaux?"

"Soon" Little scalawag bitch, "So Tiffany, you mentioned you checked on Troy and Sadie. Isn't Troy, Sojourn's ex-husband?"

"Yes. He was in a car accident."

"Wow. You know tragedies have a way of repairing estranged relationships, maybe it'll do some good for Sojourn and Troy."

"I'm sure she's probably feeling closer to him, she's a bit protective and guarded right now."

So she is feeling protective over him, guarding him, this would be the perfect time to incite a jealous rage and show Rick her ugly side.

"How is he responding?"

"I hope he doesn't. Anyway, I see my car. I'll see you later Shannon. Congratulations!"

"Thanks Tiffany!" I call off as she runs away and I circle back around to talk to Rick.

As I turn around I see him approaching me in the parking lot.

"Are you forgetting something Shannon?"

"What are you talking about Rick?"

"You came out here for your phone. Remember?"

"Oh, yes. Silly me, I had it the whole time. Right here in this suitcase of a purse. I just couldn't find it until I felt it vibrate."

"Shannon..."

I interrupt before he has a chance to finish his sentence, "Rick, we'll both be first time parents, you have a right to be a bit nervous. I'm nervous too."

"Shannon, how do you know this is my child? We only had sex once."

"It only takes one time Richard, you're my only boyfriend. I haven't been with anyone else. Remember Jason broke up with me."

"Wait a minute, slow down. I'm not your boyfriend. I'm still married. Married to Tiffany who you've already shared this information with!"

"Rick you don't even live in the same house, Tiffany is divorcing you."

"I'm still married Shannon!"

"Well now you're expecting, we both are. Babies are a blessing from above, so stop treating this as if it is a curse!"

Rick's anger still has not subsided.

"Rick, don't I take good care of you at work, I'll do the same as a life partner and mother. Don't worry."

"Life partner? What are you talking about Shannon? I'm married, I have a life partner."

"Well convince Tiffany of that, and while you're at it, make sure Sojourn knows also. She has a life partner she's working hard on protecting and restoring to his proper place right now. Haven't you noticed how this tragedy has brought them back together? She loves Troy and everyone can see it, it's time you see it too."

"Shannon, I'm not convinced that it's my child. Are you keeping it?"

"Of course Rick, I don't believe in abortion."

"You aren't on the pill?"

"Rick pill maintenance is so hard. I keep forgetting to take them."

"Why didn't you tell me this?"

"Would it have mattered?"

"Yes!"

"Rick, I didn't forget to take them on purpose. I get so focused on work and covering your back, that there are times that I forget to take them. It's hard to remember to do this everyday."

"Shannon. You're irresponsibility is a high price to pay for my life and yours – if this is my child."

"Rick my body doesn't produce sperm! I can't get pregnant all by myself. So before you start talking about responsibility or lack thereof, remember you're the one with the sperm and you're also the one telling me that you're married! You are no one to give me a talk on responsibility!"

I see frustration beginning to overwhelm him. His body is tensing up and I see the stress seeping through his skin as if it is poision contaminating his thoughts and sound reason.

"Rick regardless of how you see this or how I feel about this, I'm keeping this child. At my age, it may be my last chance to have one. This is both a blessing and a joy for me. You're a great guy, good looking, great career and great set of brains. I couldn't ask for a better father for my child. Even if it was an accident, I'm pleased."

"I feel like you set me up Shannon, as if you are manipulating me, I can't prove it, but I feel it in my gut."

"Rick, why would I manipulate a man that I care for so deeply, I have never betrayed your confidence or your trust. You have no right to accuse me of something like that."

"Care for me deeply? When did all of this happen Shannon! We work together that's it. Caring for my professional needs is your job. Caring for my personal needs is not!"

"Are you going to be there for me and this child?"

"I need a DNA test before I answer that question."

"Before you answer what question Rick?" Sojourn sneaks up behind me and sends me a scowling look as she speaks to Rick.

"Sojourn." How dare she look at me with attitude? She just doesn't know, I'm about to destroy that heifer.

"Are you talking about the DNA test on Sadie's twins? If so, what business is that of your secretary?" An obvious meager attempt to minimize and demean me by trying to refer to me as the hired help.

"It's none of her business Sojourn, or mine. Tell me how you're doing."

"Yes, Sojourn how are you doing? Rick asked me to let everyone know at work that you needed some extra time off. I hope the time away has been a good for you." I say with a sarcastic bite, dressed in an empathetic gown. Sojourn looks at me like she wants to say thank you, but instead cuts her eyes back to Rick.

"Rick, Carlo is resting and they're going to release Troy to come home, I'm going to get the car and drive it up to the breezeway. Troy's mother is bringing the boys and I'm going to go home and lay down. I've had a pretty eventful day and need to give my mind, heart and body a minute to catch up. I need just a moment of rest so I can recharge and tend to Troy, Carlo and the kids."

"Can I do anything for you?" Rick asks like a lovesick puppy.

"Unless you can transform into a pillow and a mattress, I think not."

She tries to look at me with kindness, but instead quietly rolls her eyes and walks off to her car. Heifer.

"Shannon, we'll finish this talk later. I need to clear my head."

Rick walks off and I turn to find Troy's room. It's time we had a talk. A baby is growing inside of me. God is so good. I travel until I find Troy's room and walk in on him as he is preparing to go home.

"Hi Troy."

"Hi. Do I know you? You look familiar."

"Yes. You do know me. We fucked. Remember?"

He studies my face as if he is trying to remember me.

"Why are you here? You've came back for more?"

"No. It wasn't that good the first time."

He gives me a soft scowl. What an arrogant ass.

"What do you want? Why are you here?"

"What would Sojourn do if she knew we fucked?"

I watch his face harden as he finally begins to understand why I'm here.

"I recorded it all on my cell phone." I play a portion for him.

"You set me up?"

"Yes. Our encounter genuinely started as a unique experience but when your friend spoke to you and I found out who you where and who your former wife was; I figured I could use this to my advantage if you were a willing participant and you were. My lucky day."

"What do you want?"

"I want the same thing you want. I want Sojourn out of Rick's life and totally in yours. I want you to do whatever it takes to win her back."

"I don't know why you want that, or how you know her, but what you're asking isn't all that easy to do. Do you know how long I've been trying?"

"Sojourn went to get the car, she'll be back shortly and I'm sure you want me gone by then so you don't have to explain to her who I am or why I'm here. So listen closely. I expect you to come up with a plan. If you don't, my plan is to make her insanely jealous by exposing our encounter. That can't be good for you, but it will be great for me. So figure out how you can make this great for you and great for me. After all we want the same thing."

"I love Sojourn. I'm going to work on putting my family back together, regardless of what you do, don't do, say or don't say. I don't like people who attempt to threaten me to get what they want, even if what we want is the same thing."

"Well, look at this way. You're not helping me get what I want; I'm helping you get what you want. However you see it, get her back in *your* life!"

I pull out my compact and straighten my hair. I glance up to address Troy one last time, "Trust me – if you fall short, I can handle it. So take care of it so I don't have to."

I smile back, "By the way, you have incredible potential. You have a nice package and sensational sexual energy, but no rhythm. Why don't you work on that too?"

Chapter 29

Tiffany

I walk into Sadie's room to check on her. She has always been transparent with her words and her expressions. Today, though, I see discontent. I hope it's not the baby blues.

"Sadie, how you doing girl?"

"I'm good, I get to go home today."

"You too?"

"Yeah."

"What's wrong girl? And don't lie, I can already see it on your face."

"Tiffany, I don't know. Carlo doesn't want a DNA test, Troy does, Sojourn does and in a way, I want to know also."

"So get the test."

"I'm scared girl, I don't want to lose Carlo. He feels so distant after the accident."

"How is he distant Sadie? It seems to me he wants you by his side."

Sadie raises her voice and tears begin to escape and run away from her eyes, "It's just different, Tiffany! I can feel a difference!"

"Sadie, calm down girl. Ok. Ok. Tell me what's different."

"When I talk of a future with us, he usually can go there with me. Now when I talk about a future, he avoids the discussion. He tells me to slow down, one day at a time."

"Sadie, sometimes you do hurry things, I don't think what he is saying is too out of the ordi..."

She interrupts me almost yelling, "It's different Tiffany!"

I'm in shock. I try not to let the worry show on my face, but she is definitely on edge.

"I'm listening Sadie. Talk."

"Tiffany, if I lose him. I don't know what I'll do."

"What do you mean Sadie?"

"I love him Tiffany. I can't let him slip out of my hands"

I want to ask her how she knows that he's slipping, but I resist, because I don't want to send her over the edge again, so I continue to listen.

"I know you care about him, Sadie. It shows."

"We got into a fight at the Coffee Bean a while back. I never told this to anyone, but he threatened to fight me for custody."

Her tears silently crawl from her eyes as if they are running away from her, trying desperately to escape a torturous prison.

"I pleaded with him not to. Not to leave me."

"What happened Sadie?"

"He stayed."

...But for how long? Slithers across my mind, but I dare not share this thought with her.

I look into her eyes, and see a desperate fear and the look scares me.

"Sadie, honey, you have to pull yourself together. You were a grown woman before you met him and you'll be a grown, fully functioning, independent woman long after he's gone...if he leaves."

"No Tiff, I was a grown lonely woman before he came, and I'll be a grown, fat, mother of two that is broken-hearted and lonely after he leaves."

My heart begins to cry, for Sadie; as if I mourn with her – wait! No! That's her grief painting that picture, it's not her reality.

"Sadie, stop it! Just stop it! Look at me. Richard and I are married and he is gone. I'm still alive, I still have life! I have to stare at my pain every day and I hate it! But I'm still here. I'm still here girl. If I can do it, God knows you can!"

"I'm not you Tiffany."

"Don't do me. Do you."

"How do you do it, Tiff?"

"Sadie, I blamed her, then I blamed him, then I blamed myself and after all the finger pointing, I decided to just live life. Live it for me. I just went back to basics and it started with me."

"Tiffany, I can't bear being alone again."

"You can be married and be alone, Sadie. You just have to start loving you. A man can't make your loneliness go away. You have to begin with enjoying your own company first. Then whether a relationship makes it or not, you don't become lonely in a relationship either – because you enjoy your own company. "

"He's going to leave me Tiffany. I can see it now. I know it's going to happen."

My eyes fall on her like a huge set of arms trying to squeeze love into her heart.

"Being a good woman isn't enough, is it?" Her words land on me like anvil and it hurts. If being a good woman isn't enough what is?

"I don't know Sadie. How can we tell if what is good today will be good tomorrow? Maybe it's more of a matter choice. Do you believe in the person enough to choose to work through the difficult times or to pack up and run as far away as you can?"

I can't help to reflect on my own choices as I reflect on hers.

"I'm willing to work Tiffany, I love him that much."

"I hear you girl, but you can't do the work alone."

I look at her with love and my glance tries to penetrate her pain, "If you want the DNA test, get it. Just don't make that man the center of your world like I made Richard. "

"Tiff, what if it's another woman. What if it's just like what you experienced with Richard?"

"Why do you think it's another woman Sadie?"

"It has to be Tiffany! It just has to." Her words trail off and attempt to survive, searching for air in a riptide of sorrow, "If it's not another woman, than it's me, something must be wrong with me!"

Tears run from her eyes as if in a marathon, they run in packs, droves and they don't stop. It's like her hurt has no end.

"Sadie." I whisper as I reach for her hand. She doesn't look at me, just continues to cry. Damn. I hate that I understand this, but I do. I cried just like this over Richard until I just ran out of tears. I don't know what to say. A piece of me knows she needs to cry this out, another piece of me feels she needs to stop blaming herself, but another piece of me feels like she could be blowing all of this out of proportion. None of the pieces come together to form a sentence. My thoughts are shooting out in all directions. So I say nothing. I just hold her hand and help her cry.

"Tiff?"

"Yes Sadie?"

"Is Sojourn in Rick's life or Troy's."

"I don't know."

I look at Sadie, "But Sojourn or not, Richard or not. I am and I will continue to be living for me!"

I release Sadie's hand and lean back in the hospital chair as if I am both the client and the therapist in a session, "I looked in the mirror, saw my faults, and said to myself, 'You're beautiful, just as you are.' Whether that's good enough or not good enough, I don't know. But what I do know is that it's worthy of a second chance at life, a second chance at love and peace."

I break my blank stare and glance at Sadie. She doesn't comment but her tears continue to run this marathon silently; as if they are trying to pace themselves more slowly now, but they are still running the race. The quiet in the room feels as soft as a mother's lullaby and we allow it to cradle our thoughts as we securely reflect on our lives.

Chapter 30

Richard

If I could find a cave and crawl into it, I would. I can't believe I messed around and got Shannon pregnant. *Shit!* Now I've got to deal with this woman for the rest of my life. Not to mention the wrath of Tiffany and Sojourn. I'm in a crappy apartment, an estranged marriage and in a relationship with a woman whose affections are as fleeting as the wind. The only good thing happening in my life right now is a new job opportunity. I don't know where to go, so I aimlessly drive, hoping the melodic sounds of jazz will run my problems away. After hearing Shannon tell me in front of Tiffany that she's pregnant. I feel lost, pissed. How do I keep making a fine-ass mess of everything? I feel like a total fuck-up.

When I finally pull things into focus, I look up and find myself in the driveway of my home with Tiffany. Why did I drive here? Tiffany hates me. I hate me. Damn! How did I do something stupid like this? I know better.

I just sit in the driveway not sure what to do or where to go. I put my car in park, throw on a track of John Coltrane, recline my seat as far as it will go and close my eyes. I turn the music up as loud as I can, hoping that the music will pound the stress and frustration out of my body. I hear the car door open, drawing my attention away from the music and as I look up, I see Tiffany. She opens the passenger side door and sits with me. She doesn't say anything; she doesn't turn my music down. She just places her left hand on my leg and the warmth from her touch calms me. I place my hand on top of hers and I feel her recline her seat back and de-stress with me. My heart whispers, *"Thank you."*

The entire album plays and I look to Tiffany, "Do you want to take a drive with me?"

I look into her eyes and see that she is hesitant. I pray she doesn't say no.

"Yes. I would like to go on a drive with you Richard."

I feel air fill my lungs in relief. I don't believe in grown men crying, but her kindness moves me. I start the car and drive. I drive in silence with the music playing and Tiffany's hand resting on my leg.

I drive until I hit beachfront in Galveston.

"Come on Tiffany, let's take a walk."

I still see her holding back, but that's ok. It feels good just being with her right now. We walk to the beach and stand just on the edge where the sand meets the water and we allow the water to wash on shore around our ankles, then retreat back into the gulf.

I hold her hands and look into her eyes, "I'm sorry I hurt you."

She listens with her heart and she puts her hand on my cheek and says, "Thank you for that."

We begin to walk along the shoreline when she asks, "Richard, what are we doing here?"

"I don't know Tiffany."

"Richard, what do you want from me? You've moved on. I need to also."

My heartbeat quickens at the thought of her moving on without me.

"Tiffany I made some mistakes when I was living life without you. I don't deserve your forgiveness and don't know if I have completely settled things in my heart, but what I do know is that I don't want you to experience the pain I carry, by embracing life without me."

"What are you saying Richard, it's ok for you to screw around with Sojourn, but not for me to date as I please?"

"We're still married, Tiffany."

"...and you're still screwing Sojourn, Richard!"

This is not going in the direction I want it to. I love her, but I love Sojourn too. Is it possible to love two women at the same time? What's wrong with me?

"Richard, regardless of how I feel about Sojourn, she is nothing more than a woman too. The difference is, she is not the woman for you. I am," she pauses, "was."

She looks at me with both fury and forgiveness, "and until you figure that out, we're fini..."

"...don't finish that sentence, Tiffany."

She stops. "Don't finish that sentence, please. Tiffany, let's just finish our walk. Just for this moment, let me enjoy the company of my wife. We can argue tomorrow if you wish, but just for tonight, hold my hand and walk with me."

I watch as one single tear rolls down her cheek, her face says I love you. I love her too.

"Ok Richard, we can finish the conversation later. Let's walk."

Chapter 31

Carlo

"Say brother, I got my walking papers today."

I wake, drowsily to Troy's voice. It takes a second for my eyes to focus, but I see him in a wheelchair with Sojourn standing by his side.

"Walking papers, huh?"

"Yeah, man. I'm going home."

"Why are you still in a wheelchair then?"

He laughs, "How you doing buddy?"

"Well if the Lord says the same, I'm going home tomorrow."

"You're doing that good?"

"Either that or the insurance is doing really bad man." Laughter escapes my mouth.

"I hear ya."

"I need some words with you man."

"Yeah what is it?"

"I'm your buddy, but not your brother-in-law. Sojourn's not my sister or your wife. After the accident man, I just have a need to be me. An honest me, no more charades."

"Cool. Do you man, but what does any of that have to do with Sojourn?"

"Carlo, Troy and I wanted to see the twins before we left. Is that ok?" Sojourn nervously interrupts. Her eyes scream with anxiety. I know she wants me not to have this conversation, but no time is a good time for this, so it's best just to get it over with.

"Sojourn, why don't you go and ask Sadie about the twins. She's leaving today also. I believe her friend Jessica just got into town and is taking her home." If Sojourn leaves, I can have this talk.

"Carlo, I have a better idea! How about you call her on the phone in your room, it would save me a trip."

I acquiesce, "ok."

As I dial Sadie's number I hear Sojourn in the background.

"Troy, the boys are really excited to see you get home. We've really got to hurry. You're mom has cooked you a 'Glad you're alive and welcome home dinner' and you know she doesn't want the food to get cold."

"Well you're the one who asked for the twins to be brought up."

"How about we just go to the maternity ward and leave from there. We can save Sadie the trouble and save time."

"Alright that's fine. I do want to see them. Carlo, don't worry about it man, we'll go down there."

I hang up the phone. I look at Sojourn with discontentment. She knows what I'm trying to do. I just feel it's best to be honest. Honest about everything. It doesn't matter if there is an 'us' or not, what matters is I don't have to live a lie.

"Carlo, if you get out tomorrow, let me know."

I look at her with a quiet anger, "Yeah, ok."

"Alright Carlo, we'll see you."

"See you, Troy."

I watch as Sojourn wheels Troy out of my room and I overhear her say, "Troy, just a minute, I left my purse in there."

She walks back in and closes the door.

"Look, Carlo! You had a spiritual near death encounter not me! I have to live with the decisions you make and I'm not ready. I've got enough crap happening in my life right now and don't have any more room for drama. Think about that the next time you feel the need to clear the air!" Her words softly glide across the room in a whisper and punch me in the gut with the force of a sledgehammer.

"Sojourn, the longer we wait, the more dangerous life games become for everyone."

"Carlo, I need to get through today. Troy is going home, his mom and kids are anxious to see him. You are not going to ruin that with your 'Honesty Tour'!"

"I'm going to 'do me' Sojourn. I've got to stand by truth."

"You know while you were up there - that place in between death and life, did your spiritual guide tell you that there's a time for every-thing? A time to talk and a time to shut the hell up! Well guess what time it is now?" Her words grab me in a chokehold.

It's a time to talk runs across my mind, but I understand, "Ok Sojourn, for now, I'll shut up. Go."

She throws her purse on her shoulder and like a whirling tor-nado, spins out of the room.

"I love you, Sojourn."

"Carlo, we're still in the shut the hell up time." I watch as she leaves, closing the door behind her.

My phone rings.

"Hello?"

"Hey honey. Did you just call?"

"Yeah. Sojourn is on her way down there to see the twins. Is Jes-sica taking you home?"

"Yes. As soon as she gets into the house and settled, she's going to pick me up and take me home."

"Carlo?"

"Yes?"

"Do you love me?"

"You're a good woman, Bella."

"I asked you if you loved me."

"Bella, you are an important part of my life."

"Do you love me, Carlo?"

"Yes."

"Say it."

"Bella, that's enough for today."

"Why can't you say it, Carlo?"

"Sadie! That's enough. I don't want you upset when Sojourn and Troy walk in."

"Why would I be upset, unless it is because you don't love me anymore? Is there another woman Carlo?"

"Sadie. When they leave come up here and we'll talk."

"No. We can talk now. I'll tell them to leave."

"Bella. Stop this. Stop. Are you trying to force me to have a conversation that I don't want to have? It's not working."

"Carlo, I need to know how you feel and I need to know now. The rest of the world can stop until I get my answer."

"The world will not stop and I'm one man that will not be controlled or made to do something that I don't want to do."

"What am I going to do, Carlo? Tell me!"

"I'm not having this conversation Sadie, it ends now. I'm hanging up."

"Carlo. Wait please."

"Sadie, I don't understand what's wrong with you. Why are you so emotional?"

"I need to know how you feel. I feel like dying."

"Sadie. I love who you are and what you have been to me. I'm not sure how I feel about 'us'. I don't know what I want or need right now."

"Are you breaking up with me, Carlo?" I hear desperation screaming through the phone and it grabs both my cheeks with force and steals my complete attention.

"Sadie. I don't know what I want or need. That's it, nothing more. It's not a break up and it's not a promise."

I hear Sojourn's voice in the background, "Sadie. What's wrong?"

I hear Sadie's voice crackling from tears penetrating the surface, "Carlo's breaking up with me, it's another woman."

What? What is wrong with this girl? What is she doing?

"Sadie! Sadie!" I yell through the phone trying to get her attention.

"Carlo!" Sojourn demands. She must have grabbed the phone from Sadie!

"What did you tell Sadie? Didn't I tell you to shut the hell up?"

"No Sojourn, you didn't." I hear Troy in the background; "You didn't tell him that in my presence. What the hell is going on? What does he need to shut up about?"

I don't hear anything. Silence.

"Give me the damn phone, Sojourn." I hear Troy yell.

"Carlo, those words you had for me earlier, you better get the rest of them out right now!"

Shit. Two things I should have done when I had the chance. I should have told Troy when he was in the room and hung the phone up on Sadie when I had the chance.

Chapter 32

Tiffany

"Richard, it's getting late. We should get back home." My words try to run back in my mouth, why in the world did I say we and home in the same sentence?

"Tiffany, this has been one of the most beautiful moments in our relationship."

"Yes. Richard it has."

"I've made a fine mess out of my life, I don't even know how to fix it."

"Richard you always find your way out of everything, including our marriage."

"Ouch, Tiff. I guess I deserved that. Do you think I can find my way back?"

"Richard, it's too late for that."

"It's not too late Tiffany. We're still married."

"I've already filed for divorce Richard."

"What?"

"I talked this over with Troy. I'm using the same attorney he had."

"Troy? What's going on with you and Troy Tiff?"

"The exact same thing going on with you and Sojourn."

"Sojourn and I were a mistake Tiffany."

"Well, whatever happens with Troy and I, I can guarantee one thing, it'll be done with intent, not by accident."

"If Troy touches you Tiffany, I'll hurt him! You're still my wife."

How dare he get jealous after what he has put me through? How dare he try and tell me anything about my life after he abused and misused my heart. I look into his eyes and see that he's hurting too. Just as much as I am.

"Richard. We have to move on."

"Tiffany, I'm not ready to move on without you."

"Richard, where is all of this coming from? I came to your room while you were waiting for your mistress to arrive."

"Tiffany, I don't need you to remind me of the mistakes I've made. My mistakes attempt to destroy me little by little each day."

I feel for him, but when I needed him, he was too busy shoving his dick up Sojourn's skirt. Now that he's in pain, he wants me to help him through. Selfish, ignorant man. I want to forgive him, but I hate him as much as I love him."

"Rick want do you want from me?"

"I want to ask for a second chance, but I'm afraid of messing up again and losing you forever."

What makes him think he hasn't already lost me forever? He acts like he is totally oblivious to the pain he has caused me. As if our break up was a little boo-boo a band-aid can cure. I went through hell and came back. I'm not doing it again! Who I am kidding? I still love this man. But what the hell does love have to do with anything? He betrayed me. Lied to me, abandoned me –all for a piece of ass on the side. Then he wants me to pity him. It is so hard trying to be open minded with him.

"Richard, what do you mean afraid of messing up again? As if slipping your dick inside of another woman happens by accident. You're clothes don't accidentally fall off and you don't accidentally slip and fall inside a pussy."

"Tiffany, what do you want from me?"

"Nothing."

He looks at me, with so much pain in his eyes. He won't cry, he never does, but you see it.

"Richard, I want to trust you. I want to have what we had before, but recapturing the past is impossible."

"We can build a future together Tiffany. A new start."

I don't know. We sit in silence, I want to believe him, but I don't trust him. My phone vibrates and I see a text message from Troy. He wants to see me. I quickly respond and focus my attention back on Richard.

"Richard, let's just take it one step at a time. No promises on anything."

"Ok."

"...and"

"and what?"

"No promises with Troy. I won't lie to you about what's happening, and I'm not going to try and hide it."

"Tiffany I forbid you to see him."

"Then let's call it off now."

"No. No. I don't want to know about it Tiffany."

He stops and looks me in the eyes, "No. My position stands. I don't want that man touching you."

I don't respond. I do want to save this marriage, but I don't agree with the terms.

"What about Sojourn?"

"I'll work on that."

"So let me get this straight, you'll work on Sojourn and I'm to avoid Troy?"

"Tiffany, I'll take care of it. Just give me a little space to take care of it my way."

"No dick accidents, Richard."

He smiles and throws his arm around my neck and pulls me toward him, my head lands on his shoulder blade and it feels good, but I don't trust him.

"No dick accidents." He kisses me on the forehead, "Let's go home Tiffany."

I knew I opened a can of worms. *Let's go home Tiffany.* His words torture me as they slither in my ears. I'm not ready to move that fast. He moved out of our home. He's not going to move back in that fast. He abandoned me, deserted me over that woman.

"When you drop me off at home, just call me so I know you made it back to your apartment." There, I think I cleaned that up.

"Ok. One last walk on the beach. Give me your hand my love."

I grab his hand, why is he calling me 'My love' as if he hasn't completely taken advantage of that love already. He doesn't deserve a second chance. How can I love someone so much, but feel so bitter at the same time? It's like my heart is at war."

I wonder what Troy is doing right now.

Chapter 33

Troy

Lord knows I hope I'm wrong about the feeling I have. If Carlo and Sojourn have betrayed me. I'll never forgive them. Is this what Carlo was trying to tell me?

"Give me the damn phone, Sojourn." I yell.

"Carlo, those words you had for me earlier, you better get the rest of them out right now!"

"Look Troy, something is with Sadie. She's on a complete emotional edge."

"Carlo, what in the fuck is going on with you and Sojourn? Don't try and distract me with Sadie's bullshit."

"Nothing is going on with Sojourn and me Troy, but I won't lie to you after the accident...."

"Hello? Hello? Carlo!"

I look up and see that Sojourn has disconnected the line. Now I know she's hiding something.

"Sojourn, what is it? What are you hiding from me?"

"You're questioning me? What are you hiding Troy? You've been with another woman haven't you? I saw the look in your eyes when Tiffany came in the room! So tell me Troy what are you hiding?"

Damn. Never mind Tiffany, we're not fucking but if that woman that came to my room gives that recording to Sojourn, she's going to be pissed.

"Sojourn, Tiffany is a friend, she doesn't carry the title of the other woman in my life. I told you that I was going to see other people Sojourn. You don't know what you want from me."

"Troy, we have got to get home. We can talk in the car. I may not know exactly what I want from you but I do know that I'm not interested in the Troy 'dick sharing' plan!"

Sojourn begins to wheel me toward the door to leave.

"Wait! Who's the other woman, Sojourn? Who has Carlo fallen in love with? I was right wasn't I?"

"You mean you were fishing for information Sadie? Carlo didn't tell you anything?"

"Do you honestly think I need a man to confirm what a woman knows in her heart?" Sadie screams.

"I look at Sadie as the innocent in all of this. I think you accidentally stumbled on something Queen."

"I didn't stumble, a woman knows when something is wrong with her man."

"Sojourn, take me to Carlo." I demand. I need to know what the hell is going on.

"No. No Troy, I've had enough. We are going home to have dinner with your mother and the kids."

"Sojourn, I'm not with Tiffany and you better not have fucked another man since being by side. I mean that!"

Sojourn ignores me and turns her attention back to Sadie. "Sadie, when are you going home?"

"Jessica is coming to pick me up. She and her husband Jason are just getting back from vacation and she wants to see me and the twins."

"Sadie, don't worry yourself, Queen. Pull it together for the sake of the twins."

I get out of my wheelchair and limp to give Sadie a hug. Sojourn throws a social smile to Sadie as we leave the room.

"Sadie is not your Queen. I am." Sojourn screams in a whisper as she is rolling to the entrance.

"Sojourn, we've had this talk already."

"Talk or not, you don't need to address any woman as 'Queen' in my presence. The car is parked out front Troy. Wait here."

A nurse waits with me as Sojourn opens the car door. I lift out of the chair and collide with the car seat as I attempt to sit down. I'm not as strong as I would like to be.

"Speaking of conversations in presence. What conversation did you have with Carlo out of my presence? Why did he feel the need to tell me you are not my wife and he is not your sister? Sojourn if I find out you're fucking him, I will destroy you and him."

"Troy, I have my suspicions as well and us not trusting each other is a horrible way to start a new beginning."

I grab her thigh as she is driving, "My suspicions better not be right."

"I'm not fucking him, Troy."

"You're hiding something Sojourn. You know when I talk to him I'm going to find out. Wouldn't you prefer that I hear it from you?"

"Troy, please we're almost at your mother's house. Can we table this?"

"Yeah. Go on in. I need just a minute."

"Ok."

I watch as Sojourn walks in the house. I need to relive some tension. What is wrong with me? I thought we were on speaking terms again. I thought if I prayed, talked to you – you could fix this. So many women. Names and faces I don't know, bodies I've touched. How can I be what Sojourn needs, if I can't be what you expect of me? It's always the same. I want to do right, then temptation, then the fall – and here I am again. Fallen. Damn. Pain begins to radiate through my leg. Why can't I get it right? Just once. Why can't I get it right?

I haven't touched Tiffany. Temptation was right there and I resisted. Maybe I can do it again?

I text Tiffany. *I want to spend some time with you. You up for it?*

She responds, *Ecstatically and Absolutely YES!*

I text her back, *You just made a grown man smile.*

She responds, *Looking forward to keeping that smile there.*

Chapter 34

Shannon

I watch as Rick walks into the office.

"Rick would you like me to program your appointments in your PDA?"

"Not today Shannon, why don't you come in my office. We need to talk."

I know he wants to talk about this pregnancy, but I can tell something else is on his mind today. I can read him like a book.

"Shannon, my personal life is too intertwined with my professional life."

"What are you telling me Rick?"

"I'm resigning. I need a fresh start."

Resigning? What does that mean for me, my job? Fear pumps

through my veins. What does this mean for our child? This changes everything.

"Resigning from me and this job?"

"I'm definitely resigning from this job. How do you know that you're carrying my child Shannon, how can you be sure?"

"In the past three months, I've been abstinent. I've only been with you. I've only wanted to be with you. I've dreamed of it." Oh, and one other, but he doesn't count.

"Shannon, I'm married."

"You and Tiffany are getting a divorce, I thought the only thing standing in our way was Sojourn."

"Sojourn? Divorce? How do you know any of this?"

"Rick, everyone knows about you and Sojourn. As for your divorce once it is filed, it's public record. Everyone has access to that."

"Regardless Shannon, no one is standing in our way, we are not standing together for anything except this job. We don't have a relationship." His words escape as hostile whispers, and sting like a wasp.

"Rick, we spend more time with each other than we do anyone else in our lives. I know what you need before you need it. I've been loyal to you and good to you. I've been better to you Rick than any other woman before me."

"Shannon, I'm married. Even if we divorce, I'll be married until the divorce is final!"

"Rick, I want to be happy too. I want the same dream as Tiffany and Sojourn. I want to fall in love, have babies and live happily ever after. Your divorce is my chance at that."

"Your dream will be your nightmare if you fall in love with some-one that doesn't love you back."

"You will grow to love me back."

"No Shannon. It's not going to happen."

"But it could…"

"No. It'll never happen."

"How do you explain our moment then? It was perfect."

"It was sex. You caught me at a real vulnerable period in my life."

"Shannon, build your life around a man that is in the position to give you love back."

"You'll be in that position soon Rick."

"Shannon, I've arranged for you to keep your job, and get a pro-motion. You're capable, ready and you've earned it. It should help you provide a better living for this baby also."

"Rick."

"This will be my last week here, and I'm going to all of the sites to bid farewell. So you won't see me in the office much."

"Rick, are you abandoning me? I'm still carrying your child."

"It's not here yet. We'll cross that bridge when we get to it."

"We're at that bridge NOW!"

"Shannon, I can only deal with one MAJOR life catastrophe at a time. One!"

"You see this as a catastrophe?"

"At this point in my life? YES! We didn't plan this! This was not an intentional pregnancy. Stop pretending. We're not together. We're not a family. We will never be one. This pregnancy could jeopardize everything for me. My marriage, my friendship with Sojourn, my career...."

"This child could be the best thing that ever happened to you."

"Shannon. I need to go. We'll talk later."

The plans and the future I was creating with Rick seem to be crumbling. I know Rick. I know he's just going through a rough patch. He'll come around. This baby will change things. *But what if it doesn't?* No. No. I can't think like that. I just need to go back to the drawing board. I thought Sojourn was the only variable, now I see the distance this job creates and Tiffany as two more variables. I'll fight for the formation of this family. My dreams will come true. I hear my phone ringing.

"Hello?"

"Shannon Scott?"

"Yes, how can I help you?"

"Hi. I'm Douglas Michaels. We'll be working together."

"Are you Rick's replacement?"

"I'm his interim replacement, as it stands now."

"So you'll be my new boss?"

"Not exactly. We'll be working side by side. At least that's how I look at it." That's right, Rick said I would be getting a promotion.

"I'd like to take you to dinner tomorrow night, so we can get to know each other better. Are you open to that?"

"Sure, why not?"

"Very good. I'll see you tomorrow night."

"Ok. I'll be ready."

Rick, I can't believe you're leaving me.

Chapter 35

Carlo

I flip through the television channels aimlessly, my eyes remain focused on the screen, and my mind wanders at the same speed of each click of the remote control. How do I create a world that is pleasing to me without upsetting the worlds of so many around me? What is my life going to be like once I recover? What will become of Sadie and I? My boys? What if I tell Troy how I really feel about Sojourn, and in his anger he and Sadie confirm paternity and try and take my boys from me? My finger continues to flip through channel after channel, my mind flips through thought after thought. Honesty is important to me, but at what cost? I don't want to hurt anyone. I'm not willing to sacrifice my boys, for a duty to honesty. *But what if?* I don't know if I can live a life of deception. What message am I teaching my boys? If I tell Sadie how I really feel, she'll hurt me or hurt herself. I know what I should do, but can I do it is the question? The creaking of the hospital door interrupts my thoughts.

"Bella. You managed to escape your floor again?"

"Walking is good. Are you able to walk, Carlo?"

"Yea. My head was bruised worse than my bones, but I seem to be doing ok."

"Come walk with me."

"Ok Bella."

I grab my IV tower and roll out of the bed. We exit my hospital room and begin to lap around the hospital floor.

"You're going home today?"

"Yes, with the boys. Jessica is going to take me home and help me out for a couple of days. When you get out Carlo, are you going to move in with us?"

"Sadie, one day at a time."

"Carlo is there another woman?"

"I'm not seeing another woman Sadie."

"How do you feel about me?"

"My feelings for you have not changed."

"Something has changed Carlo. I can feel it. What's changed and don't lie to me."

I pause from our slow stroll around the hospital floor and glance at Sadie. Truth is in me and I want to release it, but will I lose my boys in the process?

"Sadie, things for me are different since the accident. I want to live as I want - freely."

"What does that mean, Carlo?"

"I don't know." We continue to stroll.

"I don't know what it means, Sadie. But I want to live by principles of truth, honesty. I want to appreciate each day as a precious gift. I almost lost that opportunity - the opportunity to live life authentically, as the person that I am. I don't want live life based on someone else's opinion of me, love for me, or hate for me. I want to live based on my terms."

"What does that mean for us Carlo?"

"What it means is we try to live one day at a time and not all of the days at once. I almost didn't make it into tomorrow. Please Sadie, I need the freedom to just try and survive this day. I'll get to tomorrow when it comes."

"Let me help you out, Carlo." She says with a sweet sarcasm that stings, "When tomorrow comes I'll be home with two newborns that you claim as yours, trying to make a life for us all!"

"Sadie..."

"While you're out trying to figure out what and who YOU want to be, you selfish son of a bitch, I'll be feeding, changing diapers, comforting crying babies and rocking them to sleep - one in each arm!"

I try to interrupt her but she is not having it!

"While you are resting as one day ends so you can peacefully wait until tomorrow arrives, living in this one day at a time, I'll be getting up all through the night, during that same time period feeding crying babies every few hours, still changing diapers and rocking babies two at a time. While YOU are trying to live freely, on your terms and in your way, I'll be creating terms, routine terms, patterns for two chil-dren who, like their mother, don't quite understand what it means to exercise the freedom to explore principles of truth, honesty and the pursuit of happiness with two newborns at home! So while today is here and you still have a chance - kiss my ass long and hard, because tomorrow it'll be gone!"

We come to my door and she walks off as abruptly as a woman who just had surgery can. Did she just break up with me?

Chapter 36

Tiffany

If Hell ever had a night of magic, then that would describe my night with Richard. I can't sleep at night anymore, I drag during the day. I'm calling in. I'm not going in to work, I just can't. I'm too tired. Last night with Richard felt wonderful, but each moment of hope and reconciliation were burned away by the fire of pain that rages in my heart. Richard was here with me, not because he wanted me, but because he needed a friend. I gave that to him, and it gave me the chance to feel love's embrace, even if it was packaged in worthless hope. Hope that never finds a home is hell. I just don't understand Richard. How can I love someone who has hurt me as much as he has? I feel a vibration on my hip and reach down and grab my phone.

I look at the caller ID and it's Troy. I know I should feel happy to hear from him, but I feel numb.

"Troy."

"Well hello, lovely lady."

"Troy, you certainly know how to put smile on my sad little face."

"Nice to return the favor. You've supplied me with plenty."

"I could really use a shoulder to lean on."

"Well Ms. Tiffany, you're in luck. I have two shoulders and neither was damaged in the car accident. My shoulder is all yours. Everything else is a gamble. Can you come pick me up?"

"I can't handle any drama, Troy."

"My shoulders are drama free."

"Where's Sojourn?"

"Oh, I see. She's at home."

"In that case I'm on my way."

I hang up the phone with Troy and my smile is frolicking around in the sweet aftertaste his words left on me. Hmmm. Lovely lady, huh? My smile slowly stops dancing, I wish I felt lovely. I wish I could feel anything right now. The quiet numbness in my heart silences my frolicky smile and fills my face with emptiness. I'm afraid to get to close with Richard. I don't want to fill this emptiness up with the same garbage I've been dealing with. I just took love's trash out.

I refuse to let pain fool me again! Pain has many disguises including decency and honest intentions, but when the disguise is revealed, and deception, selfishness and betrayal emerge, pain will devour me. Completely. The new Tiffany will die and all progress made will be lost."

I pull up to Troy's mother's house and I feel a breeze of giddiness graze my skin and the corners of my mouth coyly raise, forming a smile.

I watch as Troy comes out of the house with a walking cane. He kisses his mother on the cheek and hobbles to the car.

"How you feeling big boy?"

"Broken."

"Me too."

He looks at me and pats me on my leg as I'm driving.

"Where to Troy?"

"I thought we'd go to my church, sit in the courtyard, talk and pray."

"Not exactly what I had in mind, but my life at this point is not exactly what I had in mind either."

"That makes two of us."

We ride in silence until Troy's words slip out of his mouth and slide in to my ears.

"I'm tired of falling down in pain Tiffany. I want to be a better person, I just haven't got a firm grip on life yet. Maybe we can help each other."

As Troy directs me to his church, I recognize where I'm going, Richard and I visit here quite frequently.

"Richard and I visit here often."

Troy looks at me with that captivating smile, "Why are you still visiting then?"

"I don't know. Richard has a childhood friend that is a member here, they're pretty close." I turn in the parking lot, "Is this a date?"

"Tiff, let's not give titles. We're at the same place, sharing our time and space together. What difference will an official title make?"

"Troy, through a feminine eye, it makes a difference, but not the kind of difference I need right now." I help Troy hobble out of the car and we walk toward the church. I'm not sure what exactly I was feeling before we got to church, but the closer I came to the door, clarity came. As soon as I stepped out of the car onto the paved parking lot, my heart began to ache. I tried to hide what was happening inside of me with small talk and gentle smiles, but I felt as if my palms were sweating blood. *Richard left me for another woman.* I was good to him, I was honest, went to church, never cheated, worked hard with him in building our future, I gave my hopes to him, my dreams, my secrets, my fears, my body and my time and *Richard left me for another woman.* I needed him, he wasn't there, he was with her. God, I did everything by the book, and I'm still here. *Richard left me for another woman.* We approach the door of the church and Troy opens the door for me. My feet freeze. I look at my palms, no blood.

"Tiffany, what is it?"

I try to smile as if nothing is wrong, but my facial muscles don't move. I glance over to Troy still trying to pretend.

"Tiffany, are you coming in?"

"No." Crawls out of my mouth as if it is a wounded solider, dragging to safety from the war going on inside of me.

He lets go of the door, "What is it, Tiffany?"

Richard left me for another woman.

Chapter 30

"Tiffany?"

I was the good wife, not perfect, but damn it, I was good and I tried! I went to church as a believer, I was deceived. How many times have I walked through these doors with faith? I've given my tithe, offerings, and my service. Now I stare at these doors with disdain, this is my return for faith? This is my reward?

"I don't trust Him, Troy." Springs from my mouth as a tear leaps from my eye.

"Richard?"

"No." I turn my gaze to him and then look off, "God."

"Do you blame God?"

"He allowed it to happen. He could have stopped it, but He didn't."

"Tiffany, I think we should go in. We can talk to someone."

"For what Troy? How is talking to someone going to make one damn bit of difference?"

"Tiffany, watch your language. This is holy ground."

"Holy for who? I paid tithes, offerings, volunteered, came to services, prayed, sacrificed, where's my part of holy? Where was salvation when I needed saving? I was there when people needed me. Deserters! God was the first deserter, Richard was the second!"

"Tiffany, I don't have answers for you, I have questions myself but..."

"But nothing, Troy. But nothing and nothing is exactly what I'm left with. I can't do this."

"I need this Tiffany. I could have died, but I'm here, alive."

"I'm dead. My marriage could've had life, but it's dead."

His eyes approach me and reveal a bleeding heart, full of hope, faith. Worthless concepts that only create more pain. I don't want his bloody look contaminating me and my feet begin to back away.

"Go Troy. Call me when you're ready for me to pick you up. I'll come back and get you. I'm going for a drive."

"Tiffany, I don't have the answers, but I know what you're doing isn't it."

"I can't do this Troy!" My words are fueled by anger and resentment. When my words nestle in his ears I watch as the impact stings him and I walk off.

It feels like with each step I take my feet release tears. My body feels heavy, my spirit feels black, empty. I'm sad again. I was over this. I healed myself. I freed myself from this pain. Why? How did it come back? No. No, no, no. I won't fall back into that dark place. I won't. I won't do it. The shower, the shower was my portal to freedom, I just need to shower. I start the car and drive off. My foot presses on the accelerator and I look at the rear view mirror and see what looks like a shadow looming near me. Fear grips me. Nervous anxiety, rage, resentment and fear drive the car to the house at accelerated rates, erratically. The shadow quietly follows me, attempting to kill me, softly, slowly, surely. The faster I drive, the slower the pace of the shadow. I can't outrun it. It's there, every turn, every light and stop sign, it follows me. Staring at me. I pull in the driveway and look at the shadow in my rearview mirror. It's scoffs at my attempts to escape. Laughter like rolling thunder. I glance into the eyes and recognize the shadow immediately. It's my pain. I'll never forget that face, never. I'll never forget the scent of pain, the aftertaste it leaves as it affects every part of your body. *Richard left me for another woman.* I know pain when I see it. Its cruel intentions pierce my heart. I see survival pooling out of my body. Darkness overtaking me. Why won't it leave me alone? Why is it chasing me? Fearfully, I look pain in the eye.

"Leave me alone!" Marches out of my mouth with a determined, rhythmical pace, "Leave me alone!" What, is the pain deaf? Does it not hear me? "Leave me alone! Go away! I hate you!" Pain continues to stare at me, it doesn't move, it doesn't breathe, it just stares at me, tormenting me, why? *Richard left me for another woman.* The shadow grows darker.

"Please." Cries out of my mouth raising a white flag of surrender. "Please, no more." I look to God in the Heavens, and my grief screams "Do you have no mercy?" "Do you have no heart?" I jump out of the car and slam the door. I don't look back; I don't want to see the shadow standing behind me. I don't want to look in the eyes of pain. *Richard left me for another woman.* The rancid stench of pain pierces my nostrils and I know it's still there. "Damn it."

I go to the shower, shed my clothes and step in, the shadow of pain steps in with me. I close my eyes, I don't want to see it, but it's there. I place both my hands on the shower wall and drop my head. The water cascades down the back of my neck in between my shoulder blades. My tears fall and become one with water, my entire body cries. The water hits me with such force my legs buckle and I sit on the floor of the shower and cry, and I feel an embrace. Pain has sat on the floor with me and holds me as if I'm a child that wants to be held by this monster. How did I get here? Again. It hurts.

Chapter 37

Troy

I watch as Tiffany walks off. I don't say anything, because there is nothing left to say. She's gone. I walk into the church and sit in the sanctuary. Tiffany is on the edge of love and life and doesn't even know it. As much as I want to, I can't save her, when I'm too busy saving myself.

"Brother Troy."

I look up and see my friend Deacon Mitchell, "Hey. What's up man?"

"You have a cane? That's a new accessory."

I smile, "I was in a pretty bad car accident, this cane is the least of my worries."

"Well what's your primary worry then? Still working on putting your family back together?"

"Yea. No. Man, I don't know. I've done what I can. If Sojourn wants to restore this, she can come to me."

"So why are you here?"

"Seemed like a nice of place to bring a girl to keep us out of trouble."

"Where's the girl?"

"Gone. Gone. Gone."

Deacon Mitchell chuckles in laughter, "Maybe it's the cologne, man."

I look at him and smile back, "What are you wearing?"

"A combination of Heaven and earth. Muskiness and mustiness all in one whiff."

"I guess I'm a bit too musty for women. I need to clean myself up before I can be the right man for any woman, Mitchell."

"Even at your cleanest point and in all your righteousness, you'll still be a filthy rag."

"I feel that way, my brother."

"It's called humanity, man. Those days come, but they also go." He says with a chuckle.

"I'm finally on speaking terms with God, and I've messed up again. I can't leave women alone. I'm tired of asking God for second chances. I can't seem to get my feet off Hell's welcome mat."

"Man, your problem is simple."

"What's my problem brother?"

"You're self-centered and not God-centered."

I look at him, wanting to respond, because I don't feel I'm self-centered at all. Instead I force my mouth to be quiet and listen.

"It's just that simple man, stop licking your wounds, let God handle that and help another lost heart find its way back home."

I focus my eyes on the cross.

"Simple, you say?"

"Yeah. Simple."

He shifts his gaze to the cross with me, "It can't always be about you, and your pity party."

I shake my head in a guilty acceptance, "Yeah, I guess I have been self-centered."

I think about Tiffany, she needs someone right now. She's sinking into the place I just left. Isolated from God, not speaking to Him, not praying, not believing, just mad and angry. She's going to sink so low into a black pain that taking a single breath is going to feel like breathing through a straw. I reach for my cell phone and call Tiffany.

"Who you calling Troy?"

"A lost heart, trying to find its way home."

"Tiffany." I say as she answers the call.

"Are you ready for me to pick you up?"

She doesn't respond.

"You can come whenever you're ready. You alright?"

"No. You?"

"I don't know. Trying not to focus on me right now. I'm just readying my shoulders for you."

I hear her voice crackling as tears fight to escape at the same time as her words.

"I could use a shoulder right now."

"It's all yours. Come get it."

"Thank you, Troy."

"Call me when you're outside."

"Ok."

"How do you do it Mitchell? How do stay so peaceful. You were like this in college too."

"Do I look like I'm at peace to you?"

I turn and look at him and I see deep, dark circles under his eyes, worry lines on his forehead, and a veil of darkness coating his eyes, "What's up man?"

"I'm just practicing what I preach. Giving to you helps me. I don't have to think about my own problems."

I feel dumbfounded. Mitchell has always been there for me; I never even considered that he ever needed someone to be there for him. I know we've supported each other in little stuff, but he's not talking about something little. I have been self-centered, feeling sorry for myself. Not tuned in to those around me. I feel as if I've been stumbling in darkness and now the lights are turned on.

I look at him again, "What's got you man?"

"My mom has cancer. She doesn't have much time left."

My problems feel so small. I can't believe I've been so wrapped up in myself, "What can I do?"

"Be there for your friend with the lost heart."

I look at the grief in his eyes, Tiffany's not the only friend with a lost heart, "You got it."

My phone vibrates and it's a text message from Tiffany, "I'm outside."

I get up; grab my cane and Mitchell stands up with me. We grip each other in a hug and I walk out towards the door.

"I'll call you later, Mitchell."

"Yeah. Ok." he calls back not convinced. I'm very convinced. That's one phone call I'm going to make. *It's not all about me.*

Chapter 38

Shannon

I walk with a nervous anticipation of meeting my next partner Mr. Douglas Michaels. We are meeting at the little Tuscan cafe near the office. I walk in expecting to see another young up and coming professional similar to Rick. I look around and don't see anyone. I tell the hostess, I'm expecting a gentleman to meet me and she nods her head, "He's already here. I'll escort you."

I see an older, very distinguished man with salt and pepper hair stand and greet me. I'm breathless. He's gorgeous. He has to be at least 15-20 years older than me and stands about 6'8". Where does this company find these men?

"Shannon Scott, I presume."

He words waltz out of his mouth and slow dance with my ears.

"Yes. Nice to meet you, Mr. Michaels."

"Actually it's Dr. Michaels, but Douglas is fine."

"Douglas. Ok then." I answer with a flirty smile. Why am I flirting with this man while I have Richard's child growing inside of me. I'm not sure what to say or what we're going to talk about, so I guess I'll start talking about my experience.

"Douglas..."

"Yes, Shannon."

Wow, he so attentive, "This promotion will be a wonderful opportunity for me, I feel working with Richard has prepared me well. I don't have a degree in engineering, but I..."

As I'm talking I watch as he coyly grins. My words fade off as they are captivated by his smile.

"Shannon, I thought we'd spend this first day getting to know each other. We'll be working rather closely together, I'd like for us to get to know each other first. Working with differing personalities can be more challenging than working with different skill levels."

Wow. This is very different from Rick. Rick was a straight businessman. We barely had a friendship or extended conversation until the latter part of our relationship. He is actually very opposite of Richard.

"So, Shannon. Tell me about yourself." I look at him in amazement. Does he really want to know about me?

"Do you really want to know, or is this small talk?"

"Shannon. I have choices. I don't have to be here. I am choosing to be here. I'd like to know if I could work well with the team that is already in place. I really want to get to know you. If I were engaging in small talk, I would have asked you about the weather. I'm too old for games and too wise to skip the most important part of any functional organization and that's getting to know the people you work with."

I like this guy.

"It's been a while since someone really wanted to get to know me genuinely. Thank you for not being one of those people."

"Looks like you need to change the group of people you associate with."

"So are things much different for you?" I ask in curiosity

"Oh yes." He chuckles, "Yes indeed. I don't conduct business with anyone unless I get to know them, know what they're about. I don't do business with just anyone. This company has been courting with me for over two years now. I know the entire board, C.E.O., every director, manager and officer. I've invited them over, been to their homes, played golf, fundraisers, the whole nine yards. When I get into a position, it's important for me to have the relationships in place to make the decisions I need to make to get the job done."

"You're smart."

"I'm effective."

"Are you married?"

He chuckles, "No. My wife and I have been separated for years. I'd never divorce her though. I love her with all my heart."

"Wow. What's stopping you from getting back together?"

"She died a couple of years ago."

"Oh. I'm sorry Douglas. It must have been a terrible loss."

"It's always tough when something so beautiful goes, but I came back to Houston to be here for my daughter and son."

"You have children?"

"Yes."

"How old are they?"

"Probably in your age bracket."

"I bet they're beautiful."

"My daughter looks just like her mother. She's had a rough go at it lately and for the first time in my life, I'm going to do everything, and I mean absolutely everything I can for her."

"She's a lucky girl."

"No, I'm the lucky one."

"So if Houston is not home, where were you living before?"

"All over the world."

"Did your wife and children ever come visit you?"

"No."

I look at him wanting to ask why, but resist, I can tell he's reading my expression.

"I'm going to try and make up for lost time while I have it Shannon. So tell me about you."

"Well I'm single, pregnant and my job is the best thing I have going for me right now."

He looks at me with a sympathetic smile.

"My job seems to be the only thing that loves me back, so I give love tirelessly to my job. It has become my life."

"Dangerous."

"It's my stability. My reason for waking up everyday."

"...and what if you were to lose your job?"

Fear grips me. He's in a position to fire me. Should I have told him all of these things? What if he doesn't want to work with a pregnant woman? What if he doesn't like me? Rick could care less about me; he just wanted the job done. This guy cares more about me than my ability, it seems. If he doesn't like me it won't matter how good I am, I gone.

"I don't know." The words crawl out of my mouth begging for mercy.

"I lost my family and kept the job. I would encourage you do the opposite."

"Do you think I'm reckless because I got pregnant without having a steady relationship?"

"Were you?"

"Maybe, but I'm happy with the result."

"Which part? The baby or the unsteady relationship?"

I don't want to answer. How does he zero in on me like this? I feel exposed. It's time for small talk.

"So are you loving this weather today?"

He chuckles loudly, he recognized my diversion. *Recover, recover, recover.*

"Have you had enough for today Shannon Scott?"

"Dr. Douglas Michaels, I've had enough of the appetizer, shall we progress to the main course and a deeper conversation."

"Humph. You're a fighter aren't you? You don't give up easy, this will be interesting. Yes. Let's order."

Chapter 39

Carlo

I awake from a sleep to see Sojourn coming through the door.

"Ciao."

"Ciao." she answers softly.

She sits beside my bed. I sit up and look around, look at the clock; I'm going home today. She passes me a bag of fresh clothes and I go into the shower. When I come out she sits in the same spot reading a book. I watch as her eyes scan me from head to toe and feel warm as I feel her looking at me as a man and not her pretend brother.

"I think I've taken enough time off from work. I'm going back to the office on Monday. You and Troy are both home from the hospital and will recover fine. It's time to put life back in order. What's happening with you?"

"I think Sadie broke up with me."

"She did?"

"It sure sounded that way."

"Well how do you feel about it?"

"I don't know. I'll be there for the boys, but I don't want to live together right now. I don't want to live life as a lie. I need to either explore how I feel about you or shut it down."

"You're timing is horrible Carlo. Rick, Troy, the boys, Tiffany down my back, work piling up on me, Sadie, the twins, I don't have the emotional energy to explore anything."

"Do you want me to leave it alone? I will if you ask me to."

I wait for her answer, but she doesn't give me one.

"Sojourn, I love you and I love Troy. I'm not going to hide from him how I feel, but I respect that he loves you and I'll walk away and leave it alone if you ask me to."

The nurse walks in and gives me discharge instructions, papers to sign. The doctor comes in shortly after and gives me the go ahead to finally go home and Sojourn and the nurse begin to wheel me to the front door. As we load in Sojourn's car, I glance over to her, "You never answered my question, but don't. I don't want to pressure you. I need to figure things out with Sadie first. Troy can wait. Just drop me off at her apartment. I want to see my boys."

Sojourn grabs my chin, pulls me close to her and kisses me romantically. I don't want her to stop, but she pulls back.

"We can't do this Carlo. How do we stop ourselves?"

"We just stop. That's it. We suppress how we feel and live with the temptation, without giving in."

"Ok."

"Ok."

"So it's over Carlo?"

"It's over."

"Completely?"

"Completely. No turning back Sojourn, only forward movement from here."

In a way, I'm relieved that we're going to put it behind us. The costs are too great.

"Now take me to see my boys, Sojourn."

Sojourn smirks as she drives off, "They're a stunning pair."

"Have you left both Troy and Rick alone?"

"Well as for Rick, the accident took center stage in my life. Intentional or not, he takes a back seat to you and Troy. I needed to give all my attention to the two of you. We've hardly talked."

"As for Troy, I've enjoyed my time with him. I've missed him. I might even find myself falling in love with him again. I don't know. What I do know is that he's getting awfully comfy with Tiffany and the thought of that makes me queasy."

"Tiffany is Rick's wife?"

"Yeah."

"Can't be mad at her, it'd be the perfect revenge on you."

"Do you think that's why she's pursuing him, to get back at me?"

"I don't know. You need to sort all that out. I don't really know her that well. I know she's a good friend with Sadie. Rick and I have a friendship, but he doesn't talk much about her to me. Just leave all of that alone Sojourn. Leave it alone."

We pull up to Sadie's house and Sojourn exits the car with me.

We walk to Sadie's apartment and her friend Jessica opens the door.

"Hi Carlo, Hi Sojourn. Sadie," she calls.

Sadie comes out of the room, slowly with a white cloth draped over her shoulder and passes one of the twins to Jessica. She greets Sojourn first.

"Hi Sojourn. How's Troy?"

"He's recovering."

"Sadie," I interrupt, "Jessica's holding Gianni, where's Valentino?"

She approaches me as if she is going to greet me with a hug when she stops. She gives me a look like I've done something wrong and I'm trying to figure out why she is greeting me with hostility. She reaches for the white burp cloth on her shoulder. I glance over to Sojourn and watch as her expression changes to shock. I look back at Sadie, and before I can ask what is going on, she rubs the white cloth on face across my lips. She examines the cloth and looks at Sojourn and then back to me. "You forgot to wipe your sister's lipstick off, you slimy snake in the grass." I see Jessica going to the back to put the baby down, my mouth begins to form words, without any idea of what they are about to say and in what seemed like one second split in half. Sadie balls up her fist and punches Sojourn right in the face. I lunge toward Sojourn trying to catch her fall to the floor, but on my way to catch her, Sadie knees me in the groin area and I fall to the floor opposite of Sojourn. Damn that hurt. Shit.

"Sadie!" I yell.

"Now what do you have to say Mr. Yearning for Truth and Honesty. Say something now!"

"Sadie," Jessica interrupts, "Sit down before you hurt yourself, you just had surgery."

I stand up and don't know what to say to Sadie. My mouth tries to put words together, but my thoughts are flying all over the place and none of them land on my tongue to share with Sadie.

"Sojourn, while you're peeling yourself up off that floor, let me tell you something about me. I will kick your little skinny ass. I don't handle bitches like a lady as Tiffany and Jessica would. I handle them like a bitch. Now get out of my house!" Sadie yells and is breathless by the time the last words leave her mouth. Sojourn gets up holding her eye, looks over to me and doesn't say anything. She just leaves.

"Sadie. Why did you do that?"

"I don't know! Why you think you can come in this house and bring that little bitch in here with your face full of lipstick, disrespect me and not expect me to respond?"

She looks to Jessica, "I told you it was another woman. I told you. I just never suspected his sister. You sick and twisted..."

"Sadie." I interrupt, "Sojourn is not my sister. We're best friends."

"What do you want Carlo?"

"I want to see my boys."

"I don't know if they're your boys Carlo. I don't want you getting attached to them until I have a DNA test run."

Sadie knows how I feel about these boys; she knows how I feel about this DNA test.

"Sadie, I don't want you to do this."

"You should have thought about that while you were on your quest for freedom and truth. You should have thought about that before you were trying to see what her spit tastes like."

Sadie's words land on me like land mines.

"Sadie, I'm sorry. Can I see my boys? Please, Bella." the words bleed from my mouth.

Jessica looks over to Sadie, but doesn't say anything.

"Carlo if they're yours, then we'll discuss visitation then."

"Jessica, can you give us a moment. I want to talk to Sadie alone."

"Sure." Jessica responds, "Sadie, Gianni and Valentino are sleeping. I'm going to step out and will see you later this evening. Call me if you need anything."

I sit on the couch with Sadie. I grab her hand. Neither one of us says anything. I can't give up my boys. How do I make things right?

Chapter 40

Tiffany

As I pull up to the church I see Troy walking through the door and I don't feel any different. Showering did nothing for me. Pain was an uninvited guest, refusing to leave.

"Hey Tiffany."

"Hey Troy, sorry to mess up our first date or rather, shared time together."

"Tiffany, this was something I wanted to do. What do you want to do, with the time we have left?"

"Can we go to the Coffee Bean and Other Things? I could use good cup of coffee, nice music and a strong shoulder to lean on?"

"Wherever you take me tonight, there I'll be. So go wherever you want, I'll be there with you."

It feels like a lightning storm with torrential rains is raging inside my body. I don't even look at Troy when words flood from my mouth, slowly. Like water overflows onto the street during a storm, when it has nowhere else to go. "I still hurts, Troy. I thought I was better, over this; but I'm not. It still hurts."

I look in my rear view mirror and see pain silently sitting in the back seat. The storm inside of me is growing, it feels darker; pain smiles like the Cheshire cat.

"Work through the pain."

"How, Troy? God has abandoned me. Richard has abandoned me and everyone seems to be flowing around Sojourn. I want her to be as miserable as I am right now. I want Richard to suffer. How is it you can forgive and still love such a scandalous woman Troy? She's horrible!"

"She's human."

"She's hell."

My storm is raging and more words flood my mouth, "She's been with my husband, Troy. She knows how you feel about her. She chose to be with my husband anyway. Scandalous bitch."

"Tiffany, I'm not going to tell you that it doesn't hurt. But there's another side to her and to me too. She spent every day in the hospital with me. Leaving my side only to check on the kids and see Carlo..."

His words trail off. "What?" I ask.

"Something is going on with Sojourn and Carlo. I don't know what, but I need to talk to him. I'm definitely going to see him when he gets home from the hospital."

"How is it she gets all the men?"

"I could be here with her right now Tiffany, but I'm with you."

"I know Troy. Thank you."

I park the car and Troy and I get out. I love the Coffee Bean & Other Things. From the huge Mahogany doors with the handle shaped as a coffee bean, to the waitress at the door offering coffee shots, the music is always a soothing sound that radiates through the room. I love the cultural decor from all over the world. This is the most refreshing spot in Houston. No matter what time of day you come, it has a healing effect on you. It's warm and cozy, just like the coffee. I love this place.

"Troy it must be great to manage a place like this."

"I love coming to work, but today I'm a customer and a friend. Let's find a nice spot."

He guides me through the Coffee Bean and he finds a nice love seat, in the back corner, low to the ground.

"How's this, Tiffany?"

"Perfect."

"Good, now tell me about you. You want Sojourn to be in pain, you want Richard to suffer, you want me to stop loving Sojourn, what do you want for you, Tiffany?"

He extends his arm and offers me to rest my head on his shoulder. I accept the invitation.

"I want my pain to end."

"Do you know the story of the rainstick?"

"The musical instrument?"

"Yes, but it didn't start that way. They're formed from a cactus. A branch from the cactus falls off or is broken off and hollowed out. Each thorn is pulled off and turned around and pushed back into the cactus. The cactus stick is sealed with another piece of cactus and filled with pebbles and put in the sun to dry. Well, in ancient times it was thought that the rainstick could be played in the belief that it could bring about rainstorms."

"I never knew that. Why are you sharing this story with me, Troy?"

"Wishing storms to come in the lives of people is like building a rainstick. It hurts. I just don't see how it is possible to handle the thorns of a cactus and not experience some pain in the process. Then after all that work, you still aren't able to create storms in anyone's life. The more you shake the rainstick the more you are left with the sounds of the storm raging in your very own heart."

"Richard left me for another woman Troy. He left me to be with her. I want him to hurt. I want her to hurt. She deserves it! They both do."

"Even if they do deserve it, it won't stop your storm."

"It will Troy, I'll feel better."

"That 'I'll feel better' feeling is the quiet that comes before the beginning of something worse."

"I can't take anything worse Troy."

"Hurt breeds hurt."

"I don't want to hurt."

"Then you will have to learn to love."

"I can't do that either."

"Then you'll exist in that storm until you make a decision to end it.

Just like me. I'm ending it. No more using women to band-aid my pain."

I look towards the stage as the live band begins to play their first set. It looks dark and then I smell it. That rancid stench of pain stinging my nostrils. The shadow grows darker, larger. Pain isn't going away. I bury my head in Troy's shoulder and close my eyes, trying to shield my vision from the shadow. Troy accepts me. Why can't Richard? I feel my phone buzz and reach down to grab it. It's a text message from Richard, *I love you Tiffany. I'm sorry. I don't want to live life without you by my side.*

I love you too Richard. Do I believe him? I don't respond to his text and my phone buzzes again, another text.

"Going to the Coffee Bean tonight, before I head home, can you get out? Jess."

It'd be great to see Jessica. *Already here with Troy.*

Cool, see you in a minute.

Chapter 41

Richard

I wake up and reach for my phone. Did Tiffany text me back last night? No messages. I get up and begin to get dressed as I prepare to transition to my new job. I hear the phone ring as I'm putting on my clothes.

"Hello?"

"Yes. Mr. Young please."

"Yes, this is he."

"Mr. Young I'm calling regarding all of the information and physical examinations you submitted for insurance coverage."

"Yes."

"I'm afraid we will not be able to insure you."

"Why?"

"Your tests reflect that you have a pre-existing condition, which we do not cover."

"What? What condition are you speaking of?"

"Oh. Oh my."

"What?"

"Sir, your tests show you're HIV positive."

"What!?"

"Sir, I'm sorry."

"Are you sure? Are you sure you are looking at my records?"

"Yes sir."

The phone falls from my hand. I don't feel any breath coming in or out of my lungs. This has got to be a mistake. This has got to be a mistake. It must be. Please, please, please let it be. I'll just take the test again. Something must have gone wrong. I'll just drive to clinic and take the test again. *No. No. No.* I go online and search for a clinic as far away from town as possible. I don't want anyone to recognize me when I go. *No. No. No.* This can't be how it ends. It just can't be. Who? How? When?

I go to my car, get in and drive to some obscure clinic on the outskirts of Houston. I don't have to give my real name and they'll give a rapid test and I can get the results within minutes. I've only been with three people, Tiffany, Sojourn and Shannon. I've put all of them at risk, and one of them infected me. Shannon. Do I call her? Does she know? *No. No. No.* Please, let this be a mistake. I pull into the clinic. I'm given a number to identify me, they perform the test and I wait for the results. I don't have to wait long. They call my number and I'm terrified. I'm brought back to a room and a nurse walks in, "Your preliminary test result is positive, but we won't know for sure if you are infected with HIV until we get the results from your confirmatory test. In the meantime, you should take precautions to avoid transmitting the virus." I'm speechless. Two tests, both positive. I'm going to die. I'm going to die a horrible and sick death. I can't touch another woman. I've lost Tiffany. What reason do I have to live? I don't want to die this way. I don't want this. No cure. Death is imminent.

"Sir, there have been so many advances in HIV research. Some individuals have already been alive over 20 years with the virus. And many people with HIV die from causes unrelated to their HIV. As we continue to learn more about HIV, the lifespan of those infected with HIV will continue to increase. We still have to wait on your confirmatory test, but I suggest you begin searching for a doctor that has experience working with HIV populations." I walk back to my car and sit. Silence. Death creeping up on me. I hear a knock on my window. I turn and see Deacon Mitchell. What is he doing here?

"Rick."

I've just got a death sentence, how do I pretend that everything is normal. What is he going to think with me here? Beads of sweat peer from skin, revealing my secret. Does he know?

"Mitchell."

"Hey man. How you doing?"

I don't answer, I step out of the car and greet him. Should I touch him? We shake hands.

"Rick, you remember my mom? Margie."

"Hi Rick, very pleased to meet you. Are you the same Rick that would come visit my son when he was just a child?"

"Yes ma'am."

"My, what a handsome man you've grown into."

"Rick, we're here doing some volunteer work with the clinic through the church."

His mother looks at me, grabs my hand. She looks to her son and tells him to go on in she'll catch up with him in a minute. He nods his head, "She has a mind of her own Rick I just say yes ma'am and do it." He smiles, "Just a word to the wise."

"Rick, I remember you. I don't like to say this in front of my son, because he's still struggling in some ways, but I've been diagnosed with cancer. I've decided to live what time I have left on my terms."

"I'm sorry, Ms. Margie."

"Oh son, I don't need any sympathy right now, but I'll tell you what I do need. I'd like to have your number. Before I go, I want to have a surprise appreciation for my son and invite some of his friends. When I'm gone, I want him to know how much love and support he still has to comfort him during my transition. Take my number and when you have a chance call me and give me yours."

"Yes. I will. You seem so positive, peaceful."

"You know, I'm in the driver's seat with this illness. I've been diagnosed with cancer, but cancer doesn't have me. Cancer doesn't know anything about me. So I choose to live and be the person I was born to be. Cancer is common. Many people all over the world have it. So dying a death from cancer is common, but me, I'm one in a million. So when my time comes, it will be my life that people remember; the uniqueness of me. Cancer will be how I died, but what people remember most is how you lived. While I still have life in my body, I choose to live and help others who have an illness to live in spite of their diagnosis."

"That's beautiful, Ms. Margie."

"I want my son to know that each person that comes to his love and appreciation celebration is there to show the power of love. Cancer's not doing these things, I am. I've got a couple of loose ends to tie up and a few more life lessons to teach my boy before I go. I'll be waiting for your call, son."

"Yes ma'am. I'll call."

As she is about to leave she turns back, "Richard, and if you want to talk about anything else, call me. I've had plenty of those phone calls lately because people know I'm taking their secrets to the grave." She chuckles and walks off. Her words make me feel safe.

"Ms. Margie. Wait."

"Yes, son."

"I just found out I'm positive."

My eyes begin to well up. A man is not supposed to cry. I force them back down. Not one of those tears will fall.

"Ms. Margie, I haven't told anyone. Not a soul. I'm dying."

"We're all dying son. Each day we get just a bit closer to the last."

"I don't feel like I have a reason to live. A piece of me wants to just end it all and die on my terms."

"Son. God's beautiful child, I wish I could pick you up and carry you through this journey, but it's a private walk. A path many have walked before you and many will walk after you. You will have to decide how you will navigate through this. I can share with you my journey."

"Please."

"When I found out I had a terminal illness, something strange happened. Rather ironic."

I look to her with curiosity, anticipating what could've happened.

"I started living."

"You were already living."

"No son. My body was living. My soul was dying."

"I realized then, my body like everyone else on this earth is dying. Death started with life. The moment I was born and became life, death started its count down."

"I never looked at it like that, Ms. Margie."

"I didn't either and what a waste of time that was. I would have started living long before this." She chuckles like soft thunder. "Boy oh boy how I grappled with death, the thought of death, the feel of death, the anticipation of death. I fought death with bitterness, depression, revenge, spitefulness, tears, fists, anger, and regrets. I fought death with everything I had, son. Everything. Each time death stood right back up looked me in the face and taunted me. You can't beat me. Those words became a deadly dance with my soul. My soul started to sway to the beat. I tried to ignore death, pretend it wasn't there. Death continued to taunt me. Death's rhythmic song became my heartbeat."

"That sounds like where I am, Ms. Margie."

"But it's where you're going that's makes the difference."

She crosses her hands and guides me as we walk.

"Son, I realized it wasn't just my body dying. Who I was, was dying. That bitter, depressed woman was not who I was. So I started living. Living as the person I was supposed to be. In fact, I started living so boldly, so grandly, without fear or regret that the rhythm of life silenced the death dance. Death was still there. It was there from the beginning, but it became a non-issue. Life was such a better life partner. Life overpowered death. The only thing death could do was touch my body."

Ms. Margie smiles and shouts praises, "Death couldn't touch my soul, my spirit. I finally started living!"

She looks over to me "I live life so loud and clear and now. Do you hear me child? Loud and clear."

She laughs again, "Death still makes is presence known. But I really don't care. Life shouts back, '*See you when I see you!*' Death has lost its power; the anticipation of death has lost its sting. I have death in a chokehold, but death doesn't have me. My spirit is free. I live life LOUD!" She laughs again, her laughter escapes with boldness, as if it has a right to be there.

"I started living. Living in freedom. Death's power became weak. My life became strong. Death was held captive, a prisoner confined only to my body. My spirit, my soul and the terms on how I live my life were free. I was free!"

Ms. Margie stands in silence with me.

She finally breaks the silence, "That was my journey of discovery, determine yours. I hope you choose to live life loud son, live loud."

"Thank you, Ms. Margie."

She grabs the back of my head with her hand and pulls me down to kiss me on the forehead, "I'm going to scream some life into some of these other dying souls. Make sure you call me, son."

"Yes ma'am. I will."

I watch her as she walks away, "Oh Ms. Margie, one last thing..."

Before I can finish my statement, she lifts her hand without turning around and says, "Your secret is safe with me." and doesn't break a stride as she walks toward the clinic.

HIV Positive. That's it.

Chapter 42

Troy

Tiffany lifts her head off my shoulder.

"Jessica is on her way."

"Now all you need is Sadie and you'd have your girl mafia restored."

"Yeah, it'd be like old times. So, have you seen the twins, since you left the hospital?"

"No. Not yet."

"Do you want to see them?"

"I wouldn't mind."

"I hate this place that I'm in Troy."

"Well don't stay there."

"I don't see a way out." I wish I could tell her the way out, but my life is dark too. I watch as different girls walk by, giving me looks and nods as if I know them. I feel like fucking. I feel like fucking each one them giving me those sly grins. I guess I should be thankful Tiffany is needing me here right now. I don't see a way out either. I respond to Tiffany, "I know that place Tiffany, I know."

I look up and see Jessica. She looks like sunshine on a rainy day, fighting to break through.

"I know that place too." Jessica says as she greets Tiffany, she opens her arms to Tiffany, "Come here honey."

Tiffany shifts from my shoulder to Jessica's embrace.

"Richard hurt me so bad Jessica, in ways you'll never know."

"You all did a good job of hurting each other during the marriage."

"I never cheated on him."

"Not with a man."

"I can't believe what I'm hearing! Are you blaming me?"

"No. Of course not. Work through your guilt. Don't carry his guilt also. I'm sure he'd have no problem allowing you to carry it by blaming you for all his actions. Let him tow the weight of his own guilt. Mr. Happy Dick had no right, trying to keep the whole world happy."

I look at Jessica and chuckle; count on Jessica to always keep it real at any expense.

"Troy you know something about happy dicks don't you?"

I laugh out loud, "No. I don't no anything about that; but if I did I'd have to say, it's time to change the happy dick way of life. I have four girls on thumb street acting as my agents now. That's who I need to start bringing in all my joy."

Jessica looks at me and laughs.

I chuckle back, "It's about time I have a talk with my agents."

Tiffany and Jessica smile. I remember Jessica's touch. Even though we'd never cross that line again, I can't help but to love Jessica.

Jessica talks to Tiffany and glances towards me, "My husband's happy dick is what got us into trouble, but he wasn't the only one happily frolicking around. I have to deal with the decisions I made, but damn it, I'm not going to let him blame me for the shit he's done. We both have to live with the consequences of all those decisions, but he has to take responsibility for his decisions and I take responsibility for mine. "

"Well how are y'all doing?"

"We were doing fine, until I found out who his mistress was. Some chick that works for the mega company your husband works for Tiffany. It set us back for a minute. It still hurts some, but not enough to break up this marriage. I love Jason."

"How did you find out?" Tiffany asks.

"I went to the computer to check my email. His email account was still up, so I deleted his spam messages and was about to empty the trash for him when I saw her email in his trash account. It's what the email said that set us back."

"What did it say?"

"She loved him, thought she may be pregnant."

"Damn." I comment to Jessica, "I know how he's feeling."

"Basically, he not only had sex, but had unprotected sex. Putting both his life and my life in danger." She says. You can tell she's still angry about the entire situation.

"Well, he was careless Jessica, but if you let it go, let it go." I mention to her matter-of-factly.

"Troy, sure. I can let it go. But the carelessness? We never addressed that. He could have messed both of our lives up."

"I hear you, Jess. He may already have." I say in agreement.

"Anyway, during my 'bout in the hospital, Jason called my dad. My dad has called me every day since. Every day!"

"Wow. Jess, you've never talked about your dad, only your mom."

"There's a good reason for that Tiff, he was never around. He was always all over the world working. He'd send a paycheck home, but not much else. I guess he's trying to make up for lost time."

"How do you feel about that?" I ask.

"Ambivalent. I haven't seen him since my wedding. Although, all that is going to change because he's moved to Houston now."

"How are you handling all of this, Jessica?" Tiffany asks

"I'm handling it one day at a time."

"What's up with you and Sojourn, Troy?"

"We're at the same place. Why do you ask?"

"Sadie just punched her in the eyeball."

"What!?" Jessica just looks at me and silently nods her head yes. I don't wait to ask her why I immediately excuse myself and call Sojourn.

"Sojourn."

"Do you hate me?"

"No. I love you."

"I need you."

"Come get me, I'm at the Coffee Bean."

"I'm on my way. Thank you, Troy."

I walk back to the table, "Jessica why did you wait so long before you told me that?"

"Troy, I wasn't focused on you at the time, I was focused on Tiffany and forgot. I told you as soon as I remembered."

"Is she ok?"

"I don't know. She's on her way up her to pick me up. Jess, can you please make sure Tiffany gets home ok?"

"Of course."

I lean over and kiss Jessica and Tiffany on the forehead and begin to walk out the door to wait for Sojourn. Wait. "Jessica, do I even want to ask why this happened?"

"No. Troy you don't."

"Then I already know."

This has something to do with Carlo.

Chapter 43

Tiffany

As Troy prepares to leave, the manager comes up and approaches our table.

"Troy are you about to leave?"

"Yea."

"We just need 5 minutes of your time before you leave."

"Sojourn is on her way, so make it quick. I didn't come to work."

"I know, but I'm trying to close out this month and need your help, I can't complete inventory without you."

Troy gives her a reluctant acceptance "Tell the hostess, to let me know as soon as Sojourn comes. I'll meet you in my office. I'm leaving the door open so I can look for Sojourn. So make it quick!"

I watch as she tries to secretly grab his butt as he limps off. Is she coming on to him?

He turns to us, "Good night ladies, Tiffany sorry to cut our night of fun short."

We say goodbye and I look over to Jessica, I'm so glad she is here with me. I hope Troy doesn't get himself into trouble back there.

"What's wrong Tiffany? Talk to me. I thought you were feeling better?"

"Jessica, I got better, but slipped back into this funk. I wasn't even mad at Sojourn anymore. Just Richard, but I find myself disgusted with her and..."

Before my words finish leaving my mouth Sojourn walks in the door with a pair of dark shades on. *Why? I just want to know why.* Why did she try and steal my husband? I have to know why. I didn't feel my body moving toward her, but that question wouldn't stop pounding in my mind. The closer I came to her, the louder and more painful the pounding of the unanswered question got. Then all was interrupted when I was standing right in front of her. Everything just stopped; I stood still as I was trying to see her eyes through those sunshades. She just stares at me as if I'm nothing, like I'm not human. I can't see her eyes. Neither of us says anything. I feel pain closing in on me. Darkness.

"Why, Sojourn?" seeps out of my mouth.

"Tiffany, I'm not in the mood right now."

"You're going to answer me."

"No. I'm not." She looks to a waitress and calls her.

"You take my husband, turn my world upside down, cascade in his love and refuse to acknowledge me?"

"We've had enough of these talks, Tiffany."

The waitress approaches, "Please tell Troy I'm here. I'm ready to go!"

The waitress nods her head and leaves. I see Jessica in the corner of my eye approaching me.

"Tiffany, leave it alone." she whispers in my ear.

"Tell me, Sojourn! Tell me!"

Sojourn tells the hostess, "I'll be outside in the car. Tell Troy where I am, please," and turns to walk out the door without giving me an answer. *Why? I just want to know why.* I grab her arm to stop her from leaving and she pushes me to the floor, "Get your hands off me!" Bum rushes like a villain out of her mouth.

I get back up and a waitress is walking by, I grab her tray of drinks and throw it at Sojourn. "Looks like you need a drink!"

Another waitress walks by and doesn't realize what she's walking through and Sojourn tips her tray of drinks on me. "I'm full, knock yourself out!"

As the tray of drinks land on me all I can say is "You little bitch!"

I lunge towards Sojourn in an attempt to push her down to the ground and as she loses her balances and falls, she grabs my arm and won't let go. I end up falling with her landing right on top of her. "Why? I just want to know why, you scandalous little..."

Arms lift me up and stand me on my feet. I look and see Troy. He pulls Sojourn off the floor. "Both of you outside, now! Jessica. Handle your girl!"

"Troy, she started it! I told you she was no good." Sojourn says in tears.

"Yes, Sojourn I did start it. I started it with Troy. We were on a date. Richard told me he loves me! Who loves you now, heifer?"

"Shut up, Tiffany!" Troy booms with anger.

"Tiffany, what is wrong with you girl? What has come over you?" Jessica's words circle around me like a question mark, as if she doesn't know me.

I watch as Troy's eyes pierce me. They slice through my shadow of pain and infect me with his disappointment. My dark shadow torments me in sneers. I know we're not on a date. I just want her to hurt as much as I do. Why should she get to live happily ever after?

"Tiffany. I won't allow you to talk to the mother of my children like this. I love your friendship, but I'm telling - not asking - you to stop."

"Troy, Richard left me for her. Do you know what I'm going through because of this woman? She's not worthy of you."

"Jessica." He demands, "Take her home now."

"Tiff, come on girl. I'm staying with Sadie tonight to help with the twins, you can help us. What is wrong with you?"

"Jessica I just have to know why"

I turn and scream back, "Tell me Sojourn! Tell me!" She doesn't even turn around.

"Jessica," I scream in tears, "Make her. Make her tell me why."

Jessica doesn't answer. Darkness surrounds me as we go to Jessica's car and I fall in the seat. "Tiffany. Are you losing your mind?"

"Jessica, I hurt every day, I deserve an explanation."

"Well, apparently you're not going to get it from her."

"I deserve the happy ending Jessica, me."

"Tiffany. You are losing it!" Each of her words lands on me like a needle piercing the fabric of a pin cushion.

"She deserved it!"

"OK, so what do you deserve?"

"Happiness."

"She doesn't deserve that?"

"She doesn't need it. She took mine. Isn't that enough?"

"Look, I'm no Sojourn fan, but you looked like the wreck back there not her."

"Whose side are you on? You've been on my case since the moment you've seen me. Is she screwing you too?"

"Tiffany, I'm not going to give that comment the dignity of a response!"

"Pull the car over Jessica!"

"No!"

"Pull it over!"

"No!"

My hands pound the dashboard, my feet pound the floor my words are exploding inside of me, "Pull it over!" I reach for the steering wheel and Jessica stops me.

"Ok." Jessica swerves the car over, slams on the breaks and I open the door, squeeze through a barbed wire fence and run into an open field. Jessica runs after me. She tackles me and I fall to the ground.

My body feels on fire. Darkness surrounds me. Tears thunder

from my eyes. "WHY?" flashes out of my mouth like lightning. I feel paralyzed and my tears won't stop. I feel pain grab me and I want to fight it off, but I'm just not strong enough. I fall. My shadow pleasantly grows as darkness encapsulates me.

"Tiffany. I have you." Jessica cries with me.

"I have you, Tiffany."

"Sometimes Jessica, I feel like dying." My words somehow find a life raft and survive in my hurricane of tears.

"I know."

"My life. It wasn't supposed to be like this. I had hope. Hope. Even after knowing what he did with Sojourn, I had hope. I went to see him Jessica. I just needed a sign. One small sign of hope and I would have fought like hell to put this marriage back on track. One sliver of hope."

"What happened when you saw him?"

"He was half naked, in the dark and he thought I was her. He was expecting her. He called me to the bedroom and expected to see her."

My tears drown my words and no other words escape. Jessica finishes for me, "...fight back Tiffany. Fight back."

"It's my f..." My tears choke me.

"What? What is it, Tiffany?"

"It's my fault."

"No."

"Yes. Yes Jessica. I ran him away. I destroyed this marriage."

"It was his choice. He made that choice. You couldn't make that choice for him and you don't have the power to make choices for him."

"I should have cooked more."

"You did cook more and he made his choice. It's not your fault."

"I should have been more attentive. I should have been around more."

"Tiffany, don't do this to yourself. I told you, carry your guilt and deal with it, don't carry his. He made this choice. His choices are not in your control!"

I look into the black sky and scream, "Why God? Why have you forsaken me?" The sky is too big and my screams disappear into the night. "You answer me, God. You answer me right now! Why did you let this happen? Was I not good enough? Did I mess up one too many times? What did I do to deserve this? Answer me!"

Jessica stands with me as I wait for an answer from Heaven.

"Did you hear that Jessica? I heard something. God answered me."

"That was a cow. We're in a pasture or right next to one. Come on girl."

"Jess."

"I already know Tiff, you don't have to say anything more, if you don't want to. Come on."

We walk through the pasture in silence, and climb back through the barbed wire. Did I actually come through this? As we make it back to the car I look back into the Heavens and they look as dark as my shadow of pain.

"I need an answer Jessica, I need an answer from God."

"That's His choice. Another one of those things that isn't in your control."

"I was the good one. I deserve the happy ending Jessica."

"It doesn't mean you're going to get it."

Jessica looks toward the rear view mirror, puts the car in drive and emotionless she says, "You're right about one thing."

"What's that?"

"You're the good one."

Chapter 44

Carlo

"I'm getting the DNA test, Carlo. I've made up my mind."

"Why Sadie? Our relationship is already strained. I know the boys are mine. I know this."

"Carlo, I want to know. Decisions have to be made."

"What decisions, Sadie. If they're not mine, what do we have left to fight for, to hold on to? If they're mine, it would only confirm what I already know, but it would show just how much you disrespect my wishes."

"Carlo you know they're yours. I don't know that. I'm not as confident as you are. Don't hold it against me because I want to be as confident in this as you."

"I'm getting this DNA test, Carlo."

"And then what? Then what, Sadie? Who are you going to run to with the results? Troy? Me? You may find my body, but you won't be able to find my heart. I can tell you where Troy's body and heart will be...with Sojourn."

"Are you threatening to leave me if I get a DNA test Carlo?"

"It's not a threat." There's silence between us, I will not change my mind. If Sadie does not support me on this, it will create a wound too painful to recover from.

"I'm going to see my boys and hold my boys before I leave this apartment. A knee in the groin isn't going to stop me."

"What do you expect, Carlo? You come home from the hospital and there's lipstick from your sister on your lips."

"I expect you to talk to me."

"Explain it to me then."

I cringe in frustration. I don't want to have to give her any explanation for something that was nothing. My breaths grow deep and as I exhale my words escape, "Sadie. I've known Sojourn all my life. We've always loved each other. I thought maybe there was something more. I wasn't sure. I didn't know, but I didn't want to take things with you to another level until I knew for sure. I didn't want to hurt you, Troy, Sojourn or me. It was a kiss. That's it. We both decided, it was best if we did not explore and left things as they were. We agreed never to walk down this avenue again. We left it alone. That kiss, sealed the deal."

"So was there?"

"Was there what?"

"Something more?"

"I guess we'll never know. It's over."

"How long have you been curious Carlo? How long have you had a sick attraction to your sister?"

"We are NOT sister and brother. We grew up together and have always been close. Stop making this into something it's not Sadie."

"Carlo, I didn't call this woman your sister, you did. You were playing this sick game, not me."

"Sadie, Sojourn is a childhood friend."

"How long have you been attracted to Sojourn, Carlo?"

"I don't know Sadie. I don't know what it is I feel or felt. I'm not going to waste any time in trying to figure it out either. If there was something, there's nothing now. It's over."

"So she's back to being a demented sister?"

"No. She's a friend. A friend that you had no right punching."

"Carlo, here's what I know, if you never explore that curiosity, you'll always be curious. Deep down, when you look at her you'll always 'wonder what could have been' and you'll be susceptible to exploring once more. How can I ever trust you? How do I know you won't always have this sick attraction to her?"

"Sadie. Will you always be this reactionary? This violent? Will you always be this emotional and insecure whenever you feel threatened? Will you always turn on me, without getting the story first?"

"I don't want to be, Carlo."

"Neither do I. I'm not going to live my life always wondering 'what could have been' with Sojourn. It's over. I'm moving forward. I will keep moving forward with or without you. So instead of focusing on what may or may not be, focus instead on what is."

"Carlo, I want this DNA test. I also love you. I don't want this to divide us."

"I'm against it Sadie. I'm going to see my boys. You owe Sojourn an apology."

"What about me? What am I owed?"

"You tell me."

"I'm owed a bit of respect, honesty and.." She pauses and a sly smile appears on her face, "..and amazing make-up sex, after I heal that is."

Sadie. This is why I love her. Her personality amazes me. She always knows how to put a smile on my face and I feel the tension release like air escapes from the lip of a balloon.

"Ok, Bella. First, I'm going to see my boys."

As I walk off, I know this DNA conversation is not over.

Chapter 45

Shannon

omehow this man knows how to have a conversation with a woman and warmly persuade her to let her guards down. I can't believe how comfortable I feel with him, talking to him. This is great. His looks and personality are incredibly seducing.

"You certainly know how to make a woman feel at ease. This is a very enjoyable evening."

"I too have enjoyed our conversation. I believe in creating comfortable work environments based on trust, it increases productivity."

"So your warm persona is really all business?"

"It benefits business. It's just who I am."

"Any advice for me as I professionally grow?"

"Avoid the romantic lure of an office love affair."

My breaths stop coming. Does he know? Does he think I'm attracted to him? I am attracted to him, but how would he know that. Is he trying to tell me he's not interested?

"Did you learn that lesson the hard way?" I ask with curious anticipation hoping I will have a clue as to why he chose to give me this piece of advice.

"Yes I did." he gives me a look of relief, "But I only had to learn it once." He chuckles, "Maybe twice." He shakes his head, "Ok twice and a half, but not a third." He laughs out loud and I laugh with him.

"Cassanova, are you?"

"No. Most definitely not. I'm completely focused on this job and being what Jessica needs."

"Jessica? Who is Jessica?"

"Remember I told you I had a son and a daughter. Jessica is my daughter. She has had a real rough time since her mother passed. Her husband Jason called me out of concern. I immediately made a decision to put her first, and job second. I began talks to relocate to Houston and here I am."

He pauses with pride and I pause with anxiety. Please, please, please, please don't let this be the wife of my ex-boyfriend Jason Jones. Please, please, please. It just can't be.

"Shannon, I've never felt better in my life about a decision that I've made. I'll do anything in my power for my daughter. She deserves it. I owe it to her."

Please, please, please, don't let her last name be Jones.

"Shannon, what is it? What's wrong?"

My mind is screaming! What's wrong? Jason and I had an affair! That's what's wrong! Half the problems with that marriage are based on decisions we made. Jessica knows. She knows about me. Please, please, please don't let her last name be Jones!

"Shannon?"

"I'm sorry. I was a bit distracted. What did you say her married name is?" Please, please, please don't say Jones. Please, please, please.

"Jones." He says with a smile.

A mental clock begins ticking, despair creeps in. The count down to the moment when my demise will consume me alive has begun. Another beautiful man abducted peace from my life with a seductive smile and one word. Jones.

Is wanting love such a bad thing? Every time and every move I make toward love gives me intense moments of mortiferous silence. This could end my career.

"So tell me Douglas, I've never had to fire anyone before, if I ever did, what are reasons to fire someone?" I wonder...would he even fire me over something like having an affair with his daughter's husband?

"Well, aside from the obvious reasons to fire someone. I believe in a solid ethics policy that our entire team should operate by. Ethics are the foundation of integrity."

"What about something someone has done in the past?"

"What do you mean?"

"What if someone broke an ethical code in the past? Would you fire them if you learned about it in your new assignment?"

"Are you trying to tell me something Shannon, or are we still discussing reasons to fire someone because you've never done this before?"

"I'm still curious as to good reasons to fire someone."

"Ok. Well, has this past ethical violation been addressed?"

"No."

"Ok. If we're still satisfying your curiosity, then I would have to address the ethics violation as soon as I had knowledge of it. Just because it was in the past doesn't excuse the offense."

Damn. I'm finished.

"Shannon?"

"Yes?"

"Is your curiosity satisfied?"

"Yes. Thank you."

He knows. This awkward silence is giving me away. Hurry Shannon, fill it with something before he discovers the real reason for asking those questions.

"Ummm, well, do you enjoy the snow, because we have none of that in Houston."

"Uh. Ok. More weather talk. Well Shannon, unless you want dessert, perhaps it's time to bring a close to our wonderful dinner."

I hear my phone vibrate and Douglas looks to my phone. Why do I even bother turning the ringer off when the vibration is so damn loud. It's a text message from Rick, "I need to talk to you now. Call me." What could this be about? Maybe he realizes that he needs me to work with him at the other company and will rescue me from the wrath of Dr. Douglas when he finds out I was the other woman that almost destroyed his daughter's marriage.

"Well Shannon, dessert?"

"I think I'll pass. A moment on the lips is a lifetime on the hips." I attempt to playfully end things on a softer note, perhaps he won't discover it's me. As soon as those thoughts surface in my mind, my head dismisses them with a deep roll of the eyes and desperate head shake, who am I fooling. It's just a matter of time. Damn.

"If I may?" Douglas walks around to my side of the table, pulls my chair for me and offers his arm to guide me out of my seat. What a gentleman. Any woman would go ga ga for this man.

"Why thank you. How awfully considerate."

"My pleasure. We should do this again. We'll talk business soon. I'm taking this next week to spend with my Houston family. I want my transition here to be as smooth as the situation allows. More than likely, you won't hear from me very much this next week. After that, we'll meet together at the office and with the rest of the team to strategically plan."

"Sounds like a winner to me Doc." The corners of his mouth softly smile and I watch as his lips form words that serenade me, "Until we meet again. Adieu."

"Adieu."

I watch him as he walks to his car. Even his walk commands attention. He has a gentle swagger that looks like leaves dancing on a branch on a windy day. Tick tock, tick tock. It's just a matter of time before that sweet breeze of a man becomes my tornado. What in the world am I going to do about this mess? My phone vibrates again. Rick. *I need to talk to you now! Where are you?*

What could this be about? I text back. *Leaving a dinner meeting I can meet you now. Where?*

Come to my apartment.

Ok. On my way.

Chapter 46

Richard

I should have asked Margie if questions were taunting her as much as death was when she first learned of the cancer. Questions keep coming at me, like darts stinging on impact. Each sting sends a singe of poison that travels to my body searching for answers with no answer to be found; so the poison like the questions multiply. I don't know why I'm expecting Shannon to have any answers. I know this didn't come from Tiffany. It was either Shannon or Sojourn. I wish it weren't either of them. I hope it's not both of them infected. Did they know? Who else were they with? Damn. Why didn't I just work things out with Tiffany from the beginning? My thoughts are halted by a knock at the door, Shannon. How do I tell her? Do I tell her? Does she already know? She was the last person I was with, before her was Sojourn. So if it is Sojourn, Shannon has it. If it is Shannon, Sojourn is safe. "Rick what is it? Is this about the new job?"

"No."

I look at her, studying her as if I'll be able to tell if she has HIV by just looking at her.

"What is it Rick? You're scaring me."

"Shannon, sit down."

"Rick. Please, what is it?"

"I have HIV."

"What!?"

"You need to get tested."

Shannon sits on my couch, speechless.

"Rick, I'm pregnant." Tears fall from her eyes.

"Who will raise our child? What if the baby has HIV? Are you sure Rick?"

"Shannon. I wish this wasn't the case. God knows I wish the two tests I took were wrong. I wish this were all a bad dream, but it's not a bad dream. It's my life now."

"Did this come from me?"

"I don't know. You were the last person I was with. Before you was Sojourn."

"Does she have it?"

"Shannon!" My words come out as loud as thunder. "I don't know. I don't know anything aside from what I told you. Please!"

Shannon falls, covering her eyes and resting her entire body on the couch, crying. I can't do anything with her or for her. I'm pissed,

confused and not sure where or who to turn to myself, much less anyone else. Then my thoughts stop. I sit on a chair across from Shannon watching her cry hysterically. Why? Why? Why? Why? Why is
the only word that accelerates through my mind at hurricane speed.
Why? I can't take this. Why does my body want to kill me? I'm dying.
HIV Positive. I stand up, walk to my room, close the door and fall
across the bed. Stupid, Stupid, Stupid. Margie, how did you survive
this? How did you beat death?

I hear my door creak open.

"Richard. If this was me, I'm sorry."

"Sorry isn't a cure. Sorry isn't going to change the course of things."

Shannon starts crying again. I can't take this. She is going to have
to leave.

"I know Rick, I know. I'll leave. I'm sorry."

"You don't have to leave, just stop crying."

"What's next Rick? What do we do? What about the baby?"

"Stop asking so many damn questions Shannon! I don't have any
answers. I don't know."

I feel my eyes burning my pain onto her flesh, "You need to get
tested. You need to think about who else you've been with and they
need to be tested. You need to go to your doctor and find out about
HIV and pregnancy. I don't know Shannon, you need to go to someone who has the answers. I don't have them."

"What about us?"

"What us Shannon? Are you delusional? There is no 'us'! There
has never been an 'us'!"

"Rick we can't go through this alone! Even if there was never an 'us' before, it is an 'us' now! We're having a baby together."

"Shannon, my wife and I are going through a rough patch, but I'm still married. I love Tiffany."

"What about Sojourn?"

"Why in the hell are we talking about my love life? Shannon, I have HIV. Do you get that? You probably have HIV. There's no cure. We're dying. Not only are we dying, but you're pregnant on top of that! Who is going to be left to raise this child? Why are you concerned with my love life? Who wants to love a man with HIV?"

"Me."

This woman is crazy. All these issues we're dealing with and all she is concerned with is me. Me? Why me? Is this my punishment for all the wrong I've done? Did I have to get a death sentence?

"Shannon, you need to get tested."

"I don't want any bad news confirmed Rick."

"Woman are you crazy? Had you been tested earlier, you could have prevented passing this to me and who knows who else. Stop killing people with your damn ignorance!"

"Rick I didn't know."

"You didn't know or you didn't want confirmation because you were afraid of the result."

"No Rick, no! I didn't know!"

I look at Shannon with disbelief. I want to kill her, but what's the point she's dying anyway. She starts that damn crying again. How do I tell Tiffany all of this?

"Shannon, you need to get tested." I swing my feet on the side of the bed, stand up and straighten myself out. I need to talk to Ms. Margie again. I move to the front room, grab my wallet and look for my keys.

"Where are you going Rick?"

"I need to get out Shannon. These four walls are closing in on me. I just received a death sentence. I'm looking at the woman who could have given it to me. The same woman who claims to be carrying my child. The same woman who doesn't want to get tested and could do to someone else what was done to me. You disgust me Shannon. Ignorance. Just ignorant. I need to get out of here before I explode."

"Rick, I never would have done anything like this to you or anyone else on purpose."

"When you do it on accident, it's just as bad, Shannon."

I look at her, realizing that continuing this talk with her is a complete waste of time.

"Shannon, I have to go. If you don't get tested, then don't call me until the baby is born so I can get a DNA test."

"Don't cut me off Rick, please."

"Shannon, what is staying in contact with each other going to do? You disgust me."

"Rick please. I love you."

"Shannon! Stop! That's enough! Your love is about as ignorant as your mind! Get tested. Babies can be born from HIV parents without having the disease themselves. Keep this baby healthy and get out of my face! I can't stand to look at you."

"Rick, I'm so, so sorr.."

I feel like I'm about to lose it with her. My frustration finishes her sentence, "I know sorry."

I grab my keys.

"I'm leaving, Shannon."

She starts that damn crying again and walks out the door. I close the door behind her, lock it and dial Ms. Margie's number on my cell.

"Hello?"

"Hi Ms. Margie. This is Rick. Can I talk more with you?"

"Sure son, we are headed back from the clinic to the church, we're only going to be at the church for a moment, then we're headed home to cook dinner. You can meet me at the church and then come back to the house with us if you would like."

"Thanks Ms. Margie. That would be great. I'm walking out the door now."

"We'll see you then."

Chapter 47

Troy

Sojourn and I ride in the car together in silence. A piece of me
wants to comfort her, a piece of me wants to leave her alone. She
drives to my neighborhood and pulls up to the community park to
park the car. It's almost night, so the park is empty.

"What's going on with you, Sojourn?"

"I don't know," she softly whispers.

"What do you want?"

"I don't want you with that girl!"

"You have always had my heart and you know this. How long
have I been trying to put our family back together, Sojourn?"

"I know, Troy."

"How long?"

"Troy. I know."

"I'm tired, Sojourn. I'm not dating Tiffany, but I'm tired of waiting for you as you run to the arms of Rick."

"I'm not in his arms, Troy. Not anymore."

"What happened then?"

"Nothing. Nothing has happened. We haven't talked, we haven't seen each other. Nothing has happened. Whatever did happen is over."

"What's going on with Carlo, Sojourn?"

I asked the question, but I really don't want to know the answer. The wrong answer would kill any love I have for her or him.

"Nothing."

"Sojourn, if I found out anything contrary to what you're telling me, I don't think I could recover from the lies and deception, not from you."

She doesn't respond.

"Is there anything else you need to tell me Sojourn, because if not, then I'm finished. I won't ask about the fight with you and Sadie, I won't ask anymore about what's going on with Carlo, I'm just going to leave it alone and move forward."

"There's nothing with Carlo. What's going on with Tiffany?"

"Tiffany and I are friends. She needed a shoulder to lean on tonight and I gave that to her. Obviously you know what she's going through. Whatever beef you have with her and she has with you, you all need to settle it!"

"Are you lovers, Troy?"

"No. If we were, what difference would that make to you? I'm not waiting on you anymore, Sojourn."

"You don't have to wait anymore. I don't expect you to."

"What do you mean?"

"I mean I'm here. I've caught up. I want to work with you. You don't have to wait on me any longer."

"You want to put this family back together with me?"

"Yes."

I don't know what to say. All this time I've loved Sojourn, dealt with her resistance, sacrificed what I wanted for her and now she's at the same place with me. Ready to work with me, grow with me. Can I trust it?

"Say something Troy."

"Can I trust you?"

"Yes."

"Ok." I breathe. A breath of excited anticipation, skepticism and nervousness. What I have mess up again? "Ok then."

She leans over and gives me a kiss on the lips and adrenalin shocks my body. She kisses me again. I love this woman. Can I trust her?

"Troy."

"Yes?"

"Can I trust you?"

I look into the sky just beyond her glare. I want her to be able to trust me. Can I trust myself? What if she finds out about the other women? Have I beat my problem? Yes. Yes. I can beat this. I can. Please Lord, give me the strength. The urge and impulse is still with me. I don't want to fall. I want to resist.

"Troy?"

"Sojourn. I don't want to lie to you. I love you and I'll never love another as strong as I love you. You can trust that. God is still working on me in other areas, well, I'm working on me."

"What can I do to help?"

"Live life with me."

I look down at my watch.

"What is it?"

"Take me to the flower shop before it closes, but hurry. Mitchell is at the church because it's Bible Study tonight and I want to take his mother some flowers. She has terminal cancer and he's having a hard time. I figure the more smiles he sees on his mother's face, the easier all of this will be on him."

"You're really a thoughtful guy, Troy. I don't like Tiffany, but all the wonderful things she says about you are true."

"Sojourn, I'm selfish and self-centered, but I'm trying to share more. Mitchell is always there for me, it's my turn."

I see the flower shop in the distance, "What type of flowers should I get her?"

"You'll have plenty to choose from."

"When we leave here Sojourn, drop me off at the church, go to Mom's house to pick up the boys, because they'll be with you tonight and then swing back by to get me. I should be ready by then."

"Ok Troy. I'll call you when I'm on my way."

Once I get the flowers, Sojourn drops me off at the church. I have hopes of a peaceful restoration, but I need to prepare for any setbacks by moving into this slow. I walk through the church doors looking for

Mitchell and instead I see Rick, with a blank stare affixed to the cross. I approach him and silently sit next to him.

"Rick."

He breaks his stare and with bloodstained eyes he glances at me and then back into an abyss of nothing, centered on the cross.

"Tiffany's mine. You can't have her." slips out of his mouth ready to kill.

So many thoughts, feelings and responses flood my mind. I know how this man feels. I know what it feels like to see your marriage fall apart. The same man I've wanted to tear apart for so long is the same man I feel like encouraging. I've hated him for so long. Where did all the hate go?

"Tiffany is yours, and if you want my help restoring your family, you've got it."

He sits in silence and I sit with him.

"You're a good man, Troy."

"We're the same man, Rick. Making the same mistakes, trying to right our wrongs. Trying to recover. We've both hurt the people we love."

"There's no recovery for me. I've fallen too low. Way beyond the grasp of God. He's proven to me that he doesn't want to have anything else to do with me. Terminal."

"Well it may get worse before it gets better, so just prepare yourself. God wants all of the credit if it is in His will to restore your family."

"What do you mean?"

"Well he wants you and everyone else to be able to look at your life and say, 'only God could've put that family back together.' He wants the room to prove He's God."

I pause, "A good friend told me that when I was sitting where you are now."

"My future is death."

"That's the future for all of us son." Ms. Margie says as she approaches us from behind.

"Ms. Margie!" I answer in a startled excitement.

"Well hello there. Troy, I didn't know you and Rick knew each other."

"Yes ma'am. It didn't start off as a pleasant friendship, but perhaps it can end as one."

"Rick, Troy and my baby went to college together. He'd come home every chance he got with my boy." She looks back to me. "Richard and my baby are childhood friends."

So we both knew Mitch at different points in our lives.

"Ms. Margie, I have something for you."

"Now don't you flirt with me. I'm much too old for you Troy."

"Not to worry. I'm saving myself for Sojourn, but if she gives me a hard time, watch out! I'm coming for you."

She laughs with me and I enjoy seeing her smile, "I'm giving my son an appreciation and celebration dinner and hope you can invite his college buddies."

"I can do better than that, I can host it at the Coffee Bean & Other Things. You just let me know when."

"Boy, I tell you, I don't have much time on this earth left, but you better tell that Sojourn I'm coming for *you*."

"Mama, stop flirting with my friends." Deacon Mitchell joins us, and brings another person.

"Hey Troy. What's up Rick?"

Rick greets him with a solemn smile.

"Mom, this is Jason Jones."

Wait a minute. I know this brother. It's going to come to me. I know him. I've seen him at The Coffee Bean. Oh. Oh man, this is Jessica's husband. Jason greets all of us and I feel a bit uneasy. His wife and I have a history. Everyone greets each other and Ms. Margie can't take her eyes off him.

"How's Jessica?" Rick asks.

"She's good. She and Tiffany are staying with Sadie tonight." Jason answers.

"Mom, Jason is a carpenter. He helped restore some of the homes of our senior members. I invited him over for dinner."

I watch as Ms. Margie studies him, "So you're married, Jason?"

"Yes ma'am."

"Have you met his wife, honey? Jessica did you say?" She asks as if she already knows the answers.

"Yes." Mitch answers, "On many occasions."

"Is that right?" Ms. Margie questions.

Jason interrupts, "Deacon was our counselor when we were in couples counseling."

"Hmmm." Ms. Margie answers.

"Ms. Margie." I interrupt, "I have something for you. I want to give it to you before I forget."

I reach down and pick up the cactus plant.

"Wow! A cactus."

"Yes ma'am. When you give a gift of a cactus, it symbolizes endurance."

She reads the card, "May your love and spirit endure with us all until the end of time."

"Why thank you, Troy. You tell that little Ms. Sojourn to get on her j-o-b. You are my kind of man!"

"Mama! Stop flirting. You're embarrassing me." Mitch says with a wink and a smile toward me. I'm glad this gift put a smile on his face. He's going to need as many as he can get. This transition is going to be tough on him.

"Well Jason, do you have a picture of your wife, I bet I've seen her around the church."

"As a matter of fact I do. I just took a picture of her with her dad on my phone a couple of hours ago."

He passes the phone to Margie.

"Well, look at that." Ms. Margie says in a whisper.

"Do you know her, Mom?" Mitchell asks.

"I know who she is. I know her dad very well, but she looks more like her mother."

"He's been gone for a while, he knows you too." Jason responds, "But he's living here now. Next time he's over for dinner Mitch, why don't you and your mom come and meet him?"

"You can invite him over tonight." Ms. Margie responds passing the phone to Jason and looking to Rick, "Rick, when we get to the house, why don't you come spend some time with me and help in the kitchen. Mitch, Jason, I hope that's alright with you. I'm going to share my secret recipes with Rick."

Rick smiles with sadness surrounding him, "Yes ma'am."

"It's not alright with me Mom, I wanted you to leave me the secret recipes. Rick you can't have my place in the will now." Mitchell says with a melancholy laughter.

"I'm sure he'd love to come over." Jason answers.

I look down to see my phone vibrating, it's a text from Sojourn. *I'm on my way.*

Ms. Margie looks to me, "Troy set up that thing up for me that you mentioned earlier, in three days around 5:00pm. Can you do that for me, son?

"What are you talking about mom?"

"When you become the person I'm talking to, then you'll know what I'm talking about. Until then. Ten." she flashes up the number ten with her fingers to Mitch

"Ten?"

"Yes. Ten. Tend to your own business!"

We all chuckle, Ms. Margie has spunk.

"Consider it done Ms. Margie. Here is my card, my cell number is on the back. Call me anytime. I'll let you know if Sojourn falls off her game."

"Watch it now!" She says with a smile. As I walk off toward the door to greet Sojourn, she slaps me on the behind. I can't help but laugh. I call back, "Alright Ms. Margie, I'm saving myself." Mitchell's mom is a mess, I'm going to miss her too. I walk toward the door and see Sojourn in the car with the boys.

Chapter 48

Tiffany

"I need to run home and get a change of clothes. I have one for you also. Sleeping over with Sadie should be fun. My dad is at the house with Jason, so you'll get a chance to see him."

I'm trying to listen to what Jessica is saying, but my heart cries are drowning out all sound.

I know I'm not myself. What is happening to me? Why can't I snap out of this? I feel like fighting the world with both fists and finishing things off with a head bunt to knock myself out.

We walk into Jessica's house to be greeted by her father and husband, Jason. I manage to peer through my shaded glaze to sense Jessica's simultaneous comfort and relief as she is greeted by her dad for the first time in years. She lightly embraces him and he holds on to her as if this will be his last embrace. She gently moves as if she is politely letting go, but he holds on. He whispers in her ear, "I'm sorry. It's my turn to take care of you now that your mother's gone. I'm here, for good. I love you Jess."

Jessica doesn't move. He doesn't let her go.

"It's ok Father," she answers like kind words that you would exchange with a stranger.

"I love you sweetness." he whispers.

"Dad."

"I love you." It's like his words have a gravitational pull and Jessica can't resist anymore.

"Daddy, I needed you. Momma died and I was alone." Her words emerge from the bellows of her stomach in a misty shower sprinkling the pain from her heart on everyone in the room.

She relaxes and sinks into his arms. His arms don't greet her anymore, they comfort her.

He pulls back and looks at her, "We've got a journey ahead of us. I know you have questions. I'll answer all of them."

She nods her head as tears, in perfect alignment, walk single file down her face.

"Ok. Daddy. We'll talk. I want to understand. I want to know. I want to know why."

"You won't like some of the answers Jess, but they'll be honest answers."

She doesn't respond, he responds for her, "I miss her too."

She falls back into his arms as if she is relieved that he understands her.

"Daddy, this is my friend Tiffany."

"Tiffany. My pleasure to meet you."

A certain sweet charm surrounds him.

"Hello." I answer

Jason, who has silently been witnessing all of this with a smile adds, "Tiffany was with Jessie and I at the hospital when Jessica was admitted last year."

"Well, you are a dear friend indeed." He asserts.

"Yes, and a friend in need," Why did I say that? I guess I'm just tired of bottling up all this pain. tired of holding all this crap in. Who cares anymore?

"Tiffany and her husband are going through a difficult time right now, Daddy."

"Jason, do you think Mitchell, our marriage counselor, can help Tiffany?"

"Yeah. Sure. Why not?" Jason responds so affectionately to Jessica. Jason and Jessica are just great together, that marriage counselor can't fix what God allowed to be so messed up with my marriage.

"I'm going to go to Bible study. I'll see him tonight." Jason adds.

Bible study? Wait a minute? A church counselor? Yeah right. God turns his back on me and sends a church counselor to talk to me. Forget about it.

"I don't know Jessica, one step at a time." My words come out with razors, shredding all hope.

Jason looks at me as if I have the power to control darkness, "Tiff, when you're ready, let me know. I'll talk to him. Deacon Mitchell is a great guy. We're great friends now. He did a lot for me and Jess."

Whatever. Whatever. Whatever is all that circles in my mind.

"What is Mitchell's last name?" Jessica's father asks.

"I don't know. What's his last name Jason?" Jessica asks.

"Well his mom is Mother Margie Madison, so I assume he's a Madison," Jason looks to Jessica's dad, "We never asked him his last name."

"I didn't know Mother Madison was his mother." Jessica responds with curiosity.

"I know Margie." Jessica's dad answers with an unreadable emotion.

"Do you know Mitchell?" Jason asks

"No, not really, but I'd like to."

"I'll bring him over for dinner one night, he's a great guy." Jason responds.

"I'd love to connect with him. I haven't seen his mother in a very long time."

"Daddy, Jason, we're leaving. Catch up with you two later."

"Ok sweetness. Goodbye, Tiffany."

Finally, out of happy zone, back in the arms of my only comfort right now, darkness.

"Jess, your dad seems really nice."

"I guess."

"Was he bad to you growing up?"

"No. He was always good to me, always showed me love. He just was never here. Never."

"Oh." I respond, not sure what to say next.

"When momma was dying, where was he? I took care of her myself. I did everything. When I was grieving, I was grieving alone.

Where was he? When you go through something like that alone, a telephone call expressing love is about as valuable as a two headed nickel. Completely worthless."

"I get that. It holds about the same value of someone saying 'I love you' while screwing another woman at the same time. Worthless."

Jessica gently chuckles, the kind of chuckle that feels like swallowing a mouthful of tacks, "Yeah, I guess you do get it. Why don't they?"

"Jason gets it, Jessica. You're lucky he gets it."

"He gets it now. Honestly, he got it then. We both messed up. Our marriage counselor helped. He can help you and Richard too. That's if you want help."

"Of course I want Richard, Jess. I love him. That's why I married him. I don't know how to love him and the pain he caused me at the same time. How do I love him with the memory of what he did with Sojourn? I hate what he did. How can I love a man, but hate what he has become at the same time."

"So what, Tiffany. You live and you die. In between those two points, we make mistakes and we recover, that's life. Or we make mistakes and we don't. That's death. Don't get too comfortable in your darkness, honey. It's alluring, it's deadly, sometimes you think it's the only answer."

Can she see my shadow of pain, my darkness following me? How does she know?

"Can you see it Jess, my darkness?"

"Girl, yes. I can smell it. I see it. I went through it. Darkness almost became my life. I was in it. Dead. Somehow, light managed to break through and when I opened my eyes, light flooded me. When I was able to focus, I saw you and Jason in my hospital room. I know darkness and I can tell you it's not relief, it's not a happy ending, it's just more pain. Don't get comfortable in it. I'm talking to Mitch about you and Richard and I'm not taking no for an answer!"

"Well, I guess we're going to counseling then."

"Yes ma'am you are. That's what friends are for. They save each other."

We pull up to Sadie's house.

"Are you ready to save this crazy woman in here? These baby blues are about strangle the life out of her."

"We're going to have to team up on Sadie."

"Don't I know it. Come on, let's get in there."

Chapter 49

Carlo

I lay across the bed and play with both my boys. "Do you remember me boys? Do you remember playing with Pappa before you were born?"

I place my finger in each one of their hands. I remember this touch. I remember my boys during that brief moment where I was both dead and alive. "I remember you. I came back for you."

My boys. *My* boys. I forbid Sadie from getting a DNA test, but I can't stop her. Troy won't be hurt at all if they're not his, but it would ruin me. "I know you're mine. I know this. I love you Gianni and Valentino. Pappa loves you."

Sadie walks in the room, but doesn't speak.

After her quiet observation, she finally releases words. "Need some help?"

"No. I'm just enjoying this time with my boys."

"Jessica and Tiffany are coming to stay the night to help me with the boys."

I guess she's telling me to get ready and leave. Why do I have to leave my boys behind? I have just as much right to be with them as she does. I feel a fight coming on, how can I avoid this? I don't want to fight with Sadie and I won't begin the habit of fighting in front of my boys. How is she going to tell me to leave and leave my boys behind?

"Are you asking me to leave, Sadie?"

"Do you want to hang around a bunch of women?"

"I want to hang around my boys. Let me keep them tonight."

"No. You're not set up, Carlo. Just stay here for the night. Jessica and Tiffany can sleep in the front room."

"Ok. Fine. Can I at least put them in the stroller and take a walk around outside for some fresh air?"

"Carlo, it's so early, but if you insist, just keep them completely covered and don't let anyone around them, breathe on them, cough on them or touch them. Keep them covered, away from people."

I turn to look at my boys. "Are you ready for some fun boys?"

Sadie smiles. "Here Carlo," she passes me bottles.

"Feed them, give them some fresh diapers and a fresh set of clothes and blankets. Let me know before you take them out. After they eat, they may fall asleep or fall asleep during the walk."

The doorbell rings.

"That's Jessie and Tiff, I'll be in the front room if you need me."

"Ok. Go. I got this."

I turn to my boys and sing.

"Ninna nanna di pace che invento

Pensando a un bambino

Che è arrivato stanotte dal mare col freddo che fa

Trasportato sulle ali del vento

Da un paese lontano, fin qua

Con in tasca il ricordo più dolce di un'altra città."

I turn around and see Sadie, Tiffany and Jessica standing behind me.

"What does that mean Carlo?" Tiffany asks.

I sing it again for my boys in English

"Lullaby of peace that I invent

Thinking of a baby

Arrived tonight from the sea with the cold it does

Transported on the wind wings

From a faraway Country to here

With a sweeter memory of another town in his pocket."

I smile back. "Trust me, it's much easier to sing in Italian."

"Is there more?" Jessica asks.

"Yes. More for them, for you, no. Enjoy your time with Sadie. I'm going to enjoy these moments with my boys."

"Well, Sadie. I think that's our cue to leave." Jessica sings.

"Sadie," I call out before she leaves, "My position stands. I forbid you to get a DNA test. These are my boys."

"Carlo, I'm going to spend some time with friends. We'll talk about this later."

As Sadie walks out, I dial Sojourn and put my earpiece in my ear.

"Carlo."

"Hey Sojourn. How are you?"

"Ok. Depressed. Hopeful."

"Sorry about what happened with Sadie."

"It wasn't your fault, Carlo. I don't blame you. In fact, I really don't blame her. I don't blame Tiffany for hating me either. I understand."

"What do you mean?"

"We all have vulnerabilities and vulnerable moments. Rick was going through a rough patch and found solace in me and I in him, it led to an affair. It made our situations worse, not better. Tiffany is going through a rough spot and found her comfort in Troy. You almost died and when you came back to life, I was the piece of comfort that reached back to you. If we would have explored it, it wouldn't have lasted either. I went through this with Rick. I know how the story ends. I've come full circle, Carlo."

"Where's that place?"

"With Troy."

"So you are going to work things out with Troy?"

"We were young and didn't know what we were doing when we married, then we were older and didn't know what we were doing and divorced. Let's hope we know what we're doing now that we're trying to put this thing back together."

"No matter what, I love you lady."

"I love you too. I'm almost at the church getting ready to pick up Troy."

"He's going to address this with you and me at some point."

"...and when he does, we'll tell him the truth. It was nothing but vulnerable moments getting the best of me. I'm with my boys Sojourn, I love them completely. If Sadie insists on this DNA test, it'll kill me."

"We'll talk Carlo. Ciao."

"Ciao."

I hang the phone up with Sojourn, finish dressing my boys and load them in the stroller. Dressed, packed, and ready to go. I go to open the door and turn back around to grab their pacifiers. I hear Sadie's voice creep through the small opening through the cracked door as I am looking for their pacifiers. I love her. She infuriates me sometimes, but I love her.

"You guys don't have to stay tonight. Carlo is going to be here."

"Are you sure?"

"Yea, I'd like to save you all for a night that I'll really need you when Carlo isn't here."

I smile as I find one pacifier and look for the other. I'm glad it will be just me and Sadie tonight, maybe we can work on this trust issue, and this whole relationship thing in general.

"Tiffany, Jason just sent me a text he's at Mother Madison's house for dinner, my dad is going too. Come with me?" Jessica asks.

"Sadie are you sure you don't need us tonight?" Tiffany asks.

"I'm good, besides that, my home DNA test came."

"What are you going to do with that Sadie?" Jessica asks.

"When Carlo goes to sleep, I'm going to swab his mouth, swab the babies mouth and send it in. He'll never know. That way I can know who the father is and no one will know I ran a DNA test." Sadie says in a loud enough whisper.

"You better hope he is a sound sleeper, Sadie." Tiffany chimes in.

"Sadie, stop being so 007, just do it and let him know." Jessica demands.

"If I do, he'll break up with me. I have to do it this way. This is the only way we can both have peace. If you guys leave, it'll give me the space I need to do this."

"What if he catches you?" Tiffany asks.

"He won't." Sadie responds with confidence, "He can't."

"Ok sweetie. Tiff and I are leaving then. Call on us on the cell if you need to, we'll be at Mother Madison's eating dinner."

"Ok. See you later." Sadie responds.

Enough of this! Enough! I can't believe Sadie. Enough!

I leave the twins in the room and close the door. I don't want them to hear me with their mother. I walk out of the room and Sadie is lying on the couch.

"Give me the damn swabs, Sadie!"

"What? Carlo, I'm sorry, I ..."

"Give it to me!" I yell. My words storm out of my mouth and in a whirlwind she gets up and gives me the swabs.

She hesitates in passing it to me. I grab it from her hand and rub it all around my cheek walls. I look her in the eye as I hold it up for to reach over and grab it. She doesn't move.

"Take it!"

"That's ok Carlo. Really."

"Take it Sadie! You want to know. You want peace. Take it!"

She doesn't move.

"Sadie!" My words arrest her. She surrenders and takes the swab and places it in the container, and back in the plastic bag. I go back to the bedroom, push the twins out.

"These are my boys Sadie! My boys!" I exclaim and swab Gianni and Valentino's mouth with swabs, "How long before we get the results?"

"Three days."

"I want to see the results with my own eyes Sadie! I'm taking the boys for a walk. I'll bring them back, and then I'm leaving. I don't want to see you until you have the results in your hand!"

"Carlo please. It doesn't have to be this way."

"Three days, Sadie!"

I walk out the front door and my frustration slams it shut. Why does it feel as if this is my final walk with my boys? I've got to hold on.

"Gianni and Valentino, no matter what. No matter what, I'm your Pappa."

I walk my boys with broken spirits. Please Lord let my words be carried to you on the wings of mercy and on the back of hope, "Don't let a DNA test take my boys from me."

Chapter 50

Shannon

I leave Rick's apartment and sit in my car. Everything is lost. Everything except my unborn child. This could be lost too. I can end this. I can end all of this. I'm not as strong as Rick. I can't maneuver my way out of this. I need to talk to him again. I need to know for sure. I grab my phone and see I have one missed call, with a voice message. Who could this be?

"Ms. Scott, this is nurse Lynn from calling from Dr. Cartman's office with the results from your last visit with. We ran all of our tests and the doctor needs you to come in to discuss the test results. Please call as soon as you get this message. Thanks."

Oh no. I forgot about all the labs they ran. I can't run from this anymore. I'm too afraid to face the truth. I drive to the doctor's office and hope they'll see me. I need some answers.

The first face I see is Nurse Lynn.

"Hi Ms. Scott. I'm helping train our new receptionist. You got my call?"

"Yes."

"Well have a seat. I'll call you back in just a minute."

"Ok."

I'm nervous, scared and act as if doing as I'm told and being polite will change the news I'm about to hear.

"Ms. Scott."

As soon as I hear my name being called, I quietly get up and follow the nurse to a room.

"Doctor Cartman will be in shortly."

"Thank you."

I sit on a chair and watch the door hoping for a miracle.

"Good Afternoon, Ms. Scott. You caught us just before closing. I'm glad you came in."

"What's wrong with my lab work?"

"Your HIV test came back positive."

Darkness.

"Shannon, there have been so many breakthroughs in HIV/AIDS research that you can live a long life with HIV. Early treatment is helping many people with this infection live longer, healthier lives."

"How long?"

"Well, if you follow our medicinal diet and make some lifestyle changes, you can live long enough to see the child your carrying turn into an adult."

"Will my child have HIV?"

"There's a chance. But your OB/GYN can work with you to eliminate as many risks as possible."

"I'm scared."

"Well, that will make you normal. It's scary right now because you don't know anything about HIV or how to fight it. Start reading, researching, learn as much as you can about this and it won't become as scary anymore. Understand it."

The doctor pauses and waits for my next question.

"I feel so lost."

"Shannon, you will need to talk to all your present and past sexual partners. They'll need to get tested. You will need to make sure all future partners are aware that you are carrying the HIV virus before you have sex."

"What do I do next?"

"I'm going to recommend you to an OB/GYN and a physician that specializes in working with HIV patients. We may have a cure in the next twenty years, stay hopeful. Encourage others to support HIV research. It's through research that science experiences breakthroughs."

"This is going to be hard, Dr. Cartman."

"Don't let this take over your life. Learn to live with it. Learn to live life without fear. You're going to have a child to raise. Your courage is going to be that child's greatest life lesson."

"I don't know if I want to live with this."

"You need to talk to a counselor. Let someone you can trust help you sort through all of this."

"Ok."

The doctor gives me a list of referrals and that's it. I'm out the door. Alone trying to fight for my life. What I really want to do is give up. I'm not that strong. I get in my car and drive. Drive and drive. I look up and see a church. I've never been here, but maybe there's a confessional or something or someone I can talk to. I don't want to walk in the front door and make a grand entrance so I walk through a side door, and immediately bump into someone.

"Oh. Excuse me. I'm looking for the confessional."

I'm not sure what to say, the words just topple out of my mouth.

He pauses, smiles and looks to me, "Are you looking for someone to talk to?"

"Yes. Privately." A tear rolls from my eyes. Please. No water works now.

"Ok. Come in here. I'll be right with you. Let me go and tell the people I'm with that I'll join them later. Will you wait here for me?"

"Yes."

He trots off and I sit, and look around. This must be the church office. He must work here.

Waiting for him to come back only took fifteen minutes, but it felt like an eternity. When he comes back he smiles.

"I was worried you were going to sneak back out that door. I'm so glad you stayed. Let's go to one of the rooms in the back, we can talk privately there."

"I've never been to confession before, I'm not sure how it works."

"This is a Baptist church. We don't have confessionals."

Oh. I feel stupid.

"We celebrate all denominations though. So it's ok."

He must have read my face. We walk into a room with a conference table and couch and he offers me a seat. I sit on the couch and he sits across from me. He reminds me of someone, but I can't recall who.

"Would you like to offer me your name?"

"No."

"May I offer you mine?"

"Yes."

"Most people call me Mitchell. I'm a Deacon at the church."

"Does that mean you're the pastor?"

"No. It means I serve. I help the pastor and the ministry in service."

"I guess you can tell I haven't been active in the church."

He laughs, "We have church goers that aren't very active either. I can help you with that if you would like."

"I just got horrible news, I'm afraid."

"I can see that."

"I don't have anyone to turn to. I feel so alone."

"Life has a way of making us feel like that sometimes."

"You talk as if you understand me."

"My mom is dying. I never really knew my father. When she dies, I'm sure I'll have my battles with loneliness to fight too."

"I'm dying."

He doesn't say anything. He looks at me as if he is not shocked by what I just said. He just nods his head in acceptance.

"I'm dying and I'm pregnant. I feel like ending it all. My life and my unborn child's."

"How do you plan to end it all?"

"I don't know. I haven't thought that far. I'm just scared. Death seems an easy way out."

"Short cuts always seem easy. How far have shortcuts in life gotten you so far?"

"Not far at all. It was through hard work, that I found the greatest success."

"I wonder why?"

"I don't know. Maybe because I cared more, invested more so when victory came. It was sweet."

"If you worked hard through the situation you're in now, will your victory be sweet?"

"I can't experience victory. I'm dying."

"So is my mother, but her fight for life makes every day of her living sweet. She's still alive."

"What is she dying from?" Oh no, did I intrude, maybe I shouldn't have asked, "I'm sorry. Do you mind me asking?"

"No, I don't mind at all. Cancer."

"It's not the same."

"What's not the same?"

"I have HIV. People will run from me."

"You fear people won't accept you when they learn of the HIV?"

"Yes. People don't run from cancer patients. They hug cancer patients."

"You think people don't hug HIV patients?"

"Yes. HIV is shunned. It's scary. People with HIV are looked at funny. Treated differently, fired from their jobs."

"They are also sons, daughters, mothers, brothers, sisters, fathers, cousins, nieces and nephews that are loved dearly."

"I'm not any of those things. Especially the loved dearly part."

"You don't feel loved?"

"No."

"You're carrying love inside of you right now."

"My baby."

He sits in silence. How do I survive with the disease and raise a child? How do I not pass this disease to my child? How do I do this, go through this? So many questions. My eyes land back on him. Praying he has the answers.

"I don't know how to get through this." I whisper.

"You don't have to go through this alone. Just take one step at a time."

"I don't want to step at all. I don't want to move. I want to die. I have to talk to everyone I've had sex with and tell them to get tested. Do you know how hard that's going to be?"

"No. Tell me."

"I have three men I need to talk to, well maybe four; but the fourth one we used a condom, I think he's safe. One has already talked to me, I found out from him. He's HIV positive. The other is my married ex-boyfriend. I don't even want to think about those complications and the other is a man I met from Atlanta. It was one night and we never saw each other again. I have his phone number though. Before my ex-boyfriend I was in monogamous relationship for 13 years. We broke up when he didn't ask me to marry him and moved to Bermuda. That's it."

"So you have two people to talk to."

"Yeah."

"I have to go to more doctors. Get more tests. Deal with the father of this child."

"Will he be supportive?"

"No."

"Where do you want to start?"

"I don't."

"What if not starting isn't a choice, and you were forced to start, then what?"

"Well, then I would call and find a good doctor."

"How about you consider calling a good doctor and we won't call it a start, we'll just call it a phone call."

I smile, counseling was a good idea. Stopping here by accident was a great idea.

"Ok." I respond.

"Ok. I'm going to give you my card and contact information. Please call me, stay in touch. I don't know your name or how to reach you so I'm depending on you to stay in touch with me. My mother and I go counsel HIV patients and other terminally ill patients often, I'll get you some other numbers of professional counselors, if you ever need that. Ok?"

"Ok."

"I want you to come see me again Sunday. We have three church services and we can talk after any one of them. Call and let me know which service you are able to attend and I'll save a special seat for you. We'll talk more after the service."

"Ok."

"Are you a woman of your word?"

"Yes."

"So you will call me?"

"Yes."

"Ok. I look forward to it."

"Well, lady with no name, may I escort you to your car. I'm going to go and spend some time with my mother."

"Yes. Of course. Thank you Mitchell."

"It wasn't me, and it wasn't coincidence. It was God. Thank Him."

"Ok. Well, thank you God."

Chapter 51

Richard

As we prepare to go to Ms. Margie's house for dinner, Mitch runs to the back office to lock up and we all gather our things. Troy leaves and I begin to really appreciate him. He could have taken our talk in a totally different direction. He's good for Sojourn. She deserves some goodness. I walk down the hall looking for Mitch so we can leave. I see him moving toward me.

"Rick?"

"Yeah, what's up Mitch?"

"Can you take my mom to the house and help her get everything started. Tell her and Jason I'll catch up with them. Someone just walked in and looks like they need some help. I won't be long. Just get things started for me and explain it to my mom, she'll understand."

"Yeah. No problem."

I turn around head to Ms. Margie.

"Ms. Margie, do you mind riding with me? Someone just walked in and needs some help, so Mitch said he'll catch up with us in a bit."

"Great, now where's that fancy car you drive?"

"Right this way."

I open the door for Ms. Margie and help her get seated.

"Ms. Margie, this is hard, you're the only person I can talk to."

"Talk away baby. It's going to the grave with me."

"I'm married. I had one affair. Two affairs. Both of them are over. I'm not sure what to do. My wife isn't going to want me now that I have HIV and one of the women I was with told me she's pregnant with my child. This is too much Ms. Margie. I feel like I'm suffocating."

I look to her hoping she can force breath into my lungs.

"Son, when I found out I had cancer. Cancer was my every thought. I lived cancer, until I decided to treat the cancer and start living. I couldn't make the cancer stop attacking my body. So I decided to live anyway."

"So what are you saying, Ms. Margie?"

"Live. Continue living. You'll just have to live with HIV also. It's not as if you have a choice anyway. So the question is, do you still try and reconcile with your wife? What do you do about this baby?"

"I don't know Ms. Margie. I hate this place I'm in. I don't want this child. It complicates things for me."

"Honey, this child isn't even here yet, so don't blame your complications on this child."

We arrive to Ms. Margie's house, and I help her get out of the car.

Jason pulls up right behind us, "Ms. Margie, my wife and her friend are going to come over also, is that ok?"

"Sure. No problem. I have plenty of food and Rick is here to help."

I look to Jason, "Tiffany is coming with her?"

He looks to me and nods his head yes, as if he can see right through me. I'm not surprised if he knows all my problems. Tiffany has probably told Jessica everything and I'm sure Jessica has shared with Jason.

"Jason, make yourself at home. Rick and I will be in the kitchen. Let your guests in when they arrive. Mitch should be pulling up shortly."

"Jessica's dad is in the neighborhood, he should be here any minute."

"Ok. We're in the kitchen." she answers.

I walk her to the kitchen and the minute we walk in my questions begin again.

"How do I explain any of this to Tiffany? Ms. Margie"

"Grab that pot of dumplings in the refrigerator and put it on the stovetop on medium heat, honey. Is that the same Tiffany that is on her way over here?"

"Yes."

"Talk to her honestly. Look in the refrigerator. There's a pan of dressing and chicken, put that in the oven to warm up and put the oven on 350."

I follow all her directions.

"Boil me a pot of water and let me show you how to make hot water cornbread. Make sure you wash your hands real good. A good cook is a clean cook."

"Yes ma'am."

She walks to the refrigerator and pulls out a pot of greens and puts them on the stovetop.

"A long time ago, I was in the same situation you were in. Except I was one of the women you were having the affair with."

"Did he give you a STD?"

"No, he gave me a child."

"Mitchell?"

"That's his boy."

"Did you love him?"

"Still do, but we didn't stay together."

"Did he stay married?"

"Yep."

"Did he tell his wife about you and the baby?"

"Yep."

"What happened? Did he help with Mitchell?"

"Oh yes, in many ways. None of it made a difference to Mitchell though."

"How did he help?"

"He sent a check every month. A big check. It helped us through some hard times. He paid for Mitchell's college and graduate school."

"Mitchell never talks about his dad."

"He doesn't know him. He wouldn't remember him even if he tried. He doesn't even know what he looks like."

"I never knew that. All those times I saw him with a man growing up I thought that was his father."

"Nope. That was his uncle."

Ms. Margie grabs my hand to get my attention, "Ok. This part is hard, the water is hot. We're going to mix some of the hot water with this meal and pat it into cornbread patties. Then we're going to fry the cornbread in this hot oil in this iron skillet. Ready?"

"Ok."

"Ok."

I look up and see Jason.

"Ms. Margie, this is Jessica's father Douglas Michaels." Jason says. Introducing him.

"Well I'll be, it's been years Dougie."

"Yes it has, Margie."

"Go on and put that one in the grease now. Let them brown and don't mess this food up. You're not too old for me to tan that hide now."

"Yes ma'am."

I watch as she gives Jessica's father a hug.

"Excuse me," Jason says, "Jessica lost. I'm going to go and meet her and let her trail me in."

"Ok." I answer as Ms. Margie and Jessica's dad seem to be catching up.

"Rick, meet Douglas Michaels, Mitchell's father."

What? Wow. Does Mitchell know his dad is going to be here? Wow.

"You're ready to let the cat out of the bag, Margie?"

"Rick and I keep lots of secrets with each other. You can let the cat out when you're ready, but the sooner the better for me. Mitchell is going to have lots of questions for the both of us and I want to answer them before my time runs out."

"Jessica doesn't know she has a brother, Margie."

"Well you'll have a chance to tell them both tonight."

Ms. Margie looks back to me.

"Move fast with that cornbread son, don't let that water cool off. You have to shape them while the water is hot."

"Yes ma'am."

"Rick here is in a similar situation you were in during our time. At some point you should counsel him. I love this boy, I don't want him to turn out like you. Tell him different."

He chuckles, "I'm here now Margie. I'll be here for Mitchell when you're gone. If he'll have me."

He looks to me, "Son, we'll talk. You're going to learn a lot from just being here tonight."

"Mitch looks a lot like you." I tell him.

"Does he?" he asks.

Oh yeah. He hasn't seen him.

"You'll recognize him the moment you see him."

Ms. Margie moves furiously around the kitchen, heating food up, getting serving items, preparing a place for everyone to sit. This is going to be an interesting night.

"Margie, if you don't slow down. You're going to go tonight and that's too soon."

"Well all this work isn't going to get done by you just looking at it. Help me out then."

"Margie. I haven't seen you in over a decade. I'll help you. Let me see you once more. Come here."

He still loves this woman.

She comes and gives him another hug.

He kisses her and I pretend not to look. He kisses her on the lips, and not one of those greeting kisses. This kiss has purpose, as if it were carrying a message. An apology kiss floating on the wings of love.

Ms. Margie pulls back, "Boy! If you don't stop looking at me and pay attention to that cornbread, we can't eat tonight! Nobody likes burnt cornbread!"

"Yes ma'am."

Mitchell walks in the garage door and all I think is uh oh. He walks to his mother and wraps his arms around her waist from behind and kisses her on the cheek.

"Hi Mom."

"Hi baby."

"What's up Rick?"

"Cooking man, cooking."

He looks to his dad. Can't he see his face in that man? Ms. Margie and I both watch.

"You must be Jessica's father."

He nods his head yes. He's speechless. Mitch looks just like him. Mitch can't interpret the expression on his face and he's then diverted by Jason, Jessica and Tiffany.

"Hi Daddy." Jessica says in a politely warm greeting.

"Richard." Tiffany acknowledges me. I look to Ms. Margie. She messages me to relax.

"Hi Tiff. Hey Jess."

"Tiff, this is the marriage counselor I was telling you about. Deacon Mitchell Madison."

Mitch walks over to Tiffany and shakes her hand.

"Actually, it's Mitchell Michaels. Hi Tiffany, we've met through Rick before. Good seeing you again."

"I didn't realize this was who you were talking about Jessica. Yes, we have met. I didn't know you were a counselor."

Mitch smiles, "I'm not. I've just morph into whatever the church needs me to be."

"Well I didn't know your last name was Michaels, that's my maiden name." Jessica's words burst out as playful laughter.

Bingo. Bingo. Bingo. Mitchell still hasn't picked up that Jessica is his sister and Douglas is his father. Ms. Margie is sitting on edge watching all of this on pins and needles.

"Well everyone sit around the table, there's plenty of food for everyone. Rick is fabulous in the kitchen. Bring that cornbread, Mitchell bless the food and let's eat!"

Mitchell quietly stares at his dad trying to put all of this together and studying his mom.

"I never knew you could cook, Richard." Tiffany says with a gentle smile.

"Oh he's a natural, honey, throw that man in the kitchen more. Let him start cooking for you." Ms. Margie exclaims in support of me. I love her.

Mitchell offers a perfect blessing over the food and his dad beams with pride bringing a smile to his mom's face. He's picking up on these cues. He just doesn't know what it all means yet. He doesn't say another word. He just watches as his mom reacts to every word Douglas says. She even blushes at times.

"Who are you?" soars from Mitchell's mouth interrupting all conversation with no apologies. I sip on my tea, curious as to how all this is going to unfurl. He looks directly at his dad.

"He's my father Mitch. What's wrong?" Jessica asks with a bit of fear.

"Daddy?" her words curl around him like a cat.

"Who are you to my mother?" He demands as if he is a soldier protecting a fortress.

His dad grabs a napkin and wipes his mouth. I can't believe Jessica and Mitch have not put two and two together, they look just like that their dad.

"Daddy." Jessica says with a sense of urgency, expecting an answer.

Jason is silent. Ms. Margie looks as if she is going to explode if Douglas doesn't say something. There's no easy way to say this. He's just going to have to get it out. I guess that's what I have to do with Tiffany.

"You're mother and I dated years ago, before you were born..."

"Oh for goodness sake Dougie! He's your father, son."

"Margie, I was going to tell him."

"Daddy?" Jessica questions.

He looks to Jessica, "This is one of the answers to a few of the questions you were going to ask me later dear. You have a brother."

Mitchell is speechless. He pushes away from the table and is about to leave in disgust.

"No. Son. Don't leave."

"How are you going to call me Son? You come now? Just as my mother is dying! Are you kidding me? Do you have any idea how old I am?"

"You were born September 21 at 2:23am. It was a cool September that year. You were 2 weeks early. Long and plump. As a baby you were a crier. You cried all through the night. You were always a deep thinker, never really allowing anyone to see how deep of a thinker you were. Your sister on the other hand was a good sleeper and always told everyone exactly how she felt about everything her entire life. You graduated in the top half of your graduating class. An under achiever. You love basketball and learning. You attended Moorehouse, then Stanford for graduate school and you just graduated from Harvard's doctoral program. You did all this before you turned 30 years old. You are 33 years old."

Mitchell looks to his mom with his eyes full of confusing tears.

"Momma?"

"Baby, you need to know your father."

"Why now momma? We've gone our entire life without him! Why now?"

"Son. I can go any day now. I'm not leaving this earth until you've met this man."

"Mom, he was always a paycheck, never a dad. I don't need him. I need you."

"I'm going home son."

"No! No, momma. No! I need you, not him. Momma please."

"Son, baby, I'm leaving. Neither one of us can stop this day from coming."

"Momma. Please." whimpers out of his mouth.

"Mitchell, this man has supported us in many, many ways. Do you know how expensive your college education was? You didn't take out one loan. Not one! We've never missed a meal. You've never had to be without anything. Who do you think helped me with all of that?"

"So what? You want me to tell him thank you? Thank you for never being there? Do you know how many nights I cried in my bed wishing I had a father and not an uncle? I'd trade all the college degrees he paid for in exchange for a childhood with him."

Mitchell stands up. His father stands up and they look at each other face to face. Mitchell is almost the exact same height, just an inch or two shorter.

"Why are you here?" He yells. His words are frustrated and don't know how to land. His emotions are all over the place.

"I came for you and Jessica."

"I don't need you."

"I'm here. I want to be a part of your life."

"Why now?"

"You and Jessica both have questions. I'll answer them. All of them."

"Jessica knew you, I've never known you. Never."

"You think I knew him?" Jessica words cry, and her face looks like the reservoir of which they came.

"He wasn't there for me either. My mom is dead! I went through that alone. You are such a whimpering baby! Your mom is alive. Do you know what I would give just to have one more moment with my mom? Just one! Here your mom is still living and you're angry that he is here to support you through this? Are you completely stupid?"

Jessica begins crying and fights through her tears to finish screaming at Mitchell, "I wish he was here when I lost my mother, but he wasn't. He's here for you and your mother! Be fool enough to throw that away if you want, you spoiled little, idiotic, brat!"

She looks at her father, "I can't believe you, why couldn't you be there for me and my mother? What's so special about his mother that you decided to change your entire life and move to Houston? You couldn't do that for me? Do you love him more than me? His mother more than mine? You're a selfish old man and you sicken me!"

Douglas Michaels looks to Margie for support. She offers none. Jessica is standing up preparing to run out and Mitchell looks to her wanting to say sorry. Margie intervenes. When she stands up, everything stops. She stood up and commanded attention like a general leading an army.

"No one is leaving this room. I don't care how hard this is for any one of us. My time is near and I will be heard."

Her eyes land on Jessica like an arrow hitting a bullseye, "Sit down honey." She then sends a scolding, yet comforting glare to Mitchell, "Have a seat."

Her eyes then search and find me. She doesn't say anything, but I know she is telling me to pay attention.

"Who in this room is without mistake?" She waits for a response and doesn't get one. "Who can judge this man and not condemn themselves?"

"Jessica, I knew your mother and she knew me. It was because of our disdain for each other that you and your brother don't know each other. If she were here today, she, along with me would change the way our history was written. We could have been great friends. The pain you're feeling now is because of the choices we made when we were your age. Don't blame all of this on this man. The fault is shared."

"Why did you and my mom hate each other? If my mom didn't like you, why should I?" Jessica asks.

"We didn't hate each other. Our disdain grew from a fear of each other. Regardless, we should have put how we felt about each other to the side to do what was best for you and your brother. We didn't. We talked right before she left us. She wanted you to know Mitchell. Mitchell was gone away at school and we couldn't make it happen before her time came. It won't be long before I join her in Heaven, and when I do, I can tell her I finished the business she tried to start."

Ms. Margie turns her attention to Mitchell, he can barely look at her.

"Mitchell, I was not going to go to the other side until you knew your father. He not only came here for you. He came for Jessica and he came for me. I haven't seen him in years. I won't speak for him, he's able to speak for himself. Regardless of the decisions that he made in the past, you're a fine young man and even if his contribution was a financial one, he has a part in that."

Douglas Michael finally intervenes, "I wasn't there during the first part of your lives Mitchell and Jessica, but I will be here for the second part. It's what I live for. I know you have more questions now than you've ever had before. I'll answer them. Know that I have loved you both from the moment you were born. If you never knew that before, you'll see it now.

"You're here now to make up for the first thirty years you missed?" Mitchell words leave a bitter aftertaste as soon as they land.

"No. I'm here for the thirty years that are to come. I don't want to miss another moment."

My eyes are drawn to Jason as I watch him grab his phone and excuse himself out of the room. This may a good time for me and Tiffany to escape also. I should tell her everything. Give her an opportunity to think things over. I've tuned out all the 'dad missing in action, but here I am now' drama and focus directly on Tiffany. Her eyes lock with mine. I motion my head asking if she wants to get out of here. She smiles back, nods her head yes and quietly we leave.

Chapter 52

Tiffany

Richard and I step away from the table, and not a minute too soon. We get in his car and circle the block a couple of times and then drive slowly around.

"Tiffany, I love you. I'm sorry I hurt you. If I could take all of this back I would."

"Richard what exactly do you want from me?"

"I want you to still be my wife?"

"What about Sojourn?"

"We don't even talk anymore."

"That doesn't mean it's over."

"It's over. She's rebuilding her life with Troy."

"Is that why you want me back?"

"No, I want you back because I married you. I love you."

"Awfully convenient isn't it, Richard?"

"Tiffany if you don't want to work things out. I understand. I'll leave you alone and give you anything you ask for in a divorce settlement."

I don't know what to say. Could this really be a second chance? Can I trust him? Maybe there is a God. Maybe God does love me. I've fallen so low from grace.

"Ok Richard. Let's keep talking about it, before we make any sudden moves."

He doesn't respond. He should be as hopeful and happy as I am.

"What is it Richard?"

"There's more."

"What?"

"Shannon."

"What about Shannon?"

"Tiffany, Shannon is..."

I know he is not about to tell me that baby she is carrying is his! I know he's not going to tell me that! He better not! I finish his sentence before he can get it out.

"Don't you dare tell me she is carrying your child, you better not Richard!"

He's silent. Guilty!

"Richard how could you?"

"It was one moment Tiffany. One time. I don't know what came over me. It was the one biggest mistake in my life."

I try to understand, but how can he be so stupid!

"So, what does that mean? Are you in a relationship with her?"

"No."

"Do you love her?"

"No."

"So we have to share raising a child."

He looks to me like a wounded puppy.

"There's more Tiff."

"What Richard? What more could there be?"

He doesn't answer. I'm scared.

"Richard."

"I tested positive for HIV."

Silence. Dead silence.

"Stop the car Richard."

He pulls over.

"Don't follow me."

I get out of the car with my purse and phone in hand. I slam the door as I hear his pleas for me to stay in. I cross traffic so he can't follow me and disappear into a neighborhood. So this is it God? You brought me this far, gave me hope to restore my marriage only to tell me my husband has HIV? Are you kidding me? Why have you forsaken me? What did I ever do to you to deserve this? Must my fall from grace include an adulterous marriage, the other woman ridiculing the love my husband has for her, a love child and just when my husband comes back to me and I have a ray of hope, he tells me he has HIV? Are you serious? Really? Where did I go wrong, God? Do I deal the same ridiculous hand to others that was dealt to me? My husband is dying! My marriage is dying. My hope is dying. My soul is dying! What kind of God are you? What kind of God does this to their child?

I sit in a community park on a swing. I lightly swing back and forth, just like my life seems to swing from one extreme to the other. I look into the night sky and become a bit startled when I see a teen sit in a swing next to me.

"Hi."

"Hi." I respond.

We sit and just drift on the swing in silence. What is this child doing out here so late? Why am I worried about this teenager, when I don't even know what I'm doing here?

"Do you live around here?" The teenager asks in a soft voice.

"No. Do you?"

"Yes. Did you drive here?"

"No."

"You just came out of nowhere?"

"Yeah. I guess I did."

Ok, she's asked enough questions of me, so I ask, "What are you doing here this late at night?"

"Waiting to die."

"What do you mean?"

"I took a bunch of pills and I'm just waiting to die."

"What? Are you serious?"

"Yes."

"Why?"

"I've got too many personal problems. I can't handle all of them. I can't stand it any longer, so I'm ending it."

Is this teen serious? I look into her eyes to see if she really is drugged. Her head hangs to low for me to peer into her eyes. Are you serious God? I grab my phone and call 911.

"What's your name?"

"Kelly."

She falls out of her swing, she's really dying.

"What's your name?" she asks me as she blinks her eyes at the speed of millimeter inching by.

"My name is Tiffany. Hold on Kelly. Don't die yet; it's not your time. You're much too young to have problems that are too big to solve."

"Did God send you Tiffany?"

"What?"

"Did God send you from way up there, all the way down here to save me?"

"What?" I question her hysterically.

"How was the fall? I hope the landing didn't hurt."

"What are you talking about Kelly?"

She slips in and out of consciousness, "Are you human or an angel? Tell me the truth Tiffany. Did you fall, were you pushed or did you jump in order to come save me?"

"I'm human."

"I know. Aren't all fallen angels human when they land?"

"I was born human."

"If that's true, how did you know..." She stutters, "How did you know I was going to be here? You don't live here. You don't even have a car."

The ambulance arrives and I tell the paramedics everything that has happened. I ride in the back of the ambulance with Kelly and when we arrive to the hospital, they ask me a bunch of questions that I don't have the answer to. I'm reminded of Jessica and the time I was in the hospital with her and Jason last year. This is all too familiar. Kelly's parent's arrive and immediately go to her bedside. I notice her father is in a wheelchair. I attempt to quietly leave the room when her mother turns around, "Excuse me, you were with Kelly?"

"Yes ma'am."

"You saved her life. Thank you."

"You're very kind ma'am, but it wasn't me. It was the paramedics."

"You called them?"

"Yes ma'am I did."

"You saved her. We'd like to stay in touch with you. Would that be alright with you?"

"Yes. Of course."

"We've had a real rough time of things lately. Kelly lost her twin in a car accident last year. "We've all had a difficult time dealing with this. Her father was driving the car and was hit by a drunk driver. I can't even begin to tell you what we've gone through for the past year. If it wasn't for the grace of God, I don't know where we'd be."

How can she thank God? She lost a child, almost lost two, could have lost her husband and she still thanks God? I don't understand. I don't understand at all. I have to ask. I have to.

"How can you thank God after all you've gone through?"

"Oh I was upset, I still mourn. No one knows how much time we have on earth. So I thank God for the time he gave me with Kelly's twin and I treasure each moment I have with the loved ones I have left, before my time or their time comes. My husband will never walk again. His life and my life have changed forever. Simple things like intimacies, walking a sandy beach at sunset are only memories, but we still have each other. He's still alive and I still love him."

She pauses and glances back to Kelly, "Living through, working through and fighting though hell, to feel the grace of Heaven taught me that. Kelly hasn't lived long enough to live through enough to completely understand that. Young people are so ready to give up instead of getting through. But thanks be to God and thanks to you, she has more time to figure this out. Who knew I'd meet one of His angels."

My eyes embrace her, and I whisper, "I'm human."

"So are many other of His angels walking the Earth."

I pass her my contact information, glance down at my phone and see about fifty missed calls. I walk down the hall and realize I don't have my car. How do I get home? I take a moment and walk the hospital halls. I watch as many of these families pray for second chances for their family members. Here is my second chance and I'm treating it as a curse. How can my hell and her hope be in the same person at the same time? What are you doing, God? I stroll past doors that say Chapel. I decide to walk in and sit in the back. I watch as people go to the altar and pray. One of the chaplains moves toward the door and I recognize her as the same chaplain that I spoke with when I was in the hospital with Jessica last year. She looks up and recognizes me.

"Hello Tiffany."

"You remember me?"

"Of course. You were looking for answers."

"Yes. You told me the answers I needed wouldn't be found in the voice of man, but the word of God."

"Yes. Are you still looking for answers?"

My eyes give her an immediate answer.

"Did you search the word of God for you answer child?"

"I gave up on God."

She smiles, "Well it's a good thing He hasn't given up on you."

I don't respond, but wish she'd give me more. I can't figure this out by myself.

"Come near Him and He'll come near you." She pats me on the shoulder and walks off.

I grab my phone and call Richard.

"Tiffany, I've been calling you all night. Are you ok?"

"I am."

"Where are you?"

"It's a long story. Come and pick me up from the same hospital Sadie had the baby."

"Are you hurt?"

"Not physically."

"I'm sorry Tiffany. I'm in the car on my way."

Chapter 53

Shannon

Married man or one nightstand man, who first? I sit in darkness in my townhouse, as if hiding in the dark can hide me from my trouble. Who first? My fingers dial the first number and I hear his voice sail across the phone line. "Hello?"

"Shannon, this is awful timing. What is it? I'm having dinner with Jess and her dad."

"Jason, there will never be a good time to talk to you about this."

"What is it Shannon? What's wrong?"

"I'm expecting?"

"What?"

Then silence.

"It can't be mine, we haven't been with each other in over a year Shannon."

"It's not yours."

"Well what is it?"

"The doctor told me I'm also carrying the HIV virus."

He doesn't respond.

"You need to get tested Jason."

"Shit."

He hangs the phone up. Ok. One more call to make. I dial and the phone rings.

"Hello? Hello? Shannon?"

"Yes. Hello." I answer, even though I called him.

"I've been meaning to call you?"

"What is it?"

"I don't know how to tell you this."

I already know what he's going to tell me. It must have been him, "Just say it."

"I've been exposed to the HIV virus and you need to get tested."

Now I know why Jason hung up the phone like that. What else is there left to say?

"Shannon?"

"Yes."

"I'm sorry. I didn't know."

"Goodbye." is my only answer and I release the call from my line. I look into my purse for Mitchell's card. It'd be great to have someone to talk to about this. I'll see him Sunday in church.

I grab the list of doctor's to call and look over the names and locations. I'll begin to find a doctor first thing in the morning. I don't want to pass this to my child.

Chapter 54

Carlo

I stay with Sadie through the night to help with the twins, yet I exchange no words with her. I'm still beyond belief that she would try and sneak a DNA test from me. I don't want to hear sorry. I want to hear the results so I can move in the direction I need to provide for Gianni and Valentino. As the twins sleep Sadie goes into the bedroom with the boys and I lay on the couch. I don't want to be here. If these boys are not mine, I don't want to become any more attached to them, than I already am. My phone vibrates. It's Sojourn. What does she want at this hour?

She sent me a text, "I need to see you. It's an emergency. Please. Meet me at your apartment in twenty minutes."

I text back, "ok"

What could possibly be wrong? I walk back to the bedroom and Sadie and the twins are sleeping. I write her a note and leave it on the nightstand by her bed. I'll be back in three days is scribbled with a pencil, but she should be able to read it. I call Sojourn on the phone as I'm going to my apartment, but no answer. Everything was fine when we hung up the phone earlier. What could have possibly gone wrong in such a short time frame?

She pulls up to the apartment at the same time I do. She looks a mess. She has Sadie's fist print on her eye. Her eyes look like ripe tomatoes, and the minute she sees me she starts crying.

"Come inside. What is it mio dolce?"

"Please don't tell Troy I'm here, he'll never, never understand what I'm doing here at this hour."

"What are you doing here?

"I finally talked to Rick."

"Ok, so what's wrong? Did you tell him you're working things out with Troy?"

"I did."

"How did he take it?"

"He's fine with it Carlo. He's supportive of me and my decision."

"What is it mio dolce?"

"He has HIV."

"Do you have it?"

"I don't know. He told me to get tested. I'm terrified. I've already had sex with Troy."

"Does he know how he got it?"

"He thinks from Shannon, his devilish secretary. She probably tricked him."

"She didn't trick him into not wearing a condom."

"None of that matters right now Carlo. What do I do?"

"You need to get tested."

"Look, you may not even have been exposed to it."

"That's what he said."

"Just calm down. Get tested and then we'll decide what to do. Come here mio dolce, my sweet."

Sojourn leans on my shoulder inside my arms.

"Sadie bought a home DNA test and was going to swab me in my sleep. I overheard her talking about it with her friends. I took the swab from her and gave her my sample and I swabbed the twins. It'll take three days to get the results. I don't want to see her until then."

"Try to work through this Carlo. She just wants to make sure."

"Parenthood is not in DNA it is in the trust and confidence of the partner standing beside you. She violated that trust. Now she'll get paternity, but she won't have me as a partner anymore."

"Carlo, mio dolce, just take the next three days to think this over."

"I will. My mind is pretty made up, but I will think through this. Take me with you when you get tested. I don't want you to have to go through this alone."

"Grazi Carlo."

"Now go home to Troy, before he comes out here looking for you. Go. Ciao."

"Ciao."

Chapter 55

Shannon

"Mitchell did you tell the pastor to preach that sermon directly for me?"

He chuckles, "No. I'm glad you connected it though. Hopefully it'll help you to understand your life more completely."

Mitchell is such a nice person. I can't shake the feeling that I know him from somewhere. He looks so familiar.

"You ready to talk more, Ms. No Name?"

"Yes."

"Well where do you want to start?"

"I feel like fighting for life."

"Wow. What a breakthrough. How do you feel about your decision?"

"Better. I called the only other two possibilities and told them to get tested. I made a responsible decision even though it was hard.

Once I made that one, I felt like I had the strength to make the calls to the doctors. I read and researched all I could on the virus and while there's no cure, I could possibly live another twenty years. Who knows, science may even have a cure by then."

"Seems like you have really thought through a lot of this over the past couple of days."

"I have. I even looked up information on the Baptist religion."

He smiles, "Try not to get caught up to much in the religious practice and study more of the actual word of God in the Bible. Let the Bible be your guide."

"I will. Are you a counselor?"

"No. I help a lot of church members and they call me counselor sometimes, but I'm not. I'm just a simple deacon that helps service the church in any way I can. I helped a family member, with her marriage and she went and told everyone I'm a marriage counselor. I told her I'm not, I'm still just your friendly neighborhood deacon."

"You told me your mom is dying. How is she?"

"Are you a counselor Ms. No Name?"

My words smile as they swim out of my mouth, "No, just your friendly neighborhood friend."

His eyes smile back, "She's alive. She has the support of my father, me, my sister and her husband; a couple of other friends and family members as well."

"Are you prepared for her to leave you?"

"Is this about you or me, Ms. No Name?"

"Maybe both. Understanding death through your eyes, your mothers eyes, helps me better understand life."

Mitchell shakes his head in acceptance, "I feel like I'm being bamboozled into the client role. No, I'm not totally prepared, but I'm working on it. One of my friends from college is going to throw her a celebration of life party at his workplace tomorrow night. He told me to just give him the guest list and he's going to do everything else. I want everyone to be able to tell her how much she is loved before she goes. Too often we don't give our regards to the people we love, and when they're gone, we regret not sharing how we really feel about that person. So this will be the night everyone she knows will come to celebrate her life, while she's still living."

"Wow. I don't know her, but her fight for life has inspired me."

"It has?"

"Yes."

"What's her name?"

"Marigold Madison. Most people call her Margie or Mother Madison."

"I'd like to give her something. Would she accept a gift from a stranger?"

"I'm sure she would."

His look embraces me.

"You were her gift to me. You sacrificed precious moments you could have spent with her to help me. That moment you sacrificed gave me the hope, courage and strength to keep living."

"What are you trying to do to me woman? Are you trying to capture my heart?"

"I don't expect to have a meaningful relationship with a man anymore, but I learned from you the joy of giving. The joy of service.

Who knows, I may even become a deacon in the next twenty years."

I peer into his eyes and see a look that I've never seen in a man before. It's as if he can really appreciate what I'm saying. As if he can see me. Almost like the look Dr. Douglas gave me. Almost, but different. I don't try to read it or interpret it.

"Mitchell, I used to manipulate, scheme and do anything I had to do to get what I wanted. Pastor said today that all we have to do is present the desires of our heart to God and He will supply all our needs. I just wish I could have figured this out long before today."

"Well, you seem to have it now don't you?"

"Do I have an invite to Margie's Celebration of Life engagement?"

"How about you be my guest, Ms. No Name?"

"I'd be honored."

"Where do I pick you up?"

"Can I meet you here, park my car and ride with you?"

"Absolutely. You have my cell number. Stay in touch."

"Ok. Oh Mitchell?"

"Yes?"

"Will you still work with HIV and terminal populations, after, you know."

"I don't know. It won't be the same without my mother."

"If you do, may I join you? I would never want to replace your mother, but I think I can help others, as they also help me."

"We'll see."

"Ok."

"Ok. Bye Ms. No Name."

Chapter 56

Richard

Last night I dropped Tiffany off at home, without comment, pressure or dialogue. Today she calls me to ask me to come over to talk. This will be the beginning or the end. My phone vibrates with a text message from Sojourn, "Negative."

I breathe a sigh of relief. I didn't harm her or family. I pull into the drive way and Tiffany is standing at the door.

"Come in the house with me Richard."

"Ok."

I follow Tiffany in the house. Hoping for a fighting chance to save our marriage, but expecting that the mistakes I've made are too big to recover from. She was missing half the night and didn't want to talk to me about it all.

"I saved a life last night Richard."

What is she talking about? She paces the room as I walk and sit on the couch.

"I jumped out of the car out of my own pain Richard, I was cursing you, cursing God and hating my life. I couldn't believe God would torture me so."

"I'm sorry Tiffany. I know sorry isn't enough, I've made a mess of things."

"I felt as if God kicked me out of grace and withdrew His love from me. Just as I thought that things couldn't get any worse, they did. You told me you were dying. My prince, the love of my life dying?"

She talks boldly, no tears, no recourse.

"I wanted to die too. Then I met a girl who was dying. She asked me did I fall from Heaven to save her? I had to ask myself, did I? She asked me if angels experience hurt when they land. I was hurting horribly, but I told her I was human. She told me 'all angels on earth walk as humans.' Maybe God still loves me. My pain was my deliverance, and all this time I thought it was just plain ol' pain."

"What are you saying Tiffany?"

"Richard we had it so good. We were invincible. Life was perfect; we did everything by the book. We ruled the world. No one could touch us or tell us anything. Not even God. We went to church when we felt like it; we lived, as we wanted to. If we wanted to sin we did that too. If we wanted to give we did, and if we didn't feel like it, so what? We made bills, paid them off. We both got whatever we wanted. We were so high...."

"...but we weren't happy."

"We fell so hard from that time in our lives. We fell through adultery, disease, a love child, I threw my body at anyone who would take it, anyone who could give me the love I lost from you. That anyone was Troy, but he refused me. I felt abandoned all over again. Now look at us. Through that painful fall, you are fighting to love me, to stay with me."

"Yes."

"I love you too, Richard."

I walk over to Tiffany and hug her.

"We still love each other and we have nothing. No home together. No relationship. Every possible worst case scenario is right in front of us and we still love each other."

"Yes." My heart is crying, but no tears fall from my eyes.

"Superficial love and love for things that don't matter fell from us, and now we're left with each other."

"Will you love me again Richard?"

"Again? This is the moment that we fall in love together. This is the moment that our vows transition from words to life."

I hold her in my arms and glide into her soul through her eyes.

"Whatever time we have left on this earth Richard, I want to spend it with you."

"I love you Tiffany."

"I love you Richard."

We walk to the couch and I hold her in my arms. "Each day Tiffany, my life was getting worse, I thought God was killing me. He was really giving me a second chance, saving me."

"He gave us a both a second chance."

Tiffany begins to laugh.

"What?"

"God is a weirdo."

"What?" I answer laughing with her.

"His ways are way foreign to me, weird, strange, but hey, they worked. He saved Kelly's life and our marriage."

"The way He did it though," she laughs again, "Jessica was chasing me down in a cow pasture."

We laugh together.

"Yeah that's a bit weird."

"I'm happy with you Tiffany."

She kisses me, "I'm happy to be with you too."

Chapter 57

Troy

"Yes, Ms. Margie. Yes. Everything is ready. I'm going to send a car for you to get you here on time, you'll come in through the back and surprise Mitchell as he is coming in the front. He won't know what hit him. Will his dad be with you?"

Sojourn looks to me in excitement.

"Ok. Ok. So he'll escort you in and not me. You have me jealous, Ms. Margie."

"Well, what did she say?"

"She's ready. She has no idea that he's planning on celebrating her life, while she's planning on appreciating his. Mitchell has a stretch limousine picking her up. This is going to be fantastic. They both have a video montage of their life, which we'll show on both screens. This is going to make both of them so happy."

"I invited Carlo. Sadie wants to come. She called and apologized to me, I hope they can work through this." Sojourn looks to me for approval and support. I'm happy to give it to her.

"Me too."

"Does she have a babysitter?"

"Yes, her parents flew in from California. Her mother was in the hospital when she went into labor, so they're anxious to spend some time with the twins. Enough about Sadie. Tell me about Mitchell's surprise, this is so exciting."

"All of his childhood friends, college friends, professional friends and church friends will be here to surprise him. He had all of his mother's friends and every living relative come into Houston, staying at a nearby hotel. He chartered a bus to bring them to the Coffee Bean. He said he has one special guest that is coming who doesn't know his mother, but is giving her a token of appreciation."

"Troy this is going to be so awesome. Ms. Margie is going to flip to see all these people here."

"I have the stage ready for people to give remarks to both of them."

"I've made a sash, tiara and a crown for both of them to wear. I can't wait Troy. This is so exciting. I love you."

"Sojourn, everything is ready. Ms. Margie is coming through the back door. Mitchell and his guest will be coming through the front. Ms. Margie insists that she arrive first to see Mitchell walk in the front. So if Mitchell comes early, I'm going to distract him. You make sure Ms. Margie and Mitchell's dad are ready to receive them."

"Ok. I'm on it!"

"I'm going to go outside to run interference. Text me when it's ok to come in with Mitchell and his guest."

My eyes admire Sojourn, as I watch her walk off to receive Ms. Margie. My heart is thankful for that 99th chance God has given me for happiness with the woman that I love.

I go outside to get ready for Mitchell and see Jessica and Jason and Tiffany and Richard arrive at the same time. I'm always a bit nervous when I see Jason. I would hate for him to discover the one night in history I was with his wife. They've repaired their life, I've repaired mine; some secrets should just die! I'm just glad I didn't make the same mistake with Tiffany.

"Hey Jess. Jason." My words leave cautiously as I greet them.

"Hey." Jessica answers.

"Are you excited about tonight?"

"Oh yes. This is going to make my brother so happy. Has he made it yet?"

"No. I'm standing out here to run some interference until I get the signal from inside that they're ready for him."

"Need some help?" Richard asks, "That's my boy too."

"I never turn down help."

"Great, we'll wait here too." Jessica answers grabbing Jason's hand.

"Ok."

I see Mitchell's car drive by and pull in the parking lot. I can only anticipate the excitement and joy he's going to get from a night like this. This man has stood on the battleground to fight for me so often. I feel good about planning this for him and his mother.

I watch as he approaches, with his guest. Whoever she is, she is stunning. Just as I'm getting ready to greet him, I hear Tiffany whisper to Rick, "Is that Shannon, your secretary?" Rick nods his head yes.

"Did you say her name was Shannon, Tiffany? Did I hear you say that?" Jessica demands.

Tiffany doesn't say anything. "Please." Rick begs.

Jessica looks over to Jason, Jason looks like a little boy who just saw his favorite toy run over by a truck.

"Oh hell no. It's not even about to go down like this tonight. She is not about to waltz up here on my brother's arm and ruin his night or his life. That woman's madness stops here! Tonight!"

She looks to Tiffany, "This is the heifer that was sleeping with Jason. The one I told you about in the emails."

"Jessica, that's over. Just let it go." Jason demands.

"Are you defending her Jason? Please tell me if you are so I can see where I stand in your life."

"I'm not defending her Jessica. It's over. That's all. Leave it alone."

My mind is with Jason; please leave it alone before our skeletons jump out the closet.

Mitchell finally approaches the door. It only takes a second to read the expression on his sister's face. When he and his date come into full view I recognize her. Damn! This is the blackmailer. I've got to tell Sojourn about her before she tells her. Damn.

"What is it Jessica?" he asks out of genuine concern.

"That heifer on your arm isn't welcome."

"She is welcome Jessica. She's my guest, she has something to present to my mom."

Sojourn text messages me to come in. They're ready for Mitchell. I've got to put an end to this.

"Shannon what are you doing here?" Richard asks.

"She's my guest Rick." Mitchell answers before Shannon can say anything.

Mitchell looks to her, "So you do have a name, and a history I see."

"Mitchell this is the heifer that I told you about in counseling."

Mitchell looks to her, "Is this one of the phone calls you had to make."

Her eyes blink yes. Jason looks like he is ready to run. Tiffany is shaking her head in shame.

"Don't call me Shannon, I'm fine." Jason nervously petitions.

"What phone call?" Jessica's angry words march out of her mouth surrounding Jason and demanding an answer.

"What do you need to call my husband about heifer?"

Shannon remains silent.

Tiffany jumps in, "She's pregnant."

Jessica looks at Jason as if she would like to tear him apart with her teeth.

"Don't worry Jessica, it's not Jason's child, it's Richard's."

"What?" asks Douglas Michaels and Sojourn as they step outside to see what the hold up is.

"You know her dad?" Jessica asks.

"Yes, we will be working together."

"Fire her dad. Right now! Fire her!"

"Why sweetness?"

"She slept with my husband and Tiffany's too."

...and me too, quietly creeps in my thoughts.

"No." Mitchell softly demands, "Dad don't you dare. No."

"Would you like to leave Ms. Shannon?" He asks politely.

"I don't want to cause a disturbance. I will leave voluntarily. Please, allow me to give your mother a gift before I do."

"Mitchell, choose between me or her. I won't share the same space with that woman." Jessica's words soar, expecting him to respond to her ultimatum.

Sojourn whispers in my ear, "I can't stand that devilish woman." She knows Sojourn. Shit. This can't end good. Obviously, Shannon has not made many friends; after our encounter I understand why. Sojourn is going to leave me. I have to tell her the truth. Damn. God, what are you doing to me? It's as if you are forcing me to eat Hell's fire.

She looks to Mitchell, "I'm sorry. Everything they've said about me is true. I've made dreadful mistakes in life. I've paid dearly for them. I don't want you to have to pay for them too. I can give my gift to Mother Madison another time."

Tiffany is quiet but her eyes are loud and poised for an attack. Sojourn and Rick both look at her with disgust and Jason's eyes are full of resentment. I don't even know the girl, like they do – but I don't want her here either. Mitchell's eyes accept her. He accurately reads the scorn on everyone's faces and our glares mutilate her second by second.

"If any of you feel her wrongs are any greater than yours, and are above forgiveness, above a second chance at life then stay out here with us and condemn her yourself. Otherwise go inside so we may return to celebrate the life of my mother."

Without a second thought Douglas Michael returns first and shakes his head in agreement with his son. Tiffany and Richard follow. Sojourn stands by me and whispers, "I'm going to go and prepare Ms. Margie for her son. I can't stand that bitch." and she leaves. Jessica and Jason remain. Almost home free, and not one bone from the skeleton closet has popped out. Jessica looks at me, I back at her. We both acknowledge with our eyes that our lives have moved on. She glances back at Jason, doesn't turn back around and walks in. She had her second chance too. I hold the door for Mitchell and Shannon. Shannon looks at me. In the second that our eyes crossed, I remembered. I remember completely the night that we met. We both had condoms ready. She had wit and personality. I remember her blackmailing me in my hospital bed. I remember my anger and frustration with her and myself. Her eyes didn't communicate callous intentions, but almost a merciful plea. As if she was saying sorry.

"Tonight is the time for you to present your gift to my mother. You are my guest. I don't condemn you either. You've left your life of selfish mistakes. Keep moving forward."

I pass Mitchell a box with his mother's tiara and sash to present to her and he escorts Shannon inside.

I go inside and Sojourn immediately greets me once I close the door.

"Carlo is here. Sadie is here with the DNA test results."

"What are they?"

"I don't know."

I watch as all the celebrations begin, the surprises, the exchange of gifts and I'm happy, but I can't get off my mind what the results of that DNA test will reveal. Are the twins my children? I've got to tell Sojourn about Shannon, the truth.

Sojourn wait. I want to know the DNA results, but I need to tell you something.

"What is it Troy?"

"I know that woman."

"Who? Shannon!?"

"Yes." "Did you sleep with her Troy? She has HIV."

Fuck. It's over. Wait. A condom. I wore a condom. She's reading my face, I watch as her eyes troll along my face.

"You must've worn a condom. I've been tested and I'm negative. You're fine. Stop it with the dick! No more women Troy. Don't jeopardize what we are trying to do. I won't be able to stay with you if I don't trust you."

Sojourn grabs my arm and escorts me to the table with Sadie and Carlo. I breathe. Thank you God. What are we on, second chance number 99?

Shannon goes to the stage to present Ms. Margie her gift. Ms. Margie sits between her son and Mitchell's father holding both their hands.

"Ms. Margie. I don't have much, but what I have I offer you. I offer you perfumed oil in a flask given to me by my mother. She bought it for me when she visited Africa. I offer it to you as a reminder of what God is doing as he blesses you, empowers you and protects you on your journey to Heaven." Ms. Margie accepts it with a smile and Shannon continues.

"I've learned so much from your son over the past couple of days. I thank him for the sacrifices of time he's given to me, when he could have spent that with you. I've experienced circumstances in life that were killing me. Killing my body, my spirit, and my hope. I've made some mistakes Mother Madison, but God was kind of enough to bless me in spite of me. I carry a child and if it is a girl she will be named Madison Marigold Scott. I leave with you a namesake. A namesake that constantly reminds me to hope, reminds your son of the blessing of sacrifice and a name to remind the world to love. Love in spite of. Mitchell helped me save my life, and now I have a fresh start. Now your name will also have a fresh start. Your kindness and the gift of friendship from your son will spread through another generation. That's all I have Mother Madison. I love you and thank you."

"Come here precious." Ms. Margie opens her arms toward her and receives her gift with love.

Mitchell escorts her down off the stage, gives her a kiss on the cheek, a warm embrace, whispers something in her ear and she sits at a table alone. More statements are shared and I finally see Sadie, I need to hear the results of the DNA test.

Sadie has an envelope in her hand.

"Carlo, we can burn these results and start over, it's not important to me anymore. You are."

"Too late for that Sadie, open the envelope."

Sadie opens the envelope and reads the results. She doesn't look up. A tear falls from her face. Her mouth searches for the right words, but nothing comes out. She pauses and looks to Carlo, "I did trust you. I just had to know for sure."

"Sadie!" Carlo yells as if he is about to snap. The music barely drowns out the irritation in his voice.

She looks back to him and her eyes look like a capsized ship sinking in an ocean, "They're yours Carlo. They're yours."

He gets up from the table, and with fury in his eyes, says, "I'll see you in court."

Three breaths in one night. First breath when my secret with Jessica remained hidden, second breath came when I found out I was exposed to the HIV virus and not infected and the third breath when I found out that the twins aren't my responsibility. I look up to the Heavens, thank you for being the God of the 100th chance. You never left me. Never.

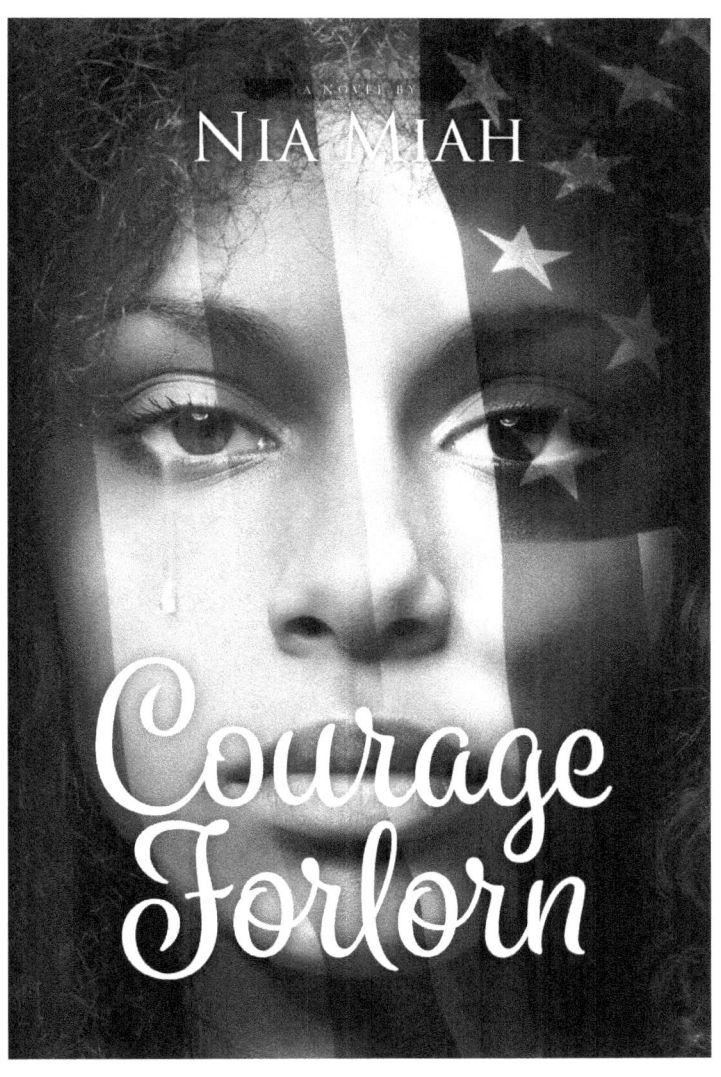

Enjoy a couple chapters
of Nia Miah's upcoming title,

Courage Forlorn

Chapter 1

Courage Forlorn

"Who are you?"

Ouch! My head feels like it is wide open.

"I'm Douglas Michaels. Are you alright? You almost started a riot back there."

I look around and there's blood everywhere. Blood on my hands, my clothes, the seat of a car, and the floorboard. Where am I?

"Are you going to hurt me?" whimpers my voice, trying to impersonate strength.

"Even if I tried, I couldn't outdo what those pigs already did to you back there?"

"Where are you taking me?"

"You need to see a doctor."

My head feels like it's trying to independently decapitate from my neck. It hurts so badly. Then there's nothing but pure blackness. When my eyes break free from unconscious captivity, I feel my body moving rapidly. *Where am I? Where is my body taking me?* My head rises off a chest, and arms are embracing me, carrying me. I want to look up to see a face, but my head feels like an anvil, so my voice secretly carries my words, "Who are you?"

"I'm Douglas. I'm trying to help you."

My eyes close again, but my ears see for me.

"Please! She needs to see a doctor!"

"Sorry sir, governor suggestions. No colored's today."

"This woman may be dying! Don't you have a responsibility to treat people who need help?"

"Yes. We are treating people today, but not colored's. Not today. The governor wants our support. We're not treating colored's. No one is."

"She needs help now!"

"Sir. I'm gonna have to ask that you leave and come tomorrow because no colored's get into the hospital today."

I hear his breaths of air desperately search the Heavens for an answer, but each one falls back from Heaven and lands warmly on my face. My body continues to rest in his arms as I feel him carry me back to the car. My mind cries for mercy from all this pain. My body is helpless. He lies me down, and in the backseat of his car the dried blood on the seat cradles me. I feel my body chase my mind, capture it, and force it back into an unconscious captivity.

When I break out of my dungeon of darkness, my ears hear before my eyes can see. Where am I?

"Big Momma, please ! Can't you do something?" Douglas's words emerge as hopeful pleas.

"Go get me a bottle of whiskey, boil my needles, and get some dental floss," orders Big Momma.

"Yes mam. On my way," Douglas answers.

"Celeste, go turn the iron on, and get some peroxide and paper."

"Ok, Momma."

"Girl, what kind of fine mess did you get yourself into?" Her question pounds my limp body. My eyes wrestle open and see an older lady with short salt and pepper hair, neatly pressed, but a bit worn from a long day. Her eyes study me as if they are trying to soothe, question, and answer me all at the same time.

"Who are you?" I ask.

"Big Momma, of course. Who else would I be?"

Big Momma addresses Douglas and Celeste as if she is calling an army to attention, "Get some wet and dry towels and a bucket of water, Dougie. Celeste, roll out a good length of that dental floss, put it between the paper, and iron it. We need to make sure it's sterile. Then bring me those needles from the boiling water and make sure your hands are clean now! Move it!"

I feel her eyes scour me up and down when she adds, "You need to drink some of this whiskey child since this is going to hurt."

Douglas scoops me up in his arms, holding me upright to swallow. I swallow and it burns my tongue and throat going down.

"Take some more child. You're going to need it." Her words are stern but feel like a warm blanket covering me. With each sip of whiskey, a warm sensation sprints through my body.

"Celeste, start cleaning that head wound with those towels while I thread this needle. I need to be able to see, so clean it good now, ya hear?"

"Ok, Momma."

"What do you want me to do, Big Momma?" Douglas asks.

"You're gonna have to keep this child still while I sew her up. Give her some more of that whiskey."

My body is screaming with pain, and the whiskey tries to muzzle the sounds, but the pain is still there. Big Momma's voice sounds like an echo, fading as it's released into the air. Black unconsciousness become my peace.

"There, that ought to do it. Get some vaseline for this wound, Dougie, and break me a small piece of that aloe vera plant. Celeste, find some clean clothes and get a bucket of fresh water so we can sponge bathe her." My unconscious darkness sneaks into my conscious awareness and steals any mental cognitive activity and darkness besieges me. Once again, I'm captive in a cell of unconsciousness.

Chapter 2

Courage Forlorn

My ears open before my eyes do, as seems to be a pattern for me.

"That governor is something else. I guess he figured he can't keep us out of the schools so he's going to keep us out of everything else. It just doesn't make any sense to suggest the state turn away every government building and hospital to Negro folks because he was forced to integrate the schools."

"I know, Big Momma. I know. I can't imagine how many families lost someone because they couldn't get into a hospital today."

"The thing about hatred is that it hurts, but it doesn't stop progression. Integration is here and that's all there is to it. We all have to get used to it."

"Big Momma, how can you not hate back? That woman who turned me away at the hospital talked to me as if I'm not even human. I wanted to just knock her out of the way and step on her as I crossed over to find a doctor."

My eyes tussle with my darkness until they finally open.

"Well, would you look a here! I think someone is trying to wake up," Big Momma says.

I look around and I'm on a couch covered with a hand-sewn quilt and pictures of family members across many generations all over the wall. My eyes focus on a couple hanging on the wall sitting with bails of cotton behind them. The ceiling is covered with gold speckled white tiles. I hear the floor creak as another body joins the room.

"My head hurts," softly sails away from my lips.

"That's because you're among the land of the living."

"Where am I?"

"Every hospital in the state of Arkansas turned their backs on me. I had to drive to Morning Star in El Dorado, where my grandmother lives. She's the only person I could think of who could help you."

"Who are you?"

"I'm Douglas Michaels."

"What happened to me, Douglas?"

"Is she going to be alright, Big Momma?" I hear a soft childlike voice ask, interrupting Douglas's answer.

"She's going to be just fine, Celeste. Go get her some aspirin and water."

"What's your name?" Douglas asks.

"Courage. Courage Forlorn."

"What kind of name is that?" Big Momma asks.

"Well, I think my last name came from the slave plantation in South Carolina where my family is from. As for my first name, my great-grandfather named me. He felt fear was man's greatest obstacle and he told me I'm fear's nemeses. Courage."

Celeste, who looks to be about 10 or 11 years old, comes back with the aspirin. Her hair is in tiny plats all over her head, barely holding their original shape.

"She sure looks better than she did yesterday," Celeste whispers to Big Momma.

"What happened to me, Douglas?"

"All on your own, you decided to integrate the malt shop and walk through the front door and sit at the counter."

"My goodness, child. Don't let courage be your curse," Big Momma exclaims.

"You decided to integrate in Little Rock on the day right after Central High School was forced to integrate. The city was already spitting mad. A bunch of us went to the same malt shop you did, but we went to the back by the kitchen where Negroes are generally served. When I saw you walking toward the front, I thought you were leaving. I had no idea you were going to walk through the front door. You almost started a silent mob, so a police officer dragged you out of the restaurant. You went with him peacefully, but he was handling you with force. I found you in an alley."

"How did you know what happened to me?"

"One of my friends from Camden, Black, can pass for white. He went into the malt shop to find out what was going on. He's a brother, but you wouldn't know it unless you know him. He got the whole story since he was bold enough to talk with the officer himself. He came out and told me what happened, so we looked for you. We searched every back road and alley until we found you.

"What did they do to me?"

"You don't remember?"

"No."

"You're pretty bruised up. You weren't this beat up when you were taken out the malt shop. We didn't see any blood. When we found you, you're scalp was ripped open and..."

"I got it from here, Dougie. Why don't you and Celeste step out and get breakfast started?" Big Momma's words send Douglas and Celeste into an obedient retreat.

"Honey, I sewed you up. I had to cut some of your hair. You're going to be sore for a while, but you'll be fine."

"Was my scalp torn up pretty badly, Big Momma?"

"Yes, but nothing that a little needle and thread couldn't fix." She gives me a soothing smile, but there's something more. I can see it on her face. Her eyes are screaming, but her mouth offers no deliverance to the thoughts that are pressing messages through her glare.

"Big Momma. What is it? Tell me, please."

"Your clothes were torn." Her words land on me as if she is whispering a secret.

What does she mean? My hands scour my body underneath the quilt. I don't recognize any of the clothes that I have on. Ow. Wait a minute. More pain? Ow. My thighs feel, sore and bruised. Oh no. No. No. No. My eyes meet with hers. Please. No.

"Were my underwear torn?"

She nods and confirms my fear.

My body pulsates with a newfound pain, and my anguished whimpers quietly burst free, the way a butterfly unobtrusively emerges from a chrysalis.

"You're going to be ok, honey," Big Momma reassures. She places her hand on my forehead, "You're going to be ok. No one knows but me. You decide who you tell and what you do."

Celeste and Douglas come back in the room. Douglas brings me breakfast. I feel lifeless. Was making a statement in the name of civil rights worth this much of a personal sacrifice?

"Courage, try to eat something," Douglas says. His words are sweet like the sound of a hummingbird.

I'm not hungry, but how do I politely say no? They've already done so much for me.

"No, thank you. I don't seem to have much of an appetite."

"We're not waiting for an appetite to come, so you're gonna eat something now, and I don't want to hear nothing else about it!" Big Momma, demands. I dare not cross her.

"No. Don't move," Douglas softly orders me.

361

"I'll feed you. Save all your energy. You'll need it to recover."

I don't want to cry, yet I feel so broken.

"Where's your family, Courage?"

"Still in Carolina."

"Should we call them for you?" Douglas asks.

"No. Please don't. They'd never understand."

"Come on, Celeste. We've a mess to clean up. Dougie can handle the rest of this.

"I watch as Big Momma and Celeste walk to the back of the house. Douglas still feeds me.

"Dougie?"

His response and sweet smile serenade me, "Yes?"

"You saved me, didn't you?"

"Big Momma had her hand in it too. Once we found you, I knew I couldn't leave you alone."

"I don't know how to say *thank you* for something like that because words just don't seem enough."

"You really don't have any memory of yesterday?"

"It's spotty. Did I see you earlier with a girl?"

I've never seen this man before today. I only asked that question to see if there is a female in his life. I don't even know why I'm even asking. I don't care. Well, maybe a little.

"Probably. If it was a girl, it was Margie. A group of us came to Little Rock supporting the NAACP's efforts to help facilitate integration. Margie is from Little Rock."

He puts the breakfast down.

"You can't change Jim Crow by yourself, Courage. I'll work with you if it'll mean you won't pull another stunt like you did at the malt shop. There's a way to do things so you don't end up dead." He leans back in the chair that sits next to the couch, "Now tell me your story, Courage. What were you doing in Little Rock?"

www.ingramcontent.com/pod-product-compliance
Lightning Source LLC
Chambersburg PA
CBHW070403260626
47161CB00001B/253